To Shaun White —
I hope you enjoy
my story.

Scott Pettit

TAHOE

By Scott Pettit

Snowball Snowboard Resort
Lake Tahoe, California

I t was six-o'clock in the morning and only the employees were enjoying the beauty of the freshly fallen snow from the night before as they were busily preparing the resort to open for the day. While they were working, they were listening to the music from a lone saxophone echoing out from the many speakers strategically placed around the entire resort. The beautiful sound of the sax was a wonderful compliment to the rising sun over the mountain peaks and served to put the employees in the perfect mental state, all by design. Along with the music and the twelve inches of fresh powder, was the intoxicating aroma of smoke from the hickory wood used in the outdoor grills as they were fired up. You could see the smoke spiraling up into the lake-blue sky from miles around. Looking down from the resort at Lake Tahoe was breathtaking. Imagining the plains of Nevada stretched out to the east only added to the allure. After only being open for business for twenty-one days, it still seemed like day one to them. It was a circus-like atmosphere of massive proportions.

Snowball was the brainchild of Hansen Giles, a forty-year old tycoon, who had learned to use his inheritance of two hundred and fifty-plus million dollars, at the ripe old age of twenty-one, wisely. Primarily, through investments in real estate, he was quickly able to double his fortune. Hansen was not good looking by Hollywood standards, but he had qualities that attracted the rich and famous to him. He stood tall at six-foot-two, somewhat lanky with dark brown hair and dark brown eyes that sparkled, giving him that visionary appearance, especially when he got excited about something. Hansen grew up surfing in Malibu at his family's summer home and frequently wintered at their palatial cabin in Aspen where he easily became an Olympic caliber downhill skier before a nearly fatal accident caused him to re-think his wildness. He loved the good life and he preferred to live long enough to enjoy it, so after he recovered from the accident, he decided to take up snowboarding. He was intrigued by the beauty of *surfing the mountain*.

When he mastered the art of snowboarding he began to formulate the possibilities of an exclusive snowboard resort. He traveled extensively to all of the major ski resorts including *Heavenly, Squaw Valley, Aspen, Vail, Taos, Sun Valley, Park City* and *Steamboat*, to name a few. He even went to *St. Moritz* in Switzerland because he wanted to learn what made each one special so he could adapt those qualities to his own resort. He chose Lake Tahoe as the location for the new resort for many reasons. Sitting lavishly in the snow-covered mountains of the Sierra Nevada mountain range, the lake itself has seventy-two miles of breathtaking shoreline, a depth of sixteen-hundred feet and has never been known to freeze. It has the aura of a beautiful blue lagoon lying in the midst of the snow-covered mountains in an area known for extremes. The average winter snow pack is twenty feet and the average winter temperature is a mild thirty degrees. The unique temperature produces some of the finest snow on the continent. With its proximity to the west coast of California, snow fanatics come by the thousands. Legalized gambling on the Nevada side adds another dimension to its lure. Lake Tahoe is a major magnet for tourists and their money. *The Lake of the Sky* has become one of the most cherished playgrounds on earth.

Hansen purchased three thousand-plus acres on the California side of the lake, at its southern end. He wanted to get close to the Nevada line so he could be near the casinos where the gambling infrastructure was already in place. Snowboarding only added to the adrenalin rush of these high rollers and, through an act of God, he was able to get the zoning approved and build his dream. He chose to name the resort *Snowball*. The logo he designed was a picture of a snowboarder surfing the top of a giant snowball rolling down the mountain. To him, the logo said everything about snowboarding and everything about his resort. It was only for the boarders, not the skiers, and he wanted *Snowball* to become their Mecca. The timing couldn't have been better because the boarders had finally inherited their money and they had plenty of it to burn. Hansen planned on making millions from sales of boards, boots, custom designed outerwear, underwear and everything else, all the way down to condoms. One of the first things he did was give free winter packages, which included everything from lodging to food, to all of the top tier movie stars, athletes, musicians and politicians around the world. He wanted the movers and shakers to be seen at *Snowball*, constantly. The only condition for the perks was that there would be pictures taken. They brought with them the Paparazzi and the Paparazzi represented free advertising in multiple mediums worldwide. He even provided a bunkhouse for the media for a nominal fee, complete with three square meals a day as well as lift passes. He wanted them to feel as special as the stars. It was the only advertising he had to do and it turned out to be the smartest move he ever made. Overnight, *Snowball* had become the new sandbox for the kiddies to play in. It quickly became obvious his venture was pure genius. No doubt.

Wintergreen Resort
Wintergreen, Virginia

Colt Salley grew up in Richmond, Virginia attending private school and later graduated from Hampden-Sydney College, a private all–boys school where he played soccer. Although life at Sydney was docile during the week because there were no girls on campus, it lit up like a Christmas tree on weekends with girls coming in literally by the busloads. Sydney pumped out a bevy of successful people and most of them already came from privileged backgrounds. It was a great place for the girls from the neighboring private schools to nab their future husbands, thus securing a lifestyle which didn't include work. Colt just happened to be the catch of all catches. He was president of his junior and senior class, captain of the soccer team and president of his fraternity. To most of his classmates, these were very coveted positions. He never sought any of them. He had movie star good looks, with somewhat long blondish hair, deep blue eyes that smiled when he talked. He had that true Virginia accent that was neither southern nor northern but unique to the breeding of his family lineage, which indicated he was a blue-blood Virginian, and loaded. Girls flocked to him like people did to Jesus. Colt could have been with anyone he wanted, including some of the boys on campus, although that wasn't his thing. It was uncanny and he never really knew how to handle it. It just wasn't what he was about.

Colt was an enigma. He liked the simple things in life like a good fire, good sipping whiskey, good conversation, a good hug and a great kiss. He never went anywhere without his chocolate lab named Burly. They were together so much they almost looked alike. He loved to hike in the mountains and he loved to watch the sunrise and sunset. He loved full moons and black starry nights. His favorite movie was *Jeremiah Johnson.* He loved good music, in particular Blackberry Smoke, and he loved to play, believe it or not, hide-and-seek with his girlfriends because it made him laugh like a kid and most of all, and he loved being a kid. After college, when most of his friends went off to med or law school, Colt decided to head to the hills. One of the first things he did when he moved to the mountains was throw his cell phone off the top of one of the many overlooks that dotted the Blue Ridge Parkway. He was tired of the bullshit phone calls from his friends who really wanted nothing more than to hang around Colt so they could get laid by the girls who weren't lucky enough to get laid by Colt. It wasn't an ego thing, it was just a fact. Although he was really good at being popular, he certainly didn't mind the solitude of being alone. He'd always believed that a mature person never got bored with his thoughts.

By profession, Colt was a snowboard instructor at *Wintergreen Resort* in the Blue Ridge Mountains of Virginia. One evening, after a long day on the slopes, he was sitting by the fireplace in his cabin, sipping on whiskey and reading *Board Mag* when he came across the article about *Snowball,* which was a resort that catered exclusively to snowboarders. He read the article four times in a row so he could absorb everything that was written. The article was very skeptical about the exclusive snowboarding resort. Colt was not. Excluding skiers was risky and could prove to be very costly, the article boasted. But Colt saw it differently. He had the same vision of success as Mr. Giles. *This is a cutting edge idea, way ahead of its time and there was no way it could fail*, thought Colt. Intrigued by the concept, he hopped on line and began to Google. What little he could dig up was enough for him to turn in his resignation the next day, effective immediately. The next thing he did was draft a long letter to a Mr. Hansen Giles.

Dear Mr. Giles,
My name is Colt Salley and I have been a snowboarding instructor/
bartender at a small resort in Virginia. When I first read about Snow-
ball I knew it was my destiny in life to be a part of this amazing
venture. Although I'm sure you are inundated with letters and appli-
cations from people like me from all over the world, I feel that I bring
something different and fresh to this unbelievable idea. I will bring
passion. Without boring you with a lot of nonsense, because I know
your time is busy, I would simply like to say that I would do anything
from washing dishes to running day camps for the children in order
to join your team. I would even be willing to invest my own money,
which is substantial (although, I'm sure you're completely covered on
that end based on your bio). If you have any questions about my sin-
cerity or character, I ask you to please contact my former employer
at Wintergreen, Josh Witherspoon. I'm confident he will convince
you that I would be an excellent hire and would completely fit into
your project. When I say former employer, I have already turned in
my resignation and am making preparations to move to Lake Tahoe
in two weeks. I certainly look forward to meeting you and hopefully
working for you. I absolutely guarantee not to disappoint you. I will
contact you in San Francisco as soon as I arrive.

I have also enclosed my resume in case you would like to inquire
about me prior to us meeting. Thank you for your time.
Sincerely,
Colt Salley

San Francisco, California

Hansen had to laugh when he read the letter from this Colt
Salley. After he finished, he stared out the window of his plush
office, which originally had been a stable for horses on his estate

called *Sunset.* Outside was a massive whiteout caused by the ever present fog rising up from the city. He preferred to work out of his home office because he found the hustle and bustle of the inner city too claustrophobic. The fog always reminded him of business, sometimes you can't see anything and then it dissipates and things become crystal clear. The fog kept him from being complacent and he actually looked forward to it. He found this letter from Mr. Salley quite interesting since he had some reservations about the management company he'd hired to run his new resort.

Because of business interests elsewhere, he was unable to be as hands on at the resort as he would like. The preliminary reports were fantastic but he would need to spend some serious time there to fully understand the operation and make the inevitable adjustments that would be needed. Despite its early success, he was still in a quandary about how to properly manage the operation. Somehow, this letter from Colt Salley had reached him at his estate which was almost impossible. *The kid must have some pretty incredible resources,* he thought to himself. *He definitely had balls.* Hansen, amused at the timing, took this as a sign that the fog was clearing. So he picked up the phone and made a call.

"Hello, *Wintergreen Resort,* how may I help you?"

"My name is Hansen Giles, and I'm calling from California. I was thinking about taking a vacation and thought a visit to the east coast would be kind of interesting. A friend of mine suggested I stay at your resort. I was wondering if you could tell me a little bit about *Wintergreen,*" replied Hansen.

"Well, certainly", replied the rather seductive sounding receptionist. "You would be seeing one of the most beautiful parts of Virginia. We are a four-season resort tucked away in the Blue Ridge Mountains. We are forty-five minutes from Charlottesville, an hour and a half from Richmond and two hours-plus from Washington. If you are interested in history then you will be fascinated to be in Virginia. *Wintergreen* prides itself as a top tier tennis resort, featuring fantastic golf, skiing or just plain relaxing if that is what you're in to. We have the best hiking trails in the state with access to the Appalachian Trail which connects Georgia to Maine. I would be happy to send you some literature which would give you more information if you like?"

"I think you sold me already," replied Hansen, knowing she was reading a script. "Just the history of your state alone intrigues me. However, I like to ski so would it be possible to talk to someone about the skiing. My friend mentioned a person by the name of Josh Witherspoon. Is he around by chance?"

"Oh-my-gosh, Josh?" She replied with a bit of a giggle. "Sorry, that was an inside joke. We always say that and he seems to get a kick out of it. Anyway, I'll be happy to transfer you to him. I hope you have a nice day and we hope you decide to come visit us. It was very nice talking to you."

"Likewise, I hope you have a nice day as well. And by the way, that was a nice sales job."

"Why, thank you. Please hold for just a second while I connect you."

"*Wintergreen Ski*, this is Josh."

"Mr. Witherspoon, my name is Hansen Giles and I'm calling to inquire about a former employee of yours. I would like to know a little more about him before I decide whether I should grant him an interview. Would you mind if I took up a few minutes of your time?"

"Not at all Mr. Giles, I'd be more than happy to talk to you about, let me guess, Colt Salley?"

"Very perceptive of you Mr. Witherspoon, must be a small world over there in your parts. By the way, please call me Hansen. I refuse to grow up and become a real adult, yet," Hansen replied to ease the formality of the conversation.

"I hear where you're coming from Hansen. I refused to grow up about thirty years ago myself. I have some awful battle scars to prove it. I just hope your memories will be as good as mine. Please, call me Josh."

"Okay Josh it is. So what can you tell me about Mr. Salley?"

"Only two words- hire him."

"Well, that was easy, I guess. Tell me why," replied Hansen.

"Because, believe me when I tell you that you will never regret it. Not even for one second. First of all, let me explain something to you, Hansen. I know who you are and I'm well aware of your project in Tahoe. By the way, I love the name *Snowball* and your logo is perfect."

"Thanks..."

"Aside from the fact that deep down inside I think you will be stealing one of my most valuable employees. I'd say, without resentment, you'll be shocked when you meet this kid. He is definitely one of a kind."

"How so..?" Hansen asked now that his interest was kicked up a notch.

"For starters, I did my homework on him just like you're doing now. Would you believe it if I told you he probably has more money than you, or soon will?"

"So what's your point?"

"Let me ask you, what type of job did he ask for? Was it snowboard patrol, cook, bottle washer or something less elaborate?"

"He seemed rather open to anything in his letter but I'll have to admit, you're really beginning to confuse me. If this kid has so much money, it sounds to me like he really doesn't want to work at all. He's just looking for another place to hang out."

"You're on the same track I was, Hansen. When he came to me, I too began to question why he was here," said Josh.

"So what cured that?"

"Well, it was pretty simple, I met him. Immediately, I knew he was for real. There are very few people in life that have a profound impact on everyone around them. Most people try, because who wouldn't? You know what I mean? Well, Colt comes by it naturally. When he walks into a room, every-body, and I mean everybody, takes notice. Women, children, husbands and even the foreign exchange employees who can't speak a lick of English look at him like he is some kind of god or something. It's the damnedest thing. Now you'd think this kid, and I say kid loosely because he is a young man, would have a huge ego. That's just the opposite. Either he is oblivious to all the attention or in some way, he learned how to deal with it. Anyway, the void he will leave behind will never, and I mean never, be filled. And the funny thing is…"

"What?"

"He works his butt off, every day. He will do anything and he will do it right, one hundred and ten percent of the time," finished Josh.

"Wow, it sounds like I should meet this guy."

"Absolutely… It would be a mistake if you let him slip through the cracks. I give you my word. I'll tell you something else…"

"What?"

"There are quite a few broken hearts around here, and not just the staff. I hope you treat him right because he's special."

"Thanks Josh, I'll definitely talk to him. I really appreci-ate your time. If you're ever out this way, please let me know before you come and I will make some arrangements for you to get the red carpet treatment at the resort. I sincerely mean it."

"I appreciate that, Hansen, but Colt already made the offer."

"I haven't even hired him yet," responded Hansen with a laugh.

"I know, but you will. Good luck with your venture. And for the record, I'm jealous. Just do me a favor."

"What's that?"

"Don't grow up. It's not worth it in the long run. Trust me."

"Duly noted… Thanks- oh-my-gosh, Josh. I have a feeling we'll be talking again," Hansen laughed. He had to get that one in.

"You know it," replied Josh as he hung up the phone, shaking his head. He'd have to talk to the staff about that nickname. *Man*, he thought to himself, *he was going to miss the hell out of Colt.*

Wintergreen

Annie-Laurie was not one to let Colt know that she was upset when he asked her to come over. She had been on the mountain a long time and her emotions were, or so she thought, battle-hardened. She had seen a lot of people come and go and was used to change. Colt, on the other hand was a different beast. One she could never conquer. Their affair had been an on-again, off-again thing for the past couple of years. She never asked for much and in return, he didn't give much. Having grown up in the valley a country girl, her only worldly experience was going off to college at nearby University of Virginia. Annie-Laurie was a very smart girl and a homebody. The homebody eventually won out. A four-year degree in economics was basically wasted when she high-tailed it back home after she graduated.

She went to work for one of the many wineries at the base of Wintergreen Mountain during the day and moonlighted as a waitress at one of the restaurants at the resort in the evenings. One of her most beautiful features was the fact that at first glance, she didn't come off as particularly beautiful. She had somewhat wavy, shoulder length brown hair, green eyes, freckles galore and a body to die for. What beauty she had was natural and she naturally knew how to exploit it. Her best quality was the fact that she was very cool. She could talk to a crowd, sip whiskey, do shooters and make love all night long. When she walked into a room, she took over. Nothing and nobody intimidated her. She had a passion for everything, including snowboarding, hiking and, of all things, chocolate labs. It was love at first sight when she met Burly, Colt's chocolate. All she had to do was win over Burly and Colt was soon to follow. Colt never tired of watching her play with that dog.

She sashayed in like she owned the place. Colt was rocking in his rocking chair covered with a reindeer skin with Burly lying at his feet. He didn't bother to get up and greet Annie–Laurie because Burly took care of that. Two seconds after she walked in, both dog and woman were rolling on the floor like two long lost lovers in the night. With a little Eagles' music playing in the background it was quite a sight to see the love that dog had for her. It made Colt happy and sad at the same time. She was not going to like what he was going to tell her. He decided to let them play it out before he talked to her. Maybe Burly would burn off some of that high energy she carried around like a badge of honor. When she finally resorted to lying on her back on the floor and let Burly lick her face to the point where she was in hysterics, Colt decided it was time.

"We need to talk."

"So I hear," she responded trying to look at him while Burly was still playing around. Reluctantly, she tore herself away and stood up to regain her composure. She walked over and sat on the floor facing him with her arms crossed over his knees. She stared at him dead in the eyes and said, "Why are you leaving me?"

"Annie, you know it's not like that. Come on, give me a break."

"Why don't you give me one?" She replied as she started running her hand up his thigh. "You know I love you."

"Let's not go there," he said while stopping her hand from getting too close. "This has nothing to do with love. I don't even know what love is. I just want some time to chase my dreams. Is that so wrong?"

"Let me chase them with you! Don't leave me alone in this one-horse town. I wouldn't know what to do without you here with me. What about Burly? He would be lost without me.

You know that. I need you and I need that damned dog of yours. I...I don't want to talk anymore. I want to make love to you. We can talk later. Okay?"

"Annie-Laurie, you're a piece of work, you know that? Your idea of making love is wild sex followed by more wild sex. You're killing me. I'm too old for that now," he said smiling as he held her face with both hands. "It will just make things harder."

"You know I have a softer side. I'll show you. Follow me..." She said as she got up and basically dragged him to the loft of his cabin.

"Annie, don't do this."

"Shut up, Colt. If you are going to leave me then you are going to do it on my terms."

"Just don't hold this over my head, okay?"

"Don't worry about me. I just want to make sure you never forget this moment."

"Now you're making it hard," he pleaded innocently.

"Really, why am I not surprised Colt?"

"That's not what I meant," he said somewhat jokingly.

"Right"

Afterwards, they both lay there side-by-side, exhausted, staring up at the ornate rafters of the cabin, listening to the occasional crackle of the wood burning down in the fireplace. Burly had waited until they were done before he came up and assumed his usual spot in the corner of the loft, near the stairs. He was used to the routine. Colt turned his head towards her and stared at her for a long time without saying anything. She just stared straight up at the rafters without acknowledging his stare.

"I have two favors to ask you," he finally said.

She tore herself away from the rafters and looked at him without responding.

"Don't you want to know what they are?" He asked.

"Not really. I'm done with you. You suck!"

He knew she didn't mean that. It was just her way of saying she would miss him, but she would let him go because she understood him.

"I want you to stay here and take care of the place while I'm gone. I'll pay for everything. I don't want to let this go."

"What about Burly, can he stay with me until you come back?"

"What makes you think I'll come back?"

"Because you're a Virginian and Virginians always come home. You know that."

"That's bullshit, Annie."

"Well if you leave the dog then I know you'll come home. I can wait. I promise."

"Let me think about it, okay?"

"When are you leaving?"

"Day after tomorrow."

"Fuck you"

"You just did."

"Colt…"

Two days later when she walked into the cabin with tears rolling down her cheeks, the first thing she smelled was dog poop. It was odd because Colt was such a neat-nick he would never allow Burly to do his business in the house. There was a note on the kitchen table. Reluctantly, she picked it up and began reading.

Dear Annie,

First of all, did I ever tell you how much I love your name? It's beautiful like you. By the time you read this I'm probably an hour or so into my journey across the country and thinking about what I have left behind. Believe me when I say it's not easy for me. I will miss you and I will miss my life there. I have to do this because it has stirred up a passion in me I never knew I had before. I have to chase it to see if it is real. I have no idea what lies ahead either out there in California or back home and I have no idea how long it will take to figure it out. I'm excited, confused, happy and sad all at the same time.

Thank you for everything! You are my lover and my best friend and I'm not sure which comes first. The only way I can do this is by knowing you are taking care of what I left behind. As you know, there are no conditions or obligations. I just want you to be happy. I'm leaving my truck for you to use. You'll need it. I'll call you when I get there.

Love you always,
Colt

PS- There is a little surprise for you in the utility room. You better hurry!

Crying hysterically, she ran to the utility room and opened the door and fell to her knees. Sitting there, with tail wagging and huge brown eyes staring up at her, was the cutest chocolate lab puppy she had ever seen. She didn't even notice the mess he'd made. They rolled around on the floor and played until he fell asleep in her arms. As odd as it would seem to others, she named the puppy Salley. She thought if Colt could live with that name then so could this beautiful, very handsome puppy. She wore him out, with love. When he woke up, she was lying there beside him, petting him. He was starving so she fed him and then they went for a long walk to Colt's favorite overlook. *Salley was going to be a fine mountain dog,* she thought as she stared into the sun setting across the mountain ridges, the sun that was setting on California.

Colt knew the puppy would buy him some serious time. Annie would give that puppy her all. He decided not to tell her that Burly was the father, yet. He thought that might be too much for her to handle. Sometimes it is so amazing how things work out. Timing is everything. Now he could focus the rest of his journey on what he was going to say in the five minutes he was probably going to get with Mr. Giles. *What was it about this concept of a snowboard resort that was powerful enough to make him walk away from the life he knew and into the world of the unknown?*

15

After driving eight hours straight, out of pure adrenalin and excitement, he pulled into this dive of a roadside restaurant somewhere in the middle of nowhere. A salty old couple were sitting at the bar drinking beer from mason jars and eating pickles that obviously came out of the nasty gallon jar at the end of the counter, next to the gallon of purple–pickled eggs. *That pretty much says it all*, he thought as he walked to a booth beside a big plate glass window illuminated by the neon sign blinking outside, telling the passer-by to keep on going. A middle-aged, somewhat attractive black woman, who looked like she just didn't make it all the way to New York City, dropped the menu down on the table and said she'd be back with his beer. He didn't even order one.

"It's a Bud, hope that's all right," she said as she placed the mason jar of draft beer in front of him along with a glass of water.

"How did you know I wanted this beer?" He asked politely, afraid she might poison his food if he sounded cocky.

"Easy, I looked at you. Let me guess. You have been on the road all day and you have a long ways to go. You're probably on your way to Las Vegas or California. Am I right?" She smiled with a motherly grin.

"Pretty much," he laughed. "I'm on my way to California. You want to come with me?" He asked jokingly.

"Nah, I'm on my way to New York. Can't you tell?"

Colt laughed out loud. "Yeah, I thought so. You have that *I'm on my way to New York*-look about you. What's your ETA?"

"Before I'm fifty," she replied. "I got ten more years to get there, but I'm in a real hurry if you know what I mean."

"I hear you loud and clear. I'm in pretty much of a hurry myself."

"Chasing a dream? Are you a gold digger?" She asked.

"I am chasing the dream."

"I thought so. I can pick-em every time. This place must be the dream-stop along the way to the golden arches. I saw three others just like you today, although, you win the pretty boy contest by a long shot. I could do you," she smiled.

"That won't get you to New York," he laughed. "Could you do me something to eat before this beer knocks me out?"

"Nah, I'm going to let the beer knock you out so I can drag you home and eat you. I'm kidding, how do you want that hamburger?"

"How do you know I want a hamburger?"
She cocked her head and put her hands on her hips. "Have I been wrong yet?"

"Medium-well, with lettuce, tomato and ketchup, and can I get fries with that?"

"Honey, you can get whatever your little heart desires. It's written all over your face. You're special, you know that? I'm psychic."

"Someone I left behind told me the same thing day before yesterday. How come I don't feel special?"

"Because you haven't caught the dream yet, sweetie, but you will. I can see it in your eyes. Like I said, I'm psychic. Your time is coming. I'm going to remember you. I'll be right back with your burger."

"Hey, what is your name?"

"Cracker, and don't ask," she said smiling as she strutted back to the kitchen.

"As in fire?" he yelled to her. She turned her head back towards him and whispered "No, as in peanut butter, but I like the way you think." He sat there staring out the window as the lights of an occasional car would blow by, heading in the same direction he was heading. *Cracker*, he thought to himself. He would remember her too. He hoped she would make it to New York, although, he doubted she ever would.

When she returned with his dinner, she had a fresh beer for him. He looked up at her as she held her hand out to silence whatever was going to come out of his mouth.

"Like I said before, don't..." She never finished her sentence. The plate glass window above his head exploded and shattered into a million tiny diamonds, raining down on him in a frenzied downpour, immediately followed by a swath of cold air. Out of instinct, he ducked as if to protect any glass from landing on his burger. He'd failed to notice the car creep up in front of the restaurant with its lights off. He'd failed to notice the window rolled down and he'd failed to notice the rifle protruding out of the opening. He remembered hearing the sounds of glass dancing on the tables and floor, the sound of a thud and the sounds of tires squealing, but he was too confused to put it all together. When he lifted his head up after the last piece of glass quit dancing on the floor, he looked around to try to put everything together. On reflex, the salty old couple had knocked their beers off the counter, crashing to the floor, and their half-eaten pickles were rolling across the counter while they sat there staring in his direction with both hands to their mouths, silently screaming in horror. The swinging door to the kitchen opened as two people scurried out into the restaurant to see what the noise was. Colt looked down to where they were all focused and gasped at the sight of Cracker lying on the floor with a gigantic red spot on her chest and an even bigger spot growing beneath her as she lay on the floor, on her back, staring lifelessly at the ceiling.

They caught the two assailants a few hours later holed up in the next town. As it turned out, it was a ridiculous case of jealously. She had broken up with her ex-boyfriend because she really was in a hurry to split for New York and he wanted her to stay with him, in his trailer, in the middle of nowhere. He simply wasn't going to let her go, no matter what. And when he pulled into the parking lot of the diner and saw her flirting with Colt, he snapped.

It all seemed so surreal. He was sitting in the local police station with the older couple and the two other people from the kitchen, and everyone was staring into space, totally lost in their private thoughts. Occasionally, there was a sob or a gasp that would disrupt the eerie silence in the room. Everyone in the room was in total shock. The reality of the situation was a long ways away and the tears would come when the shock wore off. *This wasn't happening,* Colt kept saying to himself over and over. *She has to get to New York. She hasn't caught her dream yet. She's got ten more years left.* He had only known her for five minutes and he felt like he had known her his entire life. *Cracker, I will never forget you as long as I live. Not everybody can catch their dream,* he kept thinking to himself. He silently promised her he would catch his dream, in honor of her.

Two Miles West of Nowhere

Driving *down the road again, blinded by the tragedy, Colt decided to call Annie to take his mind off of what happened. Fortunately, he'd had the foresight to get a new cell phone before he ventured across the country. He looked over at Burly lying on the front seat and wondered if he had a clue as to what just happened? What did he think about stupid humans? Burly gave him the silent treatment just like Annie-Laurie would do if she was upset with him.*

'Hello, this is Annie." She answered somewhat out of breath because she had been running around the cabin with Salley.

"So did you like my little surprise?" He asked.

"Well, I tell you what, Mr. Salley. You sure know how to get to the bottom of a lady's heart after you kick it. He's wonderful and I love him. He's soooo cute! You can't have him back either." She was serious about that.

"Annie. I hand-picked him especially for you, he's all yours. I had to match the personality, if you know what I mean."

"Then that must explain why he's constantly humping my leg. I was kind of thinking you picked him to match your personality so I wouldn't forget you."

"Anyway you want to twist it is fine with me. By the way, what did you name him?"

"I haven't named him yet," she lied, "I'm waiting to see how mad I really am at you for leaving me."

"What does that have to do with it?" He asked, trying to keep the conversation going as long as he could. He didn't want her to hang up.

"I think I will name him Judas?"

"Oh, he will surely love that. What are you doing now? You sound out of breath."

"I was lonely so I decided to go fuck your neighbor. Nice guy. Great fuck."

"That's not even close to being funny and you know it," he responded. He knew the one kink in her armor was when she was trying to make a point she would resort to using foul language to add to the shock value. He came from money, she didn't and that was her way of bringing him down to her level.

"Who's laughing? Not me, sitting here alone in this beautiful cabin, without you."

"You have Judas to keep you company, right?"

"Nice try, Romeo, but no cigar. You got that? Remember, you are still way up on my shit-list. I'm not letting this mutt you stuck on me serve as some kind of substitute," she said with a twist of humor. There was no way she could hide the fact that she already worshipped the ground Salley walked, and pooped, on.

"Annie-Laurie, why do you try to play the tough guy thing on me? I know you like the palm of my hand. Oops, sorry, that was a bad analogy. Anyway, I know you love that mutt and if I had to guess, he's probably had about three baths today and you've already arranged for a little female playmate for him so he won't get too bored when you're working. Am I right?"

"I'm not going to tell you. Come home and see for yourself."

"Baby, I've got to do this. We talked about it, remember?"

"No, I already forgot. I miss you Colt. I can't help it. But I'll get better. I promise." She was trying to control the shakiness in her voice so he wouldn't know she was crying. "So how's life on the road? Are you there yet?"

"Annie, I just left today. I saw something happen at this diner in the middle of nowhere that made me want to do this even more. " He couldn't bring himself to tell her about exactly what happened. She would be horrified for him and it would destroy her. She acted tough but deep down she had the heart of hearts and she was a real softy. "I have a long way to go before I get to San Francisco. Then I have to locate Mr. Giles and pray he'll talk to me. He might not and if that happens, I don't know what I'll do. I guess I'll have to figure out another way to get to him. What he's doing is going to be big and I really want to be a part of it."

"Colt, I understand what you're doing and I'm trying very hard to support you. I'm just so afraid I will lose you in the process. My mother always told me that absence either makes the heart grow fonder or makes the heart forget. I'm so afraid you will forget me. Please don't let that happen, okay?"

"Annie-Laurie, I will never, never let that happen. I give you my word. When a Salley gives you his word, well, you have to wonder where the hell that name like Salley came from. I'm kidding, trust me, we are going to be so good when the dust settles. Be patient, that's all I ask."

After he hung up, he came very close to ripping the steering wheel around and high-tailing it back to Virginia. It would be so easy to do. Then he thought about Cracker. He knew they'd crossed paths for a reason. As strange as it was, her murder gave him the strength to keep driving west.

Three days east of California and having driven for almost twenty-four hours straight, Colt knew he had to stop. He was done. He was fried. He looked into the rearview mirror and did a double take when he saw how red his eyes were. He wasn't sure whether that was from driving all night or crying all night. In any event, it wasn't a pretty sight. He would have to do some cleaning up just to check-in to a hotel. They might think he was a crazy man or something. So at the next rest area he pulled in and parked in the furthest parking spot he could get from the bathrooms. He dropped his sunglasses down over his eyes and reclined the front seat as far as it would go to take a short power nap. His Porsche SUV was not really equipped for long trips as one would think. It was made to drive on winding mountain roads with Burly hanging out the window. But Burly had long ago given up the thrill of the window and replaced it with a coma. Colt was tired and uncomfortable and he couldn't stop thinking about Cracker and the stupid promises he'd made to Annie-Laurie. His mind kept jumping from one to the other like a Mexican jumping bean and his emotions were ebbing and flowing like a tsunami. What sleep he could muster was extremely fitful, at best. Eventually, he was too stiff to stay there any longer, so he got out and stretched before he went into the restroom to wash his face and try to look like a human again. He was too exhausted to notice a mother almost knock her little boy out of the way on the sidewalk so she could get a better look at him while he staggered in and staggered out, looking pretty much the same. He hopped in his car and swerved down the highway looking for the first hotel he could find. Burly never moved.

He wasn't real sure what time it was when he finally woke up but it was pitch black outside. Totally disoriented, he filled the complimentary coffee maker in his room and hit the on button. Five minutes later he literally crawled out of the steaming shower and poured himself a cup. It tasted like heaven...sort of. Colt shaved about once a week. It was kind of a pain, or he was just too lazy, but he decided to rake it down before he hit the road again. He figured it would make him feel crisper and he was looking for any excuse to sip the coffee instead of gulping it. Finally, when he was done, he threw on some sweat pants and a sweatshirt to be a little more comfortable on the road. He brushed his teeth, grabbed his bag and tore out of the parking lot. He knew that no matter how fast he drove, he still wouldn't be able to outrun his mind. The next couple of days he would be buried deep in thought, both about what he was leaving behind and about where he was going.

Almost as an afterthought, he figured he'd better check in with his parents. They struggled with his earthy lifestyle but had too much class to make public their disapproval. They figured he would join the real world one day, in due time. They had money and lots of it. Most of it was inherited, passed down a couple generations with each generation successfully adding to the kitty. His parents might be the last generation to pass that success story on. Colt, being their only child was probably not going to grow the money unless he started to get serious. At least that's the way they saw it. If he didn't hurry up and get married and have children, then it would be probably be a moot point anyway. The one thing that amazed Colt was how his family could make money being philanthropists. They never had real jobs. *How can you make money when you give money away* was the million dollar question. He couldn't figure it out, but they did it and they were very good at it. They were "charity specialists" and their social life would make the privileged in Washington jealous. They went to more parties in one week than he would go to in a year and most of the ones he would attend would be the ones his parents stressed to him as being important to the family.

It seemed like every time he showed up at one of these gigs, somebody was always trying to dump one, if not two of their daughters off on him. Sometimes it would turn into a competition. It was not a natural situation for him. He would play the game to a point and then he would politely disappear, like a cool breeze, which only added to his mystique. Oddly, it made him more of a hot commodity. Everybody wanted a piece of him. *Now they were going to have to look a little harder to find him,* he thought as his mother picked up the phone.

"Colt, are your fingers broken?" She asked since it had been too long since he last checked in. "Are you having trouble dialing the numbers?"

"Sorry mom, no excuse," he responded softly. "Every time I call, you and dad are at some party. I get tired of constantly leaving messages."

"Bullshit, Colt. We have caller ID you know."

"That's why I don't have it. I like to be surprised," he said trying to divert her lectures on not being more loyal.

"That must be why you never answer your phone. Too much surprise is killing you," she joked. She was such a player.

"Mom, can we start over? We do this every time I call and I'm tired of coming up short all the time. If you'd let me win sometimes I'd probably call more."

"Sorry love, we miss you and want to hear from you. Ever since you bought that cabin you seemed to go deeper into seclusion. That's not a Salley trait. We have responsibilities..."

"I know Mom. You've told me that before." *That came out wrong,* he thought to himself. He shouldn't have cut her off.

"I don't recognize the number you're calling from. Is this your cell phone?"

"Yes, I just got it the other day. I'm trying harder to come out of seclusion, trying to be more in touch," he joked.

"Good. That's a start. Where are you calling from? Sounds like you're in your car. Would that mean you're on your way to Richmond? Please tell me yes, that would please your father so much," she began to ramble. "He's playing tennis at the club and is going to be sorely disappointed if he missed you. If he got home and you were already here, that would be fabulous. You could go to the museum with us this evening. They are having a fund-raising party for the Children's Hospital. Lots of pretty girls will be there. We can go out to dinner before..."

"Mom... Mom, sorry to interrupt, but I don't want you to get all worked-up for nothing. I'm actually heading in the opposite direction. I'm on my way to San Francisco." He said as he held his breath.

"What? Why are you going out there?"

"Business, I'm looking into a business venture that I think has tremendous potential. Who knows, with any luck, I might still make you proud of me," he added to feed the fire.

"Give me the information and I'll have your father look into it. By the time you get there you can have everything you'll need to know at your fingertips. He would love to help out," she said getting more excited by the second.

"Thanks, Mom, but I'm going to try to do this on my own. I'm pretty jazzed about it. Hopefully, it will pan out. But I'll let you know one way or the other, how about that?"

"Okay, but your father would love to get involved. It would keep him from pacing around the house all day. I wish he'd get back into golf. It takes five wonderful hours to play a round. I could use that extra time..."

"Mom, I have another call coming in. I'll call you when I get to California." It was time to move on or she would talk to him the entire way.

"Okay sweetie, but your father is going to be so upset he didn't get to talk to you."

"Tell him I love him and I'll call later. Bye now." Click. *That went pretty well*, he thought to himself. It would have gone downhill rapidly if she found out he planned on living in California for awhile. He'd done enough thinking for the day, so he popped in his *Robbin Thompson* CD. He'd let his buddy Robbin do the thinking for the next hundred thousand miles...

Kansas
Forget Kansas. It never ends.

Lake Tahoe

At the last minute, Hansen decided to jet up to the resort and check on things. Originally, it was going to be a quick in-out, and after only being there for less than an hour, he decided to stay for the night. He noticed things that weren't obvious to the people on his payroll and that bothered the hell out of him. The trash cans were overflowing; empty boxes were piled up behind the main building, which wouldn't be so bad if the main building didn't side up to the main chairlift in the village at the base of the mountain where everyone could see them. The wood-fired grills looked like they had never been cleaned, the wood was piled and not stacked, and annoying pieces of trash littered the beautiful snow. He noticed all of this by just doing a three-sixty in the center of the village. The worst thing of all was the employees were walking around like robots. They weren't smiling or engaging the boarders to make them feel at home. All added up, the hospitality part of the resort sucked and Hansen was pissed. If people felt at home, they would keep coming back and if they felt ignored, eventually the fad would just that, and die and they would take their money elsewhere. He paid a fortune for the management company to run the resort and obviously they didn't seem to have a clue about how to do it. No one wanted to take responsibility and the problem was that Hansen's hands were tied because he needed them more than they needed him. He figured he had one season to make it work, if it didn't it would quickly become a money pit.

Fortunately, it was very early in the game and he had a grace period to make the necessary adjustments. It's not like a restaurant critic where, after only one dining experience, the idiot could crush you in the review. So he knew he had time to make things right. However, the last thing Hansen wanted to do was get involved in the day-to-day operations. He was far too busy for that. He was operating on blind faith that the company he hired to run the resort was the best he could get. They had a long history of managing ski resorts so it should have been a no-brainer. Colin Diggs, the project manager, seemed like a bright guy. He was certainly smart enough to not say anything while Hansen was pointing out all the problems. He just walked around with Hansen taking notes. It was just business to Colin and that's where the two parted ways because it was a lifestyle to Hansen.

Hansen always had a plan. He would give a list of instructions with a reasonable time frame to make them happen. It was important for him to have a good working relationship with people and creating an adversarial environment never did anybody any good. That being said, Hansen could turn into a completely different person in a nano-second if he wasn't pleased, so that was the check and balance. Also, he had been smart enough in business to always have a bailout clause in case changes needed to be made immediately. That was his parachute. Unfortunately, he didn't really have a back-up this time.

After walking around with that boring punk, Colin, all day, Hansen looked forward to dining alone in his suite to have quiet time to contemplate what needed to be done. He had to be smart about it or Colin could walk, which would leave him high and dry. That was not an option at this stage and jetting back-and-forth to Tahoe wasn't an option either. Hansen's biggest problem was that, beyond himself, there was no one else he completely trusted. The minute he figured out someone wanted a piece of him, which happened on a regular basis, they were done. He never allowed himself the luxury of having a right-hand man and that wasn't a good thing when he's growing an empire. *What if he got sick or some other emergency came up to distract him?* One day off territory could potentially be catastrophic. Hiring a bunch of robots was simply pouring water into a leaky bowl. He worried about that constantly. He would figure it out eventually because he would be forced to, but at this point he really didn't have a clue. However, the early reviews on *Snowball* were favorable and that kept Hansen from doing something he would regret. He was, after all, a somewhat patient man, especially, if it was something he believed in. He truly believed *Snowball* would make it, he just knew there was a lot of work still to be done to get it right.

He spent the entire evening drawing up a list of expectations. He wanted the meeting with Colin in the morning to be a one-sided affair. If Colin didn't have the foresight to see the problems that Hansen did, then Hansen would give him a list a mile long of things to do. If Colin got at least half of the things on the list accomplished then he would be twice as far along as he would be running solo. No matter how nicely he presented it to Colin, Colin was still going to hate his guts. He decided to hold off discussing the employee situation and give Colin a little more time before he personally addressed the staff. Mixed leadership could lead to a mutiny. Hansen looked up from his notes when he heard the door open.

"You're late," he said when Colin finally strolled in to the conference room.

"Sorry, I was busy," Colin replied nonchalantly.

"That's a bold statement when I'm the boss, Colin. You didn't forget that did you? I mean, you might be running the show but I still call the shots. Is that clear?" Hansen, with both elbows leaning on the table and his face protruding directly towards Colin, could feel his eyes were bulging with anger. This was not how he planned to start the meeting but this arrogant little prick needed to be put in his place, and fast. For two dollars and a handshake he would have fired him on the spot.

"Again, sorry Mr. Giles, but we had a little situation that required my immediate attention. I would have called but I was out on the slopes."

"What happened?" Hansen asked having completely switched gears.

"One of the little starlets had an altercation with a photographer. The guy was probably Paparazzi. I really think it was a case of the girl wanting some extra attention. Turned out not to be a big deal."

"How so...who was it?"

"Which question do you want me to answer first?" Colin asked somewhat sarcastically.

"Let me tell you something, Colin... when I made my pitch to your company, they liked my idea. They wanted to work with me. Now, my idea is only going to work if people like that little starlet you seem to be annoyed with is happy. I need her to come back to *Snowball* again and again. So who is it and what happened?" Hansen demanded.

"Her name is Bobbie Creek and she's a low level country singer with a lot of potential. Problem is she wants the attention of a high level country singer because she's already a spoiled brat. The guy took a picture of her sprawled out face down on the slope after taking a rather nasty spill on a mogul. She didn't think it was becoming of her. Don't worry, I got the camera from him and destroyed the pictures. Now she's all happy and that's why I was late. Now, here I am at your disposal."

"Let me see if I have this straight," Hansen said, "you call the girl a spoiled brat, took the guy's camera and destroyed the pictures and now everybody's happy. Is that about right?"

"Yeah, not a big deal...right?" Colin smiled.

"You know what I think Colin?"

"What"

"Well, I think you're fired! Get out of my sight and don't you ever put your foot on this property again," Hansen spat off as he got up and walked out of the conference room. On his way back to his suite he placed a call to the management company and informed them what had happened. He requested an immediate replacement for Colin and also told them this was their last chance to get it right or he would find somebody else. What he didn't tell them was he was going to find somebody else anyway, he just hadn't figured that part out yet. That evening he was on his way back to San Francisco and he was distraught. For the first time he began to question his passion, that just maybe he had bitten off more than he could chew.

California Line

Colt almost completely missed it. He was so highway hypno-tized he could have driven all the way across California and into the Pacific Ocean without even knowing it. Seeing Cracker lying on the floor with a grapefruit-sized spot of blood in the middle of her chest and the continent of blood spreading underneath her was more than he could handle. He had that picture in his mind the entire trip. *It was awful* he kept telling himself. She was so nice. She had such a beautiful smile and such a wonder-ful way of dealing with people. Colt made up his mind by the time he got to California he was going to do something nice for her family if he could find them. He remembered the name of the diner so he was going to make arrangements to pay for her funeral and close out any debt that she might have had. He also sent flowers. If there truly is life after death, which he believed there is, he didn't want her to spend it worrying about unfin-ished business here on earth. In a small way she helped pave his way and he was going to return the favor.

It was the beautiful sunset that brought him back to reality. Even as a kid, he had always been mesmerized by sun-sets. It was like closing the chapter of a really good book. It gave him time to think, reflect to see if he'd been good or bad, right or wrong and if there anything that he could correct. He was a perfectionist. To him sunsets were spiritual, powerful and meaningful and they were best seen high up in the mountains, closer to the other side. Colt found peace through his decision to do something in honor of Cracker. Now he could focus on why he was crossing the California line. For some reason he new this was his destiny. There was something on the other side of the state line that was going to change his world and he couldn't wait to see what it was. One thing for sure, he was in a hurry to get to San Francisco.

He was cruising through the Sierra Nevada mountain range, heading west on Interstate 80, just north of Lake Tahoe. His Porsche was in its element now. It was all he could do to obey the speed limit. So close to Lake Tahoe, he was tempted to drop down to the southern tip of the lake to check out *Snowball* before going all the way to San Francisco. He quickly decided that was a ridiculous idea because it would have been worthless without the blessing of Mr. Giles, so he kept cruising towards San Fran. It would be late by the time he rolled into town which was just as well, because he could get a good night's sleep before making arrangements to meet Mr. Giles. He would have felt a little more confident if he actually had an appointment, but it was too late to worry about that now. Concentrating on what he would say to Giles, his cell phone started ringing. Worried it might be he parents, he almost didn't answer, but he figured he could use the distraction to help keep him awake. It had been a long, long ride and an emotional one at that.

"Hello?"

"Did you already forget about me?" She said.

"Annie, thank God it's you, I was afraid it might be my parents," he replied with a smile. "Do you mind talking dirty to me for about, let me see, four more hours? Dirty enough to get me all the way to San Francisco because I just rolled into California and I'm tired, hungry and horny. Burly feels the same. Maybe I'll put you on speaker phone so he can enjoy it too. I'm a little crispy and could use one of your notorious pick-me-ups."

"Funny, is that what you think of me, just another piece of telephone meat? Yeah, I'll talk dirty to you but I don't think it'll give you a hard on. Hell, if I was there I would probably cut your weenie off and give it to someone who knows how to use it." She snapped back.

"Do you think we should start this conversation over?"

"Sorry, I really miss you and worry I'll never see you again. Every time I look at that damned puppy I think of you," she said with a sigh.

"Was the puppy a bad idea?"

"No, it was a great idea. I love him almost as much as I love you. And I'll never let him go like I did you."

"Baby, I'm not gone. I'm just chasing a dream. When I figure it out, I'll bring you out here and show it to you and then you'll understand what I mean. Okay?"

"What am I supposed to do in the mean time? Sit and wait," she said matter-of-factly, "or just move on with my life? Please tell me because I don't know."

Colt remained silent for a while, contemplating what to say next. This wasn't what he needed to be worrying about but it was a fair question. Whatever he said could make or break their relationship, forever. It would be nice if he knew what he wanted, but he didn't. He could see spending the rest of his life with Annie-Laurie, almost. She brought out the best in him and she kept him grounded. It was like a plus and a minus, opposites attracted. He was rich, she wasn't. She was down to earth and he wanted to be. Their families would clash but whose didn't? Eh? She was beautiful in a real way, not a made-up way. She made him laugh and she made him cry. They could make beautiful babies and she would be a wonderful mother and a wonderful grandmother. The dogs obviously loved her. He looked over at Burly sleeping in the passenger seat. That dog had basically slept the entire trip; like he was going to wake up and be home and nothing had changed. Colt wondered if Burly missed Annie-Laurie. He wondered if Burly realized he had a son and would he know it if he saw him.

"Hello? Are you still there?" Annie said, bringing him back to reality.

"Yeah, I'm still here. Sorry, I'm just a little upset right now. It must be highway hypnosis. Annie, why don't we set a time line?"

"What's that supposed to mean?" She asked.

"Well, I'm not real sure. Everything seems to be so complicated. Do I stay, or do I go? What happens if I stay? What happens if I go? I really don't have the answers. I just think if we were meant to be together, this venture will solidify that and in time we'll know it. I wish we could jump ahead six weeks, twelve weeks or maybe even a year and look back to see what happened. Then everything should be crystal clear. You know what I'm saying?"

"No, what are you saying, Colt?"

"Annie, I'm not saying anything really. I guess I'm just asking for a little time to figure everything out. This move could help me find my true self. Does that make sense," he pleaded.

"No." She wasn't making it easy for him to bullshit around the subject.

"Okay, let's put the six-week card on the table. At the end of six weeks we flip it over and see what it says. Will you give me six weeks? That's all I ask."

"No, I think I'll go fuck your neighbor."

"Come on Annie, don't say that. Don't even joke about that. It's not funny. And he's ninety, you'd kill him," he replied trying to bring back some humor into the conversation.

"I'd kill you if I could get my hands on you right now," she responded. Not getting the humor. "All right," she paused. "I'll give you six weeks and then I'm going to go knock on his door, okay?" *What was she saying,* she asked herself. If she kept pushing him, she would surely push him away. That's the last thing she wanted to do. "Actually," she caught herself. "Take as long as you need. I love you. I'll wait. Gotta go…"
Click.

She dove on the bed and buried her face in the pillow and began sobbing. Salley knew something was wrong and he tried desperately to jump up on the bed to come to her rescue, but couldn't get up there. Eventually, he gave up and just sat at the foot of the bed and waited.

Lake Tahoe
Mosquito

Every time Cameron got depressed about his job or just down on himself, he would resort to watching his favorite movie *La dolce vita,* the 1960 Italian film by Federico Fellini. Paparazzo was a character in the film who was a news photographer. His named derived from a boy Fellini knew growing up who was notorious for being a fast talker. Paparazzo was the singular form of a word representing a particularly noisy, buzzing and annoying mosquito. Hence, the word Paparazzi represented the plural form. Cameron Toscanini, *Cameo the Shark*, as he was sometimes referred to by certain people, preferred to operate as a Paparazzo, going at his business alone instead of running with his fellow members of the Paparazzi. He was good at his job and earned a decent living selling his mug shots of famous people to various publications around the globe. The movie *La dolce vita* always seemed to calm him down and help him focus on what to do next. Cameron was a rather savvy businessman, invested wisely and was frugal in his lifestyle. Most people liked him because he wasn't pushy or annoying and most of his shots were unique, earning him a loyal following in the business.

On instinct, he buzzed up to Lake Tahoe from Los Angeles to check out the hot new resort, *Snowball.* Being an avid outdoorsman, he was intrigued that snowboarding had become so popular in such a short time. *How many times in a lifetime does someone invent something that ultimately becomes an Olympic sport,* he would ask himself. It was amazing. It wasn't just a craze, it was the real deal and this was the first resort just for snowboarders. Cameron was an accomplished skier, but he was dying to get on a board. So checking out the new resort was going to serve the two most important purposes in his life, business and pleasure. He'd been to Tahoe before and this was a great excuse to go back. It was a fantastic place by anyone's standards.

Cameron was a single, good looking Italian and successful. He liked people and people generally liked him which helped him immensely in his career. Nice people ultimately win in life and that's the way he chose to walk through it. But being in this business did have its downfalls. Some people flat out hated his guts and there was absolutely nothing he could do to change that. Cameron had his friends, but he also had his enemies.

Take this morning for example when that spoiled brat started screaming foul on the slopes because he snagged a picture of her sprawled out, face-first, on the slopes. Then some asshole came and took his camera, which was almost the final straw. It wasn't his fault she chose to fall in front of him. He was a beginner on the board himself. He just happened to have a sophisticated palm-sized digital camera on him at the time and it was a *Kodak moment.* He couldn't help himself. It was beautiful watching that twit eat snow. Of course the picture wasn't worth much today, but there was a possibility she would make it big time and then it would be worth a little more. He could wait. That bouncer or whatever the hell he was had ruined his day right when he was really getting into the board thing. Fortunately for him, he wasn't married, didn't own a home and basically had nowhere to go and wasn't in any hurry to get there, so he decided to swallow his pride and hang around for a while to see what other opportunities presented themselves. All he needed was clothes, cameras, laptop and, of course, his movie.

He was patient, unlike a mosquito. That was his virtue.

After he finished watching the movie, for the thousandth time, he got up from his king-sized bed, took a shower and packed his bags. Now that he'd made the decision to stay he would have to find some cheaper housing and get something to eat. Sitting at the desk, wrapped in a towel, he was going through some hotel brochures and noticed in one of the newer ones that *Snowball* provided some relatively inexpensive lodging for members of the media. *Now that's a first,* he thought to himself as he hurriedly dressed, grabbed his stuff and headed out the door. As he was driving beside the lake towards the resort, he couldn't help but notice the breathtaking beauty of Lake Tahoe. It was beyond any words in his vocabulary to describe. At that moment a joint would have been nice but he had given that up a while back. But thinking about getting high reminded him he was hungry. *Funny...* He pulled into this cute little roadside place called *The Flip Flop Inn.* Everything was decorated in the theme of flip flops, from the neon sign, doormat, door shutters, placemats and everything else you could imagine. The oddest part about it was it was in the middle of the mountains and not on a boardwalk on some beach. It was, in a sense, perfect, especially when he inhaled the aroma of pancakes and bacon. At four o'clock in the afternoon that was exactly what he wanted, breakfast.

He fell in love with the place before he even ordered and the owner made him feel completely at home. She was an adorable little lady with short, gray hair, probably in her early sixties with a business attitude that would impress Wall Street. Her employees, all three of them, looked like night skiers who worked by day to support their habits. The owner's name was Maggie and she was snapping her fingers at them, pointing out things that needed to be done immediately. These kids jumped into action for fear she would make them clean the bathrooms, which was her punishment of choice, he reckoned. Looking around, Cameron figured Maggie could easily seat fifty to sixty people at one time if she had to, but figured that was probably max for the entire day. *How often do people crave breakfast, right? Huh, probably more than not,* he mused. They had real red and white checkered linen tablecloths with white linen napkins rolled in napkin rings with fresh flowers on each table. With small, oil candles burning on each table and dim lighting, Cameron felt like he was back home in Italy, where he grew up a long, long time ago, in another life.

"What's in the back?" He asked the busboy cleaning the table next to him.

"Oh, that's a bar where we also do small parties," he replied.

"Is the bar open?"

"Nah, it opens for Happy Hour at five o'clock. Should be open by the time you finish eating."

"Thanks, I think a cold beer will go nicely after a plate of pancakes. What do you think?" He asked the boy.

"Sounds good to me," responded the busboy shaking his head and smiling.

Any good mosquito can find his way to a watering hole, Cameron thought to himself. After devouring pancakes, eggs, bacon, sausage links and homemade biscuits, he had two ice cold draft beers for dessert at the quaint little bar. He smiled happily to himself, satisfied that he'd found this special place.

Filled to the happy brim, Cameron headed over to *Snowball* to check in. He was duly impressed with the accommodations. After he checked in, he was politely directed to the media bunkhouse. He was surprised to discover that each bed was in its own stall, complete with a small plasma television, dresser and fresh sheets. The showers were located at one end of the building. A very nice oval gas fireplace was located in the center, surrounded by sofas and chairs. The entire interior was lined with cedar and it smelled woody, rustic, and cozy. There was a *great* front porch with six rocking chairs and the bunkhouse had wireless. In any other resort, it could easily cost him a hundred and fifty to two hundred dollars a night. He was getting all this, plus three meals a day at the employee cafeteria and lift passes for seventy-five dollars a night. And, he was allowed to stay as long as there wasn't a waiting list. He counted the bunk-house could sleep ten people. So far he appeared to be the only one there so he decided to hang around for a while and really get a feel for the whole package. Since he'd already been on the slopes, he would spend the next day or two learning everything he could about the resort. If there were any stars floating around he wanted to know the best angles to pick-em-off. *La dolce vita!*

San Francisco

"**I**sland Time Properties, San Francisco Office, how may I help you?"

"Good morning," this polite male voice said over the phone. "Would it be possible to speak with Mr. Giles? My name is Colt Salley, from Virginia," he added for no reason in particular.

"I'm sorry but Mr. Giles is out for the day. May I give him a message?"
Colt was devastated. It might be impossible to talk to this guy if he has a huge firewall set up. He didn't travel across the entire country to be locked out at the gate. She sounded pleasant enough, so he continued,

"I just arrived in San Francisco and I was wondering if it would it be okay if I dropped something off for him?" Colt asked while crossing his fingers.

"Sure, do you know where we're located?" she replied.

"Haven't a clue," Colt sighed in relief, which wasn't exactly true because his car had a state-of-the-art navigation system. *It could probably deliver the package for him.* "This is a completely different world out here compared to back home in Virginia."

"I'm sure," she said, "I really like your accent."

"Thank you."

"Anyway," she giggled, "here is the address. I'm not sure where you are staying, but it might be easier if you came by taxi."

"I think I can find it. By the way, what's your name?"

"Brandi"

"Nice," he said.

"Thanks"

"I do have one more question if you don't mind?"

"Sure, what is it?"

"Could I bring my dog with me? I don't have anywhere to park him and I can't leave him outside," he nicely pleaded.

"I, ah, I guess. No one has ever asked me that before. I don't care."

"Great"

Colt was sitting in his car, parked in front of the closest wine shop his navigation could give him to Hansen's office. He figured it would take him about ten minutes to get there. He wanted to get there quickly after they talked so he wouldn't be an afterthought for Brandi.

"Guard the car, Burly, I'll be right back." Burly never opened his eyes. He just took a deep breath and sighed. *It must have been that long, long drive through Kansas that did him in*, Colt joked to himself as he hopped out of the car. "Don't worry buddy, the trip is almost over," Colt said as he softly shut the car door.

"May I help you?" The clerk asked politely.

"Yes, I'm looking for a nice Cabernet to give as a gift," Colt responded.

"Domestic or foreign or does it matter?"

"When in Rome," Colt smiled as he spread out his arms, "let's go with California."

"Okay, let me see," the clerk paused, "I have a Chateau Montelena, a complex flavor of cherry, tobacco and licorice. I like to call it a *Big Red.* It goes great with steaks. I haven't found anyone who doesn't like it. It'll run you eighty dollars, which works out to about one hundred and fifty dollars in the restaurants," said the clerk while he was walking down one of the aisles to retrieve it. "Here you go," he said as he picked up a bottle off the lower rack. "I highly recommend it," he smiled.

"In that case, give me two bottles. If it's that good then I will have to drink one myself," Colt laughed.

"I hear you, brother."

"Do you have a really nice sleeve for me to put it in, and a gift card?" Colt asked, as an afterthought.

"Absolutely, I think I have just what you need. I'll put our card in the other bag in case we can help you in the future."

"Oh, I'll be back," replied Colt.

"By the way, that's a nice looking Porsche. I noticed it before you even pulled up out front."

"Thanks, you should see the dog," Colt joked as he walked out.

"Island Time Properties, San Francisco Office, how may I help you?"

"How's my number one employee doing?"

"Hello Mr. Giles. I'm your only employee," she laughed. "How was *Snowball*?"

"Not good, it's going to need some work, but we'll get it straight. Do I have any messages?"

"No sir. Things have been pretty quiet around here."

"Good. I'm almost back in San Fran so I think I will head to my office at home. There are a few things I need to research. Call me there if you need me" he said.

"Will do… oh, Mr. Giles, there is someone by the name of Colt Salley who is dropping something off for you this morning. Says he's from Virginia. He has kind of a strange name if you ask me, but he seemed really nice on the phone."

Hansen had been so distracted lately that he had completely forgotten about this guy. He still had his letter and resume in his briefcase and was pulling it out to refresh his memory while he still had Brandi on the phone. Recalling his conversation with Josh Witherspoon several days ago, he was intrigued because this Colt fellow had actually come out to California.

"Brandi."

"Yes sir?"

"When he shows up, excuse yourself for a second and go into my office and call me, okay?"

"Sure," she replied hesitantly. "Is there anything you want me to tell him?"

"I'll let you know when you call."

"Okay."

The first thing she noticed was the dog with a red bandanna around its neck as the two walked in the office. *Now that is a handsome chocolate lab,* she thought to herself. It was odd only because she had never seen a dog in the building before. She forgot this gentleman said he was bringing one along. When she finally took her eyes off the dog and looked up, she almost dropped her pen. She was staring at the most beautiful man she'd ever seen in her life. He had sandy blond hair, styled long to his shoulders and big blue eyes with dimples a mile deep. He had a ruggedly-wonderful-handsome- gorgous-lovely face, accented by a five-o'clock shadow that was to die for, all of which were completed by an incredible smile with perfectly straight white teeth. He was wearing a white dress shirt, exactly the same shade of white as his teeth, a tan hounds' tooth sport coat, blue jeans and hiking boots. She noticed all of this in about one-millionth of a second and without taking her eyes off his.

"You must be Brandi," Mr. *Beautiful Man* said.

"I sure am. And you must be Mr. Salley? I'm only guessing because of the dog," she inquired with a big smile of her own because Mr. Salley had just made her day. In fact, he just made her entire year. She had met quite a few interesting people working with Mr. Giles: from movie stars to politicians, and she was as well polished in social situations as the best of them, but no one had caught her off guard like Mr. *what was his first name again? Salley? Whaaaaaat?* "I see you found us," she said with as much composure as she could muster.

"Well, I kind of cheated. I have a navigation system in my car."

"I like your dog," she said, trying to get him to look down at the dog so she could really check him out. Unfortunately, he didn't look down so she was stuck staring into his incredibly beautiful, sensitive, loving and caring Caribbean-blue eyes. Once again, she was thinking outside of the box, or just hoping he would crawl in it. *Hers that is.*

"Brandi, I would like you to meet Burly. He's traveled all the way across the country, lying in the front seat of a very cramped car, just to meet you," Colt boasted. He was equally impressed by this beautiful brunette with dark brown eyes who had a most pleasant and seemingly genuine personality. Unfortunately, his alarm bells went off because he guiltily thought about Annie-Laurie back in Virginia. *She wouldn't like this,* he thought to himself. *Not one bit. No way.* However, he had to play the game because Brandi was the key to getting to Mr. Giles and that was why he was there. *Things could be worse,* he laughed to himself as he stared at this beautiful woman. *Maybe the most beautiful woman he's ever seen.*

Knowing she was going to have to slip down the hallway and call Mr. Giles, petting the dog provided a nice excuse for her to get up. So Brandi stood up, straightened her light pink turtle neck at the waistline, slipped her shoes on and walked around her desk and bent down to rub Burly's face. She loved dogs and she especially loved this one. *My day just became very interesting,* she happily thought to herself.

"He's so sweet," she said as she stood up and once again straightened her turtleneck at the waistline, although her basic instinct was to get down on her knees and offer Mr. Salley a nice welcome to California. "I know this may appear to be rude, but would you mind having a seat for just a few minutes. I have something I needed to do about an hour ago and I got distracted and forgot to do it. It will only take a few minutes. Okay?"

"Oh… sure, I hope I didn't interrupt you barging in somewhat unannounced," Colt said as he immediately walked over and took a seat. He had no intentions of leaving. On instinct, Burly walked right beside him, plopped down at his feet and stared back at her. Colt could tell Burly liked her. He was a smart dog. Brandi, smiled, turned and waltzed down the hallway like a runway model. Colt would have preferred if she was still barefooted because he liked that natural look, but her three-inch heels highlighted an amazing pair of legs. Both Colt and Burly watched her until she disappeared around the corner with both of them tilting their heads simultaneously to the left when she made the turn to the right. Burly looked up at Colt and as if to say *nice* and then looked back in her direction, waiting for her to come back.

"Hansen."

"Mr. Giles, Mr. Salley is here," she whispered even though there was no way Mr. Salley could hear her from all the way down the hall and with the door closed. Brandi had enough time to collect her thoughts and become curious as what Mr. Giles wanted with him.

"So, what do you think?" He asked.

"Excuse me…what do you mean?"

"So what's your first impression of him? Be honest."

"Well," she paused, "aside from the fact that I could fall in love with him, marry him, have twenty of his amazing-looking children and live happily ever after, he's a really nice guy. Oh, and did I say he was a really nice guy?" She repeated to emphasize how she really felt.

Hansen smiled on the other end of the line while listening to her. Mr. Colt Salley from Virginia obviously had made a very good first impression on her. Obviously, he passed the first test. Hansen was thinking about his conversation with Josh Witherspoon and how Josh described him. It was all adding up now. *One thing was for sure*, Hansen thought, *Colt Salley's timing couldn't have been better.*

"Brandi, I need to meet this guy and I really don't feel like coming into town. I want you to lock up the office and bring Mr. Salley out here. I'll have lunch ready when you get here," he finished.

"Do you think he'll come?" She asked.

"Oh yeah, he'll definitely come. That's why he's here. He wants to work for us," Hansen said matter-of-factly. "What do think about that? Does he have potential?"

"Well," she hesitated trying to hide her excitement, "there is definitely some potential. I think you are really going to like him. He kind of reminds me of you in some ways."

"That might not be a good thing," Hansen joked. "Bring him anyway."

"He has a dog."

"What?"

"He has his dog with him. But he's a really good dog," she quickly added. "He brought him with him from Virginia."

"Whatever," Hansen replied, not really knowing what to say. "Bring him too."

"Okay, see you in a little bit," She was already thinking about the ride to Mr. Giles' house with Mr. Salley. She hoped she wouldn't do anything out of the ordinary because she was definitely going to be tempted.

Both dog and man were smiling when she rounded the corner and both dog and man enjoyed watching her walk down the hallway towards them. She was a little flushed, but she was woman enough to enjoy their undivided attention. *And that's why she ran a thousand miles a day. Just to please them. Now, it was all worth it.*

"You're not going to believe this," she said as she approached Colt, "but while I was completing my little project, Mr. Giles called in and now he wants me to bring you out to his home to meet you. He just got back into town and would prefer not to come all the way into the city. He said he would feed you lunch?"

"What about..?" Colt said pointing down to Burly.

"He comes too," She said. "I'll call Mr. Hansen's driver to come get pick us up."

"Let's take my car," Colt said, trying to hide his excitement, "It'll be quicker and more fun." He shouldn't have said that last part. That was Burly talking, not him.

"Brandi, may I ask you a question?"

"Sure"

"What is your last name?"

"Steele, with an e," she smiled.

"Do you know my name?"

"Mr. Salley"

"Do you know my first name?" He continued.

"I forgot...sorry," she responded, shrugging her shoulders, somewhat embarrassed.

"It's Colt. Please don't feel embarrassed," he added for reassurance. "I'm not sure I mentioned it anyway."

"That's an unusual name," she added while she walked around to get her belongings. "Where did it come from?"

"It came from the fact that my last name is Salley. And with a name like that, my parents decided to throw me a bone and give me a manlier first name," he laughed. "They picked Colt for some strange reason that I'll never figure out. To me, Colt Salley sounds like the title of a really bad seventy's song," he laughed. "Anyway, it's Colt and I am very happy to make your acquaintance." It was going to be a very interesting day so he thought it best to level the playing field. He realized very quickly he had to not only win-over Mr. Giles, but he had to win her over as well. "And please call me Colt. I don't respond well to Salley."

"Okay, so Colt it is. Do you have room for me in your car?"

"I would throw everything I own into the street to make room for you," he said. "Seriously, I'm not kidding."

"What about Burly, would you throw him out too?"

"No, I would throw myself out and let you and Burly drive off into the sunset together. Truth be known, you'd probably have more fun with him."

Good answer! She thought to herself. Although, she was pretty sure she would have more fun with a one Mr. Colt Salley. *Does he have a clue how unbelievably hot he is? It is definitely time to re-name my vibrator. I might have to buy some lithium batteries as well. Longer lasting.*

She wasn't the least bit surprised he drove a Porsche, even though it was an SUV. She would've been more surprised if he didn't. After some major rearranging of luggage, short of actually throwing some bags out in the street, Colt created enough space for Burly in the back seat and they all hopped in and headed out of the city. Other than giving an occasional direction, there was mostly silence going down the road. He was thinking about what he was going to say to Mr. Giles and she was thinking about how she could sleep with him and get away with it.

"Where are you staying in San Francisco?" She finally asked.

"Nowhere yet, I checked-in to an Embassy Suites early this morning to catch a shower before coming over. I also checked-out because they don't allow dogs. I guess I'll have to figure that out later. Do you have any suggestions?"

Oh yeah, she had some suggestions! "You checked in just to take a shower?"

"Had to, you should have seen me. It was not good."

"I find that hard to..." *Oops! How did that slip out?* "I mean, I wonder why they wouldn't let you check-in with a dog. That's so unfair to the dog." It wasn't a complete recovery but it was the best she could do.

"Not everybody is animal friendly," he helped her out. "No big deal, I'll find a place. It might be some fleabag dump," he added. He almost asked her to tell him about Mr. Giles but thought better of it. She might get offended by being put on the spot so he said, "Where are you from?"

"All over," she responded, "my father was in the military. We moved around quite a bit. If I had to say one place, it would be right here. I've lived here for longer than anywhere else. It's definitely home."

"It's beautiful."

"Thank you," although she wasn't sure why she said that. She had absolutely nothing to do with its beauty.

They spent the rest of the time talking about San Francisco and Virginia. She had a minor in History with a major in Urban and Regional Planning, which certainly explained why she worked for Mr. Giles. The countryside became more beautiful the further away from the city they went. He was enjoying her good company and found it helpful to have her along. Colt couldn't tell if Brandi was Mr. Giles' co-worker, girlfriend, or Administrative Assistant. He figured it was the latter because of her degree but wasn't sure because she called him Mr. Giles so he kept the conversation casual, as far away from his personal side as he could. Occasionally, his mind would wonder to a much darker side than where it should be. The longer he was with Brandi, the further away he was from Annie-Laurie and that wasn't good. Virginia was beginning to seem like a distant memory. Eventually, they turned off the main road on to a long private drive lined with some sort of Leyland Cypress trees, as best as Colt could figure. He was enjoying her company so much he'd almost forgotten what he was going to say to Mr. Giles, so he started concentrating on his surroundings again. They continued on for about a mile, winding through beautiful tree-lined pastures and small pockets of hardwood forests. Finally, they went through a picturesque Pennsylvanian-styled wooden arched bridge over a large creek and headed uphill towards a stately antiquated mansion. It was impressive to say the least but completely different than what Colt expected. He'd figured a more modern home with all the bells and whistles that you'd typically see in homes featured in magazines, but certainly not something you would see in *Southern Living.* As they pulled around the large circular entrance to the front, they were greeted by a virtual cornucopia of animals wandering freely around the beautifully landscaped grounds ranging from chickens, a turkey, two cats and two beautiful yellow labs. Burly perked up at the scent of the animals but remained calm. Burly was a patient dog.

When they came to a stop directly in front the house, the front door opened and Hansen Giles walked down the steps to greet them. Brandi was first out of the car and walked up and gave Mr. Giles a hug instead of a handshake, Colt noticed. Colt told Burly to stay when he got out of the car because the possibly of a dog fight or maybe the chickens becoming a point of interest for him would be a bad thing when Colt was trying to make an impression.

"Go ahead and let your dog out, Colt," said Mr. Giles warmly. "If I had to make an educated guess, I would say it has been in the car a rather long time. Don't worry, my animals won't mind. They're all free out here and they don't have any pent-up anxieties to make them aggressive."

"Thank you," was all Colt could muster, hoping Burly would behave himself. The last thing he needed was a half-eaten chicken lying on the steps. Mr. Giles was right, it had been a long ride and Burly needed to stretch his legs and act like a dog again. After a series of the dogs doing circles and sniffing each other to satisfy their curiosities, they starting running and chasing each other like they were long lost cousins finally getting together at the family picnic.

"You're right, it has been a long trip," Colt said to Mr. Giles as he walked towards him to shake his hand and formally introduce himself. He did reflect that Mr. Giles addressed him by his first name and thought that was a good start. "Colt Salley, nice to meet you sir," he said. "Thank you so much for agreeing to meet with me and you couldn't have a more beautiful setting," he finished as he looked around at the surroundings for emphasis.

"Thank you," replied Hansen. "It is beautiful out here. I'm very fortunate to have found it. The problem is it makes it very hard to go to the office in San Fran, that's for sure. Sorry..." he smiled to Brandi. "Anyway, let's let the dogs run around while we get down to business." He said as he turned and headed back up the steps. As an afterthought, Colt went back to his car to retrieve the bottle of wine he bought for Mr. Giles. Following Brandi up the steps he couldn't help but notice Burly tearing off through the pasture with the other dogs. *Well, that's a good start,* he thought to himself.

"Welcome to my home," Hansen said as Colt walked into the large, elaborately furnished foyer.

"Wow!" Colt said as he looked around. "This is beautiful! It reminds me of the plantations back in Virginia," he added.

"Well, I consider that a compliment," Hansen said.

"I hope you enjoy wine, Mr. Giles," Colt said as he gave him the gift.

"I drink it like water," said Hansen as he opened the sleeve and pulled out the bottle of Chateau Montelena. "Nice choice," he said to Colt, "this is one of my favorites."

"I had help," Colt admitted with a smile.

Hansen noticed Brandi staring at Colt like he was some kind of god and had to stifle a laugh. She was right. He did have some magnetic qualities and you could feel their pull immediately. "If you don't mind, I've arranged for a working lunch in my office. We'll have this great bottle of wine with it." They walked to the far end of the front-to-back foyer and exited out the rear of the home into a breathtaking view of distant rolling hills and endless, impeccable landscaping. The winding path, through every flower known to man, eventually led them to the converted stable where Hansen's office was located.

Colt had seen a lot of palatial settings in his short life but none to this degree of impressiveness. He was in awe when he walked into the converted stable. The two-thousand square foot building had been converted into the most unbelievable office he'd ever seen. The entire room was trimmed out with three-foot wide white pine boards complete with pine beams crisscrossing the vaulted ceiling. The pine had been shellacked to a level where it looked as if it was coated with a fine layer of glass. There was a massive stone fireplace at one end of the room and a set of huge French doors leading to an outside patio, giving way to a spectacular view of a lake and rolling pastures at the other end. One side of the massive room was lined with completely filled bookshelves. In the middle of the room, there was a huge, oval shaped, pine conference table for twelve people shadowed by a multi-antler chandelier perfectly centered above it. Hansen's desk, which was accented by four comfortable leather chairs, was situated at the other end of the long room. A huge set of French doors, which allowed for natural lighting, were directly behind his desk. Hansen could sit there, stare all the way across the room into the fire burning in the fireplace or swivel his chair around and gaze outside at the beautiful landscape of California. Colt noticed lunch was already set up at the conference table, which was a welcomed relief because all of a sudden he was starving.

Hansen slid a long pocket door on the side wall opposite the bookshelves to expose a fabulous wet bar backed by mirrors. There was also a thermostatically controlled floor-to-ceiling white wine cooler to the left of the wet bar with a similar one to the right for reds, each holding approximately two-hundred bottles respectively. In a room like this, one would expect to see trophies of exotic animal heads from all around the world, but Colt was pleased to see there were none. He was an avid outdoorsman but not a hunter and he enjoyed seeing the natural beauty of the animals, not the trophy version. Hansen was opening the wine while Brandi made her way over to Hansen's desk to make a quick phone call. The fact that she didn't say anything told Colt she was just checking for messages. Colt continued to stroll around the room to marvel in its beauty and eventually settled with one foot on the stone hearth of the fireplace staring into the crackling fire and reflecting how he was lucky enough to get this far. He smiled when he realized the soft music playing in the background was the sound of Blackberry Smoke, one of his personal favorites. *How ironic,* he thought to himself.

Conversation was light and cordial during lunch, mostly

revolving around the beauty of Hansen's estate and the conversion of the stable into his office. It was kept casual so everyone could get to know each other in a relaxed way. Lunch started with a Waldorf salad, a wonderful assortment of sliced cheeses with crisp wafers followed by smoked salmon and thinly sliced London broil with fried cinnamon-apple rings on the side. It was a fantastic compilation of flavors and the wine was excellent. Dessert consisted of sliced bananas drizzled in a zebra-like fashion of chocolate and caramel syrup. There was a fresh thermos of delicious coffee served as a perfect compliment to end the meal. Colt learned that Hansen had a girlfriend who lived in Los Angeles and they traveled to see each other frequently. That erased his questions about the relationship between Brandi and Mr. Giles. At first he wasn't sure whether anything was going on between them and was comforted to realize theirs was a strictly business relationship. This worked better for Colt because there was never any room for a third wheel when a relationship was involved, whether it was business or personal. He couldn't help but notice she had flawless manners and beautiful posture. He also couldn't help but notice her catching him looking at her. He was embarrassed and hoped Mr. Giles didn't pick up on this, but he really couldn't help himself because she was quite captivating. She would simply smile at Colt and turn her focus back to Mr. Giles' conversation.

After lunch was finished, a somewhat elderly woman appeared out of nowhere with a rolling cart and politely removed the dishes from the table. She exited as quietly as she entered. *There must be a buzzer underneath the table at Mr. Giles' fingertips so he could summon her without making a production out of it,* Colt figured. Mr. Giles happened to have another bottle of Chateau Montelena in his collection, so he opened it and re-filled everyone's glasses. When Colt got up from the table he was pleased to see the labs, including Burly, were lying outside by the French doors exhausted from the miles they obviously covered in the past hour and a half. Totally full and completely relaxed, the three of them retired to the couches by the fire to discuss why, exactly, Colt had shown up in their lives.

"Well, Colt," Hansen started, "judging from your letter you want to work for me. Obviously you have a fascination with *Snowball*."

"Mr. Giles, first of…"

"Colt, I fully appreciate your southern mannerisms, being from Virginia and all, but please feel free to call me by my first name, Hansen. Everybody else does, except for Brandi here," he nodded towards her with a smile. "No matter how hard I try, I can't get her to do it so I've given up. But please, drop the mister, okay?"

"Sure, Hansen," Colt easily transitioned. "Anyway, for the past couple of years I lived near a small mountain resort in Virginia and had various jobs there. I loved the lifestyle and I loved the attitudes of people when they're vacationing. I noticed they also spend a lot of money when they play. During my time there I've become an avid snowboarder and until I read the article about you in *Board Mag,* my life was complete. I was extremely content and had no intentions of doing anything else. I have been very fortunate and have been lucky enough to be able to choose a lifestyle that fits my personality, not the opposite. But when I read about *Snowball,* I knew that in some way, shape or form I had to be a part of it. By nature, I'm very creative and have an unbelievable admiration for other people's creativity as well. *Snowball* is so far out of the box it blew my mind. What a risk! What a gamble and what a fascinating concept! I too, believe snowboarding is big enough to stand on its own. I have traveled extensively enough to appreciate your vision and I desperately want to be a part of it.

I desperately want you to be a part of it too, thought Brandi as she sat there mesmerized by the handsomeness of this man and the beautiful sounds that came out of his mouth when he talked. Occasionally, she would sneak a peek at Mr. Giles to see if he felt the same way or if he was simply bored. She was happy to see that Mr. Giles was sitting on the edge of his chair soaking in everything Colt was saying. Relieved, she would turn her attention back to her dirty thoughts. At this point, she didn't care about what he was talking about, just the fact that he was there and talking was good enough, almost.

"I hear what you're saying Colt. You're definitely making me feel pretty good about what I've done, but what do you want to do? That's what I'm confused about. How can I help you?" He asked, although he'd already figured it out. He just wanted to hear it from Colt.

"Hansen, I will do anything from washing dishes, driving a snow cat, being a bartender or becoming an investor. I just want to be a part of it, as small or as big of a part as you will let me. You planted the seed to a new species of tree and I would like to watch that tree grow. Just like what Jake Burton did when he invented the sport."

"Colt, this is where I'm confused. You have the desire to simply be a dishwasher, yet you are also willing to become an investor? That's a pretty wide spectrum of involvement. Could you be happy being a dishwasher when you apparently have some disposable assets that would make washing dishes seem somewhat mundane to your lifestyle?" Hansen asked, because everything depended on Colt's next answer. This was the litmus test to determine how real the passion was.

"I wouldn't say it if I didn't mean it," was Colt's response.

"Good answer, Colt. I'm impressed.

Yeah, great answer, thought Brandi.

"Where are you staying in San Francisco?" Hansen asked.

"I haven't gotten that far yet," Colt replied. "I'm working on it though," which wasn't entirely true. "I'm not familiar with San Francisco and I have the dog which limits me."

"May I offer a suggestion?"

"Absolutely," Colt replied.

"Why don't you let your dog stay out here for a couple of days? Judging by the way they all seem to be getting along, I don't think it will be a problem," Hansen said as he pointed to the dogs sleeping side-by-side out on the patio. "I think he'll be fine and it certainly won't bother me. I absolutely love animals.

I can have Brandi get you checked into the Hyatt downtown for tonight and then she can take you out to see the resort tomorrow. I want you to stay out there for a couple of days and I want to know what you think after you see it and experience it for the first time. After I hear what you have to say, I'll make a decision. Does that sound fair?"

This day just keeps getting better and better, thought Brandi.

Colt couldn't believe what he was hearing. In his wildest of dreams, he never thought he'd get this far this fast. Although, he knew eventually he'd get there.

"Absolutely, I'm honored for the opportunity. I can tell you one thing, Hansen."

"What's that?"

"You won't be disappointed, I guarantee that."

"I sincerely hope not," Hansen responded.

We all sincerely hope not, thought Brandi. She was already packing.

It was a pleasant trip back into the city. Colt felt very good about the meeting and was extremely excited to finally get the chance to see *Snowball* firsthand. He'd already formulated a few ideas on his own so it would be interesting to see if they would work up there. Brandi drove his car because the plan evolved where she would drop him off at the Hyatt and pick him up early the next morning. They'd agreed to take his car to Lake Tahoe, that way he wouldn't have to worry about parking at the hotel, she mentioned. When she dropped him off with his overnight bag, he left the rest of his luggage in the car so he wouldn't have to transfer it twice. He was surprised how exhausted he really was. It had been a long journey. Not one to feel particularly comfortable confined to a single hotel room, Colt decided to call Annie-Laurie before heading down to the bar in the hotel and have drink as a small celebration.

"Hey," was all she said when she answered the phone. She knew he absolutely hated that. *Hey* meant she was bored when he called, she couldn't even fake it.

"Hey yourself," he responded now that she had successfully killed his excitement. "How are you doing?"

"Fine"

"Great," he tried to sound upbeat. He was hoping for the same response but all he heard was the air whistling out of his own nose because there was nothing but silence on the other end.

"So, um, are you the least bit interested about what I'm up to out here?"

"Not really."

"Come on, Annie, don't do this to me. You know why I'm here and you said it was fine with you."

"I never said it was fine," she shot back. He could almost hear the spit hit the phone. *Or was it venom?*

"Okay, what do you want me to do, Annie?"

"Move on, Colt. I did," was her cold response."

"Move on, where? Move on to what?"

"Colt," she was crying now, "I'm not getting any younger. I'm thirty–two years old and you're twenty-nine. There is a huge difference there."

"Three years? Are you kidding me?"

"Three years is a big difference between a man and a woman when the woman is older. My clock is ticking and I want to start a family. If I waited for you to come back and for us to find each other and feel like we are meant to be together, that could take another three or four more years. I'm not waiting."

"What are you saying? What are you going to do?"

"Colt, I've had some time to think. You're a high-class guy and I'm low to middle. You can't come down and I wouldn't do well trying to move up. We get along great because of our differences but it would be like atoms colliding at the core if we merged. It would go nuclear. So what I'm going to do is seek someone at my own level, someone who I have a lot in common with. I'm going to move on with my life. I understand you more than you do yourself and I know what I'm saying is right."

"Annie, I was just calling to say hello and check in. I really didn't expect all of this," he responded. "I'm sorry but I'm totally confused."

"And I'm going to straighten you out. I'm done. It's over. Good-bye."

Click

Colt held the phone to his ear until the silence finally broke his concentration. He slowly put the earpiece down on the receiver. She was right and he knew it. It's not what he wanted to hear, but it was true. He wasn't in any hurry to start a family and he couldn't expect her to wait around until he was. It would be ludicrous for him to expect that. Besides, his mother would chew her up and spit her out like a piece of bubble gum and he could never allow that to happen to Annie-Laurie. He had family obligations he couldn't ignore either. That drink at the bar just went from a celebration to a pity party for one.

"**G**ood morning Mr. Colt Salley. How was your stay at the Hyatt?" Brandi asked while she was still sitting in the driver's seat of his Porsche. Obviously, she was planning on doing the driving to *Snowball*, which was fine with him. After several straight whiskeys at the bar last night he wasn't in the mood to multi-task by driving and talking at the same time. He tossed his overnight bag in the back and hopped in the passenger seat to settle in and move on with his life. He'd thought about Annie-Laurie all night, to the point where he was done. No matter how he looked at it, she was right and to fight it would be pure hell for both of them. He would always love her and would always have great memories of her but he needed more at this point in his life. *It's a new day,* he thought to himself, *let's roll.*

"It was good," he replied nonchalantly, "uneventful."

"You mean you didn't go out and see San Francisco?"

"I was too worn out from the long drive out here to the west coast. I think it finally hit me. I just wanted to get some rest before we got on the road this morning. Besides, I'm not much of a player. There's nothing out there that I feel like I need to see, alone," he added.

"I totally understand," she said while she was digesting all this new information he was giving her. *He doesn't like to be alone, he's not a player and he doesn't feel like there's a lot out there that he needs to see. Welcome to my life,* she thought.

She had picked up coffee and doughnuts for the ride and told him they would stop in Sacramento for lunch. So he sat back and prepared to move on. It might have been a little more difficult if Brandi wasn't so beautiful. Regardless of how he felt about Annie-Laurie, Brandi was entering his mind like water entering a sponge. He'd have to be real careful not to rock that boat. Or, so he thought. He sensed she was attracted to him but wasn't sure. He was beginning to feel guilty about Annie-Laurie and he was also feeling guilty about his attraction to Brandi so quickly. Totally preoccupied with his wandering mind, he had to ask her to repeat the question she just asked him.

"My question was…," she paused to make sure she had his attention, "so what did you see when you were staring at me from across the banquet table yesterday?" She never took her eyes off the road to look at him to see the shock on his face.

Colt moved around in his seat as if he was uncomfortable but he was really buying time to digest the question and make sure he fully understood it before he responded. Putting his foot in his mouth was a mistake he couldn't afford to make. Saying the wrong thing could bury him before he got started. She did, after all, work for Hansen. The same guy Colt wanted to work for.

"By the way, this is California, not Virginia," she added.

"What's that supposed to mean?" He asked still trying to buy more time.

"Things out here are probably a little more …progressive, you might say, as opposed to say… Virginia."

"Keep talking," Colt said, "I'm not sure where you're going with this but you definitely have my attention."

"No thank you. I think I've said enough for the time being.

Chew on that and get back to me, okay?" She said as she glanced over to him and made quick eye contact. She wasn't the least bit embarrassed or shy or remorseful for having potentially crossed the line.

"Don't you think it would be a conflict of interest?" He finally said after about three miles of silence.

"I told you this is California. All the lawyers are on the east coast," she joked.

"Okay…, what about Hansen? What would he say? I really want to make a go of this and would hate to do anything to mess it up. You understand that don't you?"

"I figured that's what you'd say. Look, Hansen has a life, I have a life and you have a life. We're all adults here. I'm allowed to do what I want and so are you. And besides, all I asked you is what did you see when you were staring at me from across the table yesterday? I didn't ask you to take your clothes off…, yet," she added as she looked over at him to get a visual on his response.

"Yet," he laughed shyly. "I caught that."

"I was just throwing you a bone. Chew on it."

Colt quit staring at her and looked straight ahead not knowing what else to say. *She was much bolder than he pictured her to be yesterday,* he thought to himself. *Wow!*
They didn't talk again until she pulled off the interstate in Sacramento for lunch. Obviously, she didn't care what he wanted to eat because she drove into town and stopped at this adorable little restaurant named *Tilly's.*

"I think you'll like this place," she said. "I stop here every time I go up to Tahoe. They have great food and it's cheap."

"I'm looking forward to it then," he replied as they got out and walked in.

"What a handsome couple," the elderly maitre de said as he greeted and seated them. They both looked at each other and said simultaneously "Thanks".

"What I saw was an extremely beautiful girl with a remarkable smile and a wonderful personality," he said out of the blue to break the silence after they'd ordered.

"Thank you," she said. "That's what I was hoping you saw. So what took you so long to tell me?"

"Well, my girlfriend just broke up with me last night so I didn't think it was appropriate to say anything yesterday."

"I'm truly sorry," she said. "I didn't mean to put you on the spot. I guess I misjudged your situation. I hope you'll forgive me."

"I forgive you," he joked to ease the situation. "It wasn't meant to be anyway. We were on different wavelengths and someone would have gotten hurt in the long run. That's life I guess," he finished with a sigh.

After lunch, which was absolutely delicious, Colt paid and they walked out to the car. Before they got in, Brandi turned and wrapped her arms around him, dropped her head in his chest and gave him a big warm hug. He hugged her back because he really wanted to even though he knew it was probably the wrong thing to do. They stood there, leaning against the driver's-side door for a long time without saying anything, just holding each other tightly. Their bodies were touching from head to toe and she could feel him getting excited. It took all of her will power to back away and walk around to the passenger side of the car. She wanted him and she wanted him to want her, she didn't want to be the life raft of despair. He stood there awhile to collect himself before he got behind the wheel.

"That was nice. Very nice," he said after he got in. Brandi didn't say a word as she stared out the passenger side window. Finally, after they got back on the road, she looked over at him and said "I hope one day I can take your pain away." He looked over as she undid her seatbelt and leaned over and gave him the softest kiss he'd ever had. He almost ran off the road but he didn't have the energy to stop her and he didn't want to stop her. He moaned softly as she stared at him to make sure she had his approval.

"Welcome to California," she said.

"It's good to be here." *It really was.* "But do you think that was a little quick?"

"I think life is a little quick," she said seriously. "I'm not a strong believer in waiting for something I want."

"I believe you," Colt said still trying to catch his breath.

The rest of the ride was pure Porsche. When they rolled into Lake Tahoe, it was late afternoon, but plenty of time to enjoy the beauty and tranquility of the area. He pulled over so they could switch seats because he wanted to take everything in and not worry about driving. She was having fun watching his animated expressions, acting like a kid, pointing to this and that, while telling her about places he's been and why Tahoe was so special. He didn't have to sell her but he was doing a good job of it anyway. She couldn't wait for him to see the resort, but she took her time because she wasn't in any hurry for the day to end.

Colt was amazed when they pulled into the resort. Instead of columns, or a big sign welcoming you, there were two giant snowballs, one on each side of the entrance. Each one was the size of a house. *It was genius because it said nothing, yet the giant snowballs said everything.* Normally, most places hit you with a parking lot before you actually get to see what they have to offer. *Snowball* was different because the road in was lined with trees on one side and on the other side it followed the contour of a huge, gentle slope which led into the village. So driving into the village, you were actually driving side-by-side with the boarders coming down the mountain, which gave you the feeling you were going into a very special place. This was designed to get you excited before you even got there. The road turned and dropped with the slope and offered an incredible head-on overview of a wonderfully rustic, picturesque, brand new log cabin-style village. Smoke was rising from the middle of the courtyard as well as from many chimneys of the surrounding buildings nestled in the small valley. One side of the village offered an incredible view of Lake Tahoe with huge decks built specifically to take advantage of the view of the lake. The other side offered an incredible view of the vast, gently flowing snowboard slopes winding their snow-covered paths up into the beautiful Sierra Nevada's. *This is like a post card,* Colt thought to himself as he remained in awe of everything he was seeing. The entrance road did not go directly into the village proper, but instead, it swung around to the left and looped up behind to a massive parking lot which was invisible to any other location in the entire resort. The second they parked a small shuttle bus pulled up behind them and the driver got out, helped them with their luggage, then proceeded to drop them off at the main lodge for check-in. The driver was a bit distant and quiet on the drive to the lodge and that bothered Colt. However, the layout was designed to keep the guests free of traffic and force them to be seen walking through the village, which gave the aura that the resort was always alive with people; who were fortunate to be there. There were giant snowballs, not as big as the ones at the entrance, strategically placed around the village. Colt counted seven of them and figured there were probably more. From the second you pulled into *Snowball,* the flow was choreographed to make you forget about everything and anything that would interrupt you from having a great time. It was like a drug.

"We have twenty-six slopes on over two thousand acres," Brandi filled him in while he was looking up the side of the mountain.

"I want to ride every one of them," he said, still staring up like a small kid looking up at a giant Christmas tree.

Because Colt was with Brandi, they were instant celebrities. Everyone, of course, knew her and they were genuinely excited to see her. They were also very excited to see him, although they had absolutely no idea who he was. He commanded quite a bit of attention and whispers amongst the staff. Brandi sensed this but Colt was oblivious to it all. He was too mesmerized by the grandeur of what he was seeing to notice the small stuff, like the people. They were escorted through the lodge and out into the beautiful courtyard where the smells of food cooking on hickory wood-fired grills immediately made them feel famished, once again, all by design. There was music echoing throughout, but it served as background to fill the silence of the festive, tranquil resort. They were escorted to two small side-by-side cabins, off to the side of the main area, located on a private knoll overlooking the entire village.

"I'm beginning to feel pretty special," was the first thing Colt said since passing the giant snowballs at the entrance. "This place is spectacular! I can't believe what I'm seeing."

"You should feel honored," she responded, "I've never stayed up here. This is Mr. Giles' private compound," she said standing in front of the cabins, "where he stays with special guests. So you must have impressed him," she finished with a tease.

"I can't believe I'm finally here. So much has happened between then and now I can't even tell you. I feel like I'm standing at the other end of the rainbow."

"You are the rainbow," she said as she blew him a kiss before following the attendant into her cabin. "I'll come get you in about fifteen minutes so we can begin the tour."

"I'll probably be standing right here," he said, while taking a time-out from relishing his surroundings to enjoy her backside as she bounced into the cabin. *What a show-stopper,* he thought to himself.

Mosquito

Cameron Toscanini, *Cameo the shark,* had finally mastered the art of snowboarding. He found *surfing the mountain* to be one of the most incredible and exhilarating sensations, short of sex, he'd ever experienced. He was quickly becoming addicted to the sport. He'd yet to tackle the higher elevation black diamond slopes designed for the more hardened risk takers, but he was anxious to get to that level. Being early in the season, his crafty mind was racing to figure out how he could spend the entire winter in Lake Tahoe. In order to snap enough photographs to remain gainfully self-employed, as usual, he had to come up with a game plan. He knew enough about the marketing plan for *Snowball* that there should be plenty of opportunities to catch the *kiddies,* as he so kindly referred to the spoiled little rich kids who drew the lottery in life, playing hard in this paradise. From his short stint here, he knew they would come in droves. He doubted that most of his peers in the business had figured out the high level of attraction *Snowball* was developing. All he wanted was one season to operate up here alone. They could have it after that and he would happily move on.

Cameron figured the best place to plant his roots would be in the main lodge where everyone checked in. That was his key to success. In order to hang around the lodge, he had to come up with a scheme to become accepted by the staff. He started taking them pastries, doughnuts and designer coffees as well as buying drinks for them when they were off work. He knew how to make people feel liked and how to make them feel important. He also knew that honesty was the key to longevity. He didn't hide the fact that he was a Paparazzo but he cushioned that by claiming he would try to include them in the background of some of his pictures so they could be seen by everyone who reads the tabloids. And that was enough for him to get his hall pass and it only took him a couple of days to pull it off. He quickly became their new best friend.

One afternoon he was sitting in the lodge by the giant stone fireplace, warming up after a chilly morning of boarding. While perusing several newspapers to catch up on events around the world, he noticed a couple being dropped off out front for check-in. His mind was a virtual *Wikipedia* of who's who and obviously this particular couple didn't ring any bells but he was intrigued by them anyway. For one thing, they might have been two of the most beautiful people he'd ever seen in his life and he had seen enough beautiful people to know they had something special going on. He was also surprised the girl was so well known by the staff. The fact that the couple was whisked past the check-in counter caused him to pull out his palm-sized digital camera with miniature telescopic lens and snap a couple of quick photos just in case they turned out to be somebody. Cameron wasn't gay but he appreciated beauty in guys because that was equally important when you're trying to sell photographs, and this guy basically took his breath away. He decided to follow them out to the courtyard and get a bead on where they were staying just in case they proved to be somebody.

Even a mediocre reporter would have easily figured out the significance of the two cabins, nestled side-by-side, nicely secluded from the heart of the village and on the most valuable piece of real estate in the entire resort overlooking the lake. They belonged to someone important. Consequently, it became a no-brainer when Jasmine at the desk told him they belonged to the owner of the resort, Mr. Hansen Giles, and he used the cabins for his entourage as well as other VIP's. The fact this couple was escorted up to the cabins elevated Cameron's interest in them even further. He could safely assume this couple was unknown, at least to the Paparazzi, because he didn't have a clue as to who they were either. But deep down inside, he felt there was a story to be told. His first impression was this guy was foreign. Cameron snapped as many photos as he could, without being outright obnoxious, to begin his new file. There would be time to become obnoxious later if the situation escalated into something.

Cameron positioned himself at the base of the path that led up to the cabins on one of the many benches spread throughout the courtyard. As they stood out front talking, the couple could only see him if they looked straight down the hill. He knew their panoramic view from the knoll would cause them to overlook him. The girl went into the cabin on the left and for the life of him, he couldn't figure out why the guy just stood out in front of the other one doing circles in the snow and looking at everything around him over and over again. One thing for sure, he could tell this mystery man really liked the scenery.

He'd seen the bellhop put the guy's luggage in the other cabin and when the beautiful woman came back out of her cabin and wrapped her arms around him from behind, Cameron began clicking furiously. *Why did they seem to be passionate about each other yet stay in different cabins? That's odd,* he thought to himself, *and he loved odd because odd made him money.* Having nothing else to do, he decided to make *Barbie and Ken,* as he named them, his project for the day. So he headed back into the lodge to get the scoop. Upon discovering that *Barbie* was Mr. Giles' administrative assistant, that piece of news took the air out of his balloon. No wonder she was staying in one of the cabins. His balloon became slightly inflated again just listening to the staff talking about the guy. You would have thought he was superman the way they were whispering to each other about him. Cameron decided that there was probably nothing worth pursuing but he would keep an eye on them because beauty attracts beauty and they might serve as a conduit to something bigger and better.

He wasn't kidding about still being there in the same spot. She had gone in to her cabin to unpack her bags and change for the colder weather. When she came out fifteen minutes later to start the tour of the resort, Colt was still standing right where she left him, taking in everything from the beauty of the snow-packed mountains, to the village below and to the lake below the village. He was freezing because he was still in the same outfit he had on that morning in San Fran, but to him it didn't matter. This place was like Disneyland for snowboarders and it definitely far exceeded his expectations. He wanted to go slow so he could remember each second of what he was experiencing. He wanted to feel everything, smell everything, hear every sound and be able to describe how it affected him as a total package. It was important to have his ducks in a row when he reported back to Hansen. It didn't take Colt very long to see areas that needed improvement, but for a new operation, he was totally impressed. *This place is hot,* he screamed silently to himself.

Suddenly, he felt the loving embrace of her arms wrapping around his waist and the warmth of her body pressed to his. She released the pressure just enough so he could spin and face her. Her scent was intoxicating. He thought it might be the French perfume called *Lou Lou,* which is his favorite, but wasn't sure. He'd find that out later.

"I was hoping that was you and not the bellhop," he joked as he stared into her soft glowing eyes. He felt like a kid at Christmas. *Is this for real,* he asked himself as he stole a quick kiss to make sure it wasn't his imagination. Her kiss was as soft and warm as her eyes.

"Why don't we go to my cabin and drink that other bottle of Chateau Montelena while I unpack my clothes," he said. "Let's take our time because I want everything we do to happen naturally just like it would for the guests. I want to feel this experience for the first time like they do," he emphasized. "Is that okay?"

"Absolutely, whatever you want. We have all the time in the world to see *Snowball.* I think you're right, makes sense to take it slow…and easy."

Brandi was a little hesitant about going to his cabin to drink wine because of what she said to him in the car on the way up. That could very easily happen again. She sincerely hoped she hadn't crossed the line and put him on the defensive but she only said it to make him feel good and she desperately wanted him to understand that. She also said it because she meant it from the bottom of her heart. The problem was she knew she was falling madly in love with him and she didn't know how to control it. But she definitely didn't want to stop it. She knew she would have to slow down and not push him away because he was hurting from a previous relationship. However, life goes on and she desperately wanted to be a part that new movement.

She knew Mr. Giles was going to hire him because he would never have sent them up here or given them his private residence if he wasn't serious about bringing Colt on board. Mr. Giles told her he was upset about the way the resort was being managed, especially after his last visit, and he was interested in finding someone to take over to do it right. He told her he'd talked with Colt's former boss and was very pleased at what he had to say about him. That explained why he wanted them to come up to his estate so he could meet Colt personally. It was all starting to make sense except she wasn't sure how she fit into the situation. After seeing Colt's passion come alive pulling into the resort, she understood what Mr. Giles was looking for. Now she had to worry that the work-thing would make it too complicated for Colt to allow her to love him. Also, she absolutely had no idea what he thought about her and that was driving her crazy. Although, she literally prayed that would change.

"So, ah, what do you think?" She asked as she sat in the rocking chair beside the bay window overlooking the village. "Pretty incredible isn't it?"

"Brandi, it's beyond incredible. It's magnificent! I'm really at a loss for words to describe what I think about this place and about how I'm feeling," he said while he was putting on Whiskey Meyers from his phone, having quickly connected to the wireless.

What did that mean? She thought. *Was he referring to his feelings about her or his feelings in general? Why was she doing this to herself? She needed to calm down because she was losing it.* "Yes, it is magnificent. I really hope it takes off for Mr. Giles. He's put his heart and soul into it, not to mention the money. This has cost him a fortune."

"I could imagine," replied Colt. He'd already done the math and had a pretty good idea of what it cost Hansen. He also knew it came out of Hansen's own pocket. It was well known that Mr. Giles preferred to operate alone and not be beholding to banks or other investors.

"The silhouette of you in that window with snow and

mountains in the background is a very nice picture. Would you mind sitting here?" he said as he patted the seat directly beside him on the sofa. "I want to get a closer look at you. Besides, I've poured you a glass of wine and I'm afraid I'd spill it if I carried it all the way over to you," he joked.

"All the way over here is such a long ways away," she chided as she got up and walked over and stood in front of him to accept the wine. "Colt, is this crazy or what?" Brandi couldn't hold it in anymore. "I feel like we're in fantasy land and someone is going to pinch me and I'll wake up. If that happens, I'm going to be extremely sad," she continued almost as if she was talking to herself. "The problem is I only met you yesterday. This is so unreal. What in the world is going on? I don't mean to act like a bimbo but I'm kind of excited and nervous at the same time."

Colt decided to let her get it all out. He too, was having mixed emotions and was trying to piece the puzzle together. His girlfriend from Virginia broke up with him, which wasn't really a surprise. Now look where he was. He, too, was excited and nervous at the same time because now all he could think about was Brandi, not Annie-Laurie. *The problem was it had only been a couple of days! In this world it seemed like a lifetime.*

"I have to ask you a question," she brought him back into the conversation. "What did you think about our little ride up today?"

"I thought lunch was great," he dodged.

"That's not what I'm talking about and you know it," she said as she sat down beside him and punched him on the shoulder. "You know exactly what I'm talking about."

"What?" He knew this was the last time he could play dumb before he actually had to answer the question. Of course he knew what she was talking about, he'd thought about it nonstop ever since it happened.

"Colt"

"I loved it," he cut her off. "And not just because it sounded great, and not just because it was exciting driving down the road and everybody else in the world would be envious of me. I loved it because I was with you. I know that sounds a little egotistical, but I really felt that. And it feels really, really good that someone cares for me." He looked down at his wine glass sitting on the table. Instinctively, he reached down to give it a swirl as he contemplated what he was going to say next. "I hope that was the beginning and not the end for us," he finished as he looked at her to read her expressions about what he'd just said.

She dropped her head to gather her thoughts. It was all moving way too fast, yet it seemed like they were in slow motion. Obviously, he liked her and didn't want this to go away. *But is this what he really wanted after just losing his girlfriend?* He must be experiencing the same confusing emotions as she but appeared to be very happy with their new so-called relationship.

"Colt," she paused, "that… was a little quick for me and I have some regrets about what I said because the last thing I want to do was push you away. I pray that's not the case. I know why you're here and I know it's not because of me. That being said," she placed her wine glass on the table and draped her arms over his shoulders and whispered into his ear "I want to make love to you right now." She stood up and walked to the center of the great room and began to undress. She took her time and let him enjoy the show while sipping on his wine. When she finally dropped her panties, she slowly turned around so he could see every inch of her perfect body from head to toe. "I think I've worked out my whole life so I could do this for you today," she said to break the silence. "Do you like what you see?"

Colt could see why there wasn't a shy bone in her body. She was absolutely stunning. With her personality and those looks, there was nothing she couldn't accomplish in life. The men in California must all be gay or dumber than dirt. *How could this person possibly be unattached?* He wanted to kid her and say *Nah, it's terrible, wouldn't touch that with a ten-foot pole,* but she didn't deserve that. She deserved his undivided attention and love. She deserved more than he could ever give her and then some. She deserved true love and happiness.

"You are everything I've ever dreamed of," he said as he got up and walked towards her. "You know I'm falling in love with you, don't you." That was statement, not a question. "Do you believe in love at first sight?"

"Not until yesterday when you walked in my office," she responded. "I fell in love with Burly right away."

"I should have known it was the dog and not me. Works every time, that's why I keep him around. You want Burly?" He asked. "Then follow me," as he held her hand a led her willingly into the bedroom.

Their love-making was the opposite of Burly. It was soft, kind, exploring and passionate. They kissed forever. They ran their fingers over each other's bodies like they were touching a Picasso. They tasted each other like they were eating dinner in heaven. It was magical. Their orgasms came quickly, slowly and often, with each one intensifying the love they were developing for each other. It was beyond fabulous, it was a *snowball*. Ironic right?

After they woke up, exhausted from the physical and mental excitement they were experiencing, they got in the Jacuzzi and washed each other with tender loving care. The scented candles in the bathroom accented the beauty of the situation and now their bodies were one.

"I'm starving," Colt finally admitted.

"You should be" she said seriously concerned, "it's after nine-o'clock. We haven't eaten since lunch. We had dinner reservations at eight. I think we missed it."

"I'm sorry," he said. "I had no idea. What do we do?"

"We get dressed and go to dinner anyway. I'm pretty sure they will hold our reservations don't you think? Besides, you're going to spend the next two hours telling me everything about yourself. I'm not going to fall in love with a stranger. Got that?" She said as she pinched his butt after she finished drying him off with the towel, underneath the heat lamp.

"Everything?"

"Everything that will make me love you more," she corrected with a smile.

"Do you mind if I use a cheat-sheet. I might have to make up some stuff."

"Just make sure it's good, cowboy, I hate to be disappointed by some rookie," she joked. " as I'm sure they say in Virginia, this ain't my first rodeo."

"This is a tough crowd. Why don't we start with you first?"

"Not happening big boy, I called shotgun first. Remember the rules?" She quizzed.

"What rules?"

"My rules," she said with furrowed brows. "The quicker you learn my rules the closer you can get to my heart." She closed with a huge kiss to make her point.

"Duly noted," he laughed. "Will I ever get to call the shots?"

"Probably not, but I'll think about it. Now get dressed because if you don't, we're going back to bed."

"Okay, works for me."

"I'm kidding. Get dressed."

Mosquito

Cameron was sitting at the end of the bar sipping a Makers Mark on ice, watching a great football game between a small college and a big-time university on the plasma behind the bar. *What a mismatch* he thought to himself. *These teams must do this so they can have a winning season and get into a better bowl game. It just doesn't seem fair for the little guy to be forced into the coliseum to face the gladiators. The sacrificial lambs didn't stand a chance. The crowd couldn't wait to do a thumbs-down and drive the sword into the chests of the unlucky ones. If he ever became a real reporter, he was going to do a running documentary about that. The number of stories would be endless.*

Burton's, rightfully named in honor of Jake Burton who invented snowboarding, was located on the outskirts of the village, but still fronted the massive courtyard. All the restaurants and bars were interspersed throughout the village, with shops and other small businesses located in between. That way there were always people milling around and seeing everything the village had to offer. Most of the guestrooms and suites were located above the shops and restaurants to keep everything as convenient as possible. All this was strategically designed to help every business become a draw for the high-rolling guests. The lit-up slopes, and lit up they were, branched out above the village to accent the picture.

Cameron was having an on again, off again conversation with Jasmine, the girl in check-in who was also moonlighting as a bartender in the evenings. He tipped her well and she took especially good care of him. In between sips, he would occasionally glance down from the television to watch her working the bar. She was pretty good at bartending and a great bullshitter. Consequently, he wasn't particularly bored. It was early in the evening, by bar standards, so there were several barstools at the bar unoccupied, including the two next to him. The restaurant side was packed. He glanced over when the front door opened and was surprised to see *Ken and Barbie* walk in. After talking to the hostess, they were directed to the two vacant stools next to him. *Small world,* he thought to himself. Instinctively, his hand touched the palm camera in his pants pocket for reassurance. Obviously, they didn't recognize him from this afternoon which was a good thing. He could make small talk like he was a normal person instead of a leech. *What a beautiful couple,* he couldn't help but think as he noticed everybody else in the restaurant do a double take when they saw them walk in. If he was an agent he would be on them like flies on shit. *Barbie* climbed onto the stool next to him and smiled and said hello and *Ken* nodded hello from the other side of her as he took a seat. Cameron nodded back and took another sip of his drink. *And this is why I like to work alone,* he toasted himself.

K & B, as he nicknamed them again, both ordered wine and she began pointing out highlights of *Burton's*. Knowing she was part of the organization, it made sense to Cameron. *K* seemed to absorb everything she was saying with keen interest and even asked a few strategic questions about the basic operation of the restaurant/bar. As Cameron nonchalantly observed them he concluded they had just had sex. It wasn't hard to figure out. With a smile here and a touch there, which weren't characteristics of a strictly business relationship, it was obvious they went a lot deeper than that. *I bet that was fun,* he thought with envy. *He was definitely going to put her in his rolodex.*

Eventually, she turned towards Cameron and struck up a conversation. Brandi didn't feel comfortable ignoring someone sitting alone at a bar.

"Are you a guest or an off-work employee?" She asked, quickly realizing that might have been too personal.

After he finished melting, he was able to recover quickly enough to give her a mostly intelligent answer, "Neither," was all that came out. "I mean both," he recovered, "sort of."

"Okay, now you have to explain," she laughed.

"Watch her, she'll bite," *K* tapped in with a smile.

Knowing she had a vested interest in the resort, Cameron decided to shoot from the hip. "Well, I'm working as a guest. I'm with the media. Does that sound better?"

"Really?" she was totally caught off guard. "That's great, I mean, what are you reporting on?"

"I'm more of a photographer if you know what I mean," he said matter-of-factly, knowing they would blow him off as soon as they realized he was a Paparazzo. He figured that by the time he finished his sip of Maker's they'd ask him to leave or they would politely excuse themselves, trying not to make it obvious they were offended to be talking to a *mosquito.*

"Do you want to take our picture?" She asked politely. *K*

just sat quietly beside her and smiled.

Cameron was taken back. This is not standard operating procedure. It's extremely rare for someone to request their picture be taken by someone in his profession. *Clearly, she didn't get it, but whatever,* he thought. *A mug shot at this distance would be priceless if it was one of the super stars. Too bad it wasn't.*

"Sure, I would be glad to take a couple of pictures of you guys. I'll email them to you if you like," as he pulled out his camera. To his surprise, they posed for several shots and bought him a drink for his troubles. At that point the hostess informed them their table was ready. B gave him her business card with her email address and phone numbers. Call me sometime tomorrow. I might have a few questions I'd like to ask you, if that's okay?"

"Sure, I'd be glad to talk to you. We can meet for a drink at happy hour if you'd like. I'm buying," he was used to saying. "I'm in the middle of learning how to snowboard, which I generally do in the mornings, so I'm free in the afternoons. I'll give you a shout. Hope you enjoy your dinner," he echoed as they followed the hostess to their table. He looked at her business card which was worth its weight in gold. *So B's name was Brandi Steele. At least he got the B right.*

"**Y**ou were mighty quiet back there at the bar, sir," Brandi said to Colt.

"Sorry about that. I just felt like this is your show, not mine, with this guy being Paparazzi and all. I figured the situation was yours to handle. I'm still an outsider you know," he emphasized. "However, I enjoyed watching him drool all over you. You humble people, you know that?"

"You're crazy," she giggled.

"Yeah, crazy about you," he said as he slid his foot up between her legs as a joke. He was surprised when they spread wider for him instead of closing in to lock him out.

"Do you want dessert before dinner?" She quizzed him,

hoping he would opt for dessert. "We can always go to the bathroom, or better yet, the coat closet," she winked.

"Let's eat," he said, impressed with her for calling his bluff. "I have to watch my calorie intake."

"Are you tired of me already?" She pouted.

"Yeah, I can't stand the sight of you. Hurts my eyes too much and makes me want to throw up. Lucky for you I can endure this type of torture. Otherwise, I'd have to leave. Let's have dessert back at my place," he added to make sure she knew he was kidding.

"What are we having for dessert?" She looked in his eyes as she softly massaged his hand.

"How about," he paused, "each other?" Like that was some sort of brilliant new idea.

"Sounds delicious to me, let's hurry up and eat. I was going to take you dancing at *The Cause* after dinner but that can wait."

"What's *The Cause*?"

"*The Cause is the cure*," she laughed. "Actually, *The Cause* is a bar and it's quickly becoming one of the hottest spots up here. Generally, after you leave you'll end up with a hangover and the only way to beat the hangover is to recognize that *The Cause is the cure* and start drinking again, kind of like *hair of the dog*. We didn't think naming the bar *Hair* was going to work, if you know what I mean. Sort of a play on words but effective marketing, don't you think? Always brings you back to *The Cause.* We have coasters, T-shirts, bandanas, you name it with the logo printed on them. We could almost float the entire resort from the sales of that stuff."

"Works for me," he said. "I wish I had figured that out a long time ago. I absolutely hate hangovers. I used to call them *overhangs*."

"I like the word *overhang* better," she smiled with approval. "Speaking of overhangs, the boarders like them too. They have a lot of money and they keep coming back for more punishment. This is their world and carrying a board is the only key. Every time I think what Mr. Giles has done here, it still completely amazes me," she said, shaking her head. "I'm very proud to be part of it. This is a pretty special place, in case you haven't already figured that out."

"Yeah, I pretty much figured that out even before I got here. I remembered the night I first read the article about *Snowball* in *Board Mag.* I read it at least a couple of times because I couldn't squeeze enough information out of it the first time. I decided to move out here that evening. It was that quick," he snapped his fingers. "My life changed overnight because of one article."

"And here you are," she chimed in.

"Yes, here I am."

"Feels like that article changed my life, too," she added as a test.

"It's amazing the power the press has over the common folk," he played along.

"Speaking of the press," she decided to change the subject away from them, "let's talk about our new friend at the bar, Mr. Paparazzo."

"I think he likes you. You should have seen his eyes light up when you sat down next to him. If looks could kill, then he would have turned to *wood* after he saw you, if you know what I mean."

"That's *stone* and no I don't know what you mean," she said as she squeezed his hand for emphasis.

"Sorry honey, I don't mean to mislead you, but that was all *wood* back there."

"Colt, I'm serious, what did you think about him?"

"He seemed nice enough, definitely acts like he likes this place," he said looking around. "I'm guessing that's what you're asking. He's here to snap the good, bad and ugly, which is all good publicity, right?"

"Absolutely, that's exactly what we want. Good publicity, especially, if a star or two gets tossed in the mix as well. Have you ever heard the saying *follow the stars?* Well, you have to know where they are before you can follow them. Unlike everybody else, we want the Paparazzi. I know it sounds crazy but it makes sense. They are our key to the world."

"I see what you mean," Colt said. *"Feed them and they will come.* Hansen's a very smart man. He knew the boarders were looking for a place to exclusively call home. And most of the Hollywood types, athletes, movers and shakers prefer snowboarding over skiing. Picking Tahoe from a location standpoint was pure genius. Look," he said, "it brought me out here all the way from Virginia and I'm none of the above."

"Thank God," she said.

"Let's head over to *The Cause* before we go home for dessert," he said. "I want to check out these boarders who play after hours. I want to see what kind of cult Hansen's created."

"You will be overwhelmed to say the least. They're a different breed, even more so now that they don't have to share their turf with the skiers. They can let it all out here. It's a pretty cool scene. I'm a little disappointed I'm going to have to wait for dessert though," she added.

The Cause

He noticed them the second they walked in the door. Actually, they were hard to miss because everybody in the bar turned their heads to check them out as soon as they entered. It was a, *who's that I wonder,* kind of atmosphere. Having already met them, Cameron decided to focus on the crowd's reaction to them. He wasn't totally surprised by the attention Colt and Brandi were getting because he too had that same initial response when he first saw them. They definitely were beautiful people and made a great looking red carpet couple. Cameron quickly surmised that everyone in *The Cause* would have screwed either one or both of them in a New York-second. Instead of running up and re-acquainting himself right away, *Cameo the Shark* let everything play out before making his move. He knew Brandi was a major player at the resort and was pretty sure Colt also represented the resort in some way. Getting to know them would be an excellent move and could be very profitable for him in the future if he could get on their good side.

He couldn't help but smile at their impact on the crowd. The people in the bar couldn't take their eyes off *Ken and Barbie* for a second. Alexandria, the bartender, lit up like a Christmas tree when she saw *Brandi*. Obviously, the two had a history. *Good information that would require more research*, Cameron thought. He also noticed Alexandria do a head–to-toe on Colt in about a millionth-of-a-second and she seemed very pleased by the way her eyes lit up when she finally finished checking him out. *The animation of her reaction to him was incredible. It was like watching a great silent movie,* Cameron smiled to himself. It never ceased to amaze him how something as simple as a person's appearance can have such a significant impact over another. He had the feeling he was watching the birth of two stars. And then it hit him like a bullet between the eyes.

The entrance was nothing like what Colt expected. There was a small, red neon sign no bigger than eight inches by twenty which said *The Cause,* over the arched doorway at the top of double-wide steps leading down to the basement level bar which was below a series of shops. Obviously, this worked well because the shops wouldn't be open late at night, so all the neighbors in business could co-exist. There was no doorman or bouncer to be seen which Colt thought was great. No one needed to be picked on before they started partying. That would be counter-productive. He was expecting loud music to blow him back up the stairs when he opened the door and walked in. To his surprise, the music was soft enough to carry on a normal conversation and the neon flashing lights weren't mind boggling. There was a long bar with huge mirrors behind it, which made the room look even bigger. There was a glassed-in cage at each end, like bookends, with beautifully made up, colorful clowns, dancing in the cages to the music. It was like Vegas on LSD. There was a computer room off to the side and lockers so people could store their laptops while they partied. The main area was occupied with tall bar tables surrounded by several tall bar stools each. The ceiling was black and made of a sound absorbing material designed to eliminate echoes and help keep noise to a minimum; conversations confidential. Smoking was prohibited so the air was cleanly scented with some sort of mild incense.

Snowboards of every color and design were hanging everywhere there weren't glass and mirrors. There was one snowboard, Colt noticed, encased in a wooden frame. It was an original *Burton Performer*, one of the first boards Jake Burton made. It had rubber bindings and a rope connected to a wooden handle with aluminum rudders on the bottom. *The Performer* resembled a surf board more than the modern boards and is why the theory of *surfing the mountain* helped transform Jake's dream into one of the most successful sports ever invented in modern times. It was a collector's item for sure. There was a life-sized picture of a skier located on the wall separating the men's and women's restrooms with a big red circle and diagonal line through it indicating *No Skiers*, which brought a smile to his face.

Colt noticed all this while he and Brandi were walking over to the bar to get a drink. He thought it was nice there weren't any bar stools lining the bar, which allowed people to come and go more freely without blocking access to the bar. He also noticed there were probably a hundred people in the main room and each one was checking them out. Actually, they were checking out Brandi and he couldn't blame them. *She commanded a lot of attention wherever she went,* he thought.

"Brandi, oh my God, where have you been?" said one of the hot little bartenders.

"Hey, Alex," Brandi said as they clinched both fists over the counter, clearly happy to see each other. "It's good to be back. I've missed you. So how is it going," Brandi asked as she looked around the room.

"Great, this place is the BOMB!" Alex emphasized. "I'm making soooo much money and I get to snowboard every day. My biggest fear is growing up and not being able to live like this anymore."

"So business is good?" Brandi asked because she was genuinely interested.

"Business is awesome!" Alex responded. "You guys definitely knew what you were doing when you created this place. Who would have thought?"

"Alex, I want you to meet someone," Brandi said as she turned towards Colt. "This is Colt Salley. Colt, I want you to meet my roommate from college, Alexandria Diaz, Alex for short. Alex was in between careers and I talked her into coming up here to help us open up *Snowball*. Sounds to me like she's not leaving either," Brandi said with a smile of relief.

"Hey Colt, nice to meet you," Alex said as she shook his hand with a *surprisingly firm handshake,* Colt thought. "I noticed you when you walked in. You look like a rock star," she laughed.

"Not even close, but I would like to be one if someone would let me. Do you have Karaoke here so I can audition?" He joked.

"Behind door number two," Alex said. "I'm not kidding. We have everything you want. You just have to find it, which is what's so cool about this place. It goes on like forever. We cater to everyone's needs and we give them their own room to enjoy what they like. We have a Hookah Bar, Disco, Punk, Rock, Oxygen, Cyber and a Sports Bar. You name it and we have it. Every bar is separate and independent of each other. You may not real-ize it, but believe it or not, we're packed right now."

"Really," Colt asked in amazement as he looked around." Where is everybody?"

"Exactly where they want to be," was her response. "Ser-iously, walk around, you won't believe it. This place will blow your mind. Before you check it out, may I fix you a drink? We have two house specials. Can you guess what they are?" She asked Colt with a beautiful smile that said if you don't get the answer right then you're an idiot.

"Well let me think," he paused, "your two specials would be *the Cause* and *the Cure.* Am I correct?"

"I like the way you think," Alex said as she looked over to Brandi. "I think he's a keeper."

"How do I know which one I want first?" asked Colt.

"That totally depends on which side of the mountain you're on. It's either party-up or party-down. Either drink will take you where you need to be. We sell more of these drinks than anything else combined. They've become the boarder's special cocktail for partying and the recipe is a secret, too."

"Let's have two *Causes*," Brandi interjected. "Alex, is any-body important here tonight?"

"Besides you two," Alex joked. "Oh yeah, we have quite a few players in the crowd tonight, with their entourages. I've sold twelve bottles of *Cristal Champagne* already. That ought to tell you something. But you know it's against the rules to talk about anybody or disclose their whereabouts in the bar, so you'll have to root them out yourselves, if you want. But believe me, there is always somebody who's somebody here. I'll tell you, it's unbelievable. It really is." She looked over her shoul-ders to acknowledge someone else coming up behind Brandi and Colt. On instinct, she started mixing three drinks instead of two. Colt turned to see if it was someone important and laughed and pointed to Cameron, the Paparazzo man.

"You sure get around, don't you?" He asked Cameron.

"Have to, it goes with the business. Let me buy those

drinks for you," he said walking up to the bar.

"Drinks are on the house," announced Alex from behind, "including yours Cameron. You spent enough money in here last night to get an army drunk," she added, "I owe you one. Did you get any good pics last night?"

"Was I really here last night?" Cameron asked dumbly. "I thought that was some kind of a dream. I better check my camera because a have no idea who I was with," he finished as he shook his head.

"Oh, you were definitely here," Alex laughed. "You were the life of the party."

"I tell you what," Cameron said matter-of-factly, "that's bullshit about the *Cause is the Cure!* I think I had about five of them last night and I'm still not *cured*. I felt like dirt all day and I just about killed myself snowboarding up on the mountain this morning. You need a drink that actually helps people like me snowboard," he joked.

"That's a great idea!" Alex responded like she really cared. "I'll play around with a few concoctions and see what I can come up with. Do you mind being my tester? I can't promise you won't fall but I'll guarantee you won't feel any pain when you do."

Colt was enjoying the banter going on between them and concluded there might be something more going on than just being bar friends, judging by the way they looked at each other. *When you like what you see, it's hard to hide it,* he thought to himself as he instinctively looked over at Brandi. He could tell she was enjoying the banter going on between Cameron and Alex as well.

"Do you mind if I join you guys?" asked Cameron. "I promise I'll behave myself."

"Please, have a seat," said Colt patting the stool next to him. It was his turn to pick this guy's brain. "How long have you been here?"

"I've been here several days. This place kind of grows on you, that's for sure."

"Do you think it'll make it? There a lot of really nice ski resorts around here to compete with."

"Good question and a legitimate one at that. As a matter of fact, that's what peaked my interest in the first place. Why would anyone come here when you can snowboard anywhere? What so special about not allowing skiers? Seems like that would be a risky venture," Cameron said. "One could lose a fortune if it didn't work. I've always heard that the best way to make a small fortune is to have a big one," he joked.

"I like that," Colt laughed. "So what do you think now you've been here awhile?" Colt asked while Alex and Brandi carried on their own conversation, which was basically about Colt. Every so often they would steal a glance at him and giggle.

"Out of curiosity, I visited a couple of the other resorts around the lake to see if they might be hurting because of *Snowball.* I was pleasantly surprised to see they were holding their own, which tells me first of all, there's room for this idea up here and it's not some kind of fad. Secondly, the boarders, or at least the more serious ones want this place to be their own. The ones who come here aren't relocating, that's for sure. So to make a short answer long, absolutely, this place is going to make it and I wouldn't be surprised to see more places like *Snowball* pop up around the world."

Good answer, thought Colt, *exactly what I wanted to hear.*

"Have you seen what some of these boarders can do?" asked Cameron. "Talk about extreme stuff. Sometimes, I just stop and watch them in awe. I mean, I know I'll never be that good, nor would I have the nerves for it at that level, but it sure is fun to watch."

"What about the people you're here to take pictures of?" Colt asked. "Are any of them any good?"

"Some of them are, but they're really here to have fun and be seen having fun. Snapping pictures of them on the slopes is actually kind of boring. Occasionally, I'll get a decent shot but I get the best ones late at night when they're all buzzed up. You catch one with red eyes or one eye shut and you've got a winner. Makes them look human and they aren't supposed to look human. Sometimes they pay me more for the pictures than I could get from my employers. Sorry, you have me rambling. What about you, do you snowboard?" He asked Colt.

"Absolutely, I love the sport. Grew up doing it on the east coast where the real boarders are," he joked.

"What do you mean by real boarders?" Cameron asked.

"Real boarders learn on ice. That's pretty much what you get on the east coast because the powder gets wet and freezes in the humid climate. When you bust your ass on ice, you know it, nothing hurts worse. So that's how you learn to board, by not busting your ass," Colt was laughing while he rubbed the hard memories. "Believe me, I had to learn fast. I love it though. When I first read about *Snowball*, I was intrigued and had to see it for myself, so here I am."

Cameron was constantly amazed at how people were so nice to him. Most people in his profession were nothing short of poison, yet everyone around here treated him like he was important. It was a really good feeling and he was becoming a celebrity of sorts himself. He hadn't figured out who Colt was but assumed he was Brandi's escort and that was good enough for him. A guy that good looking fit right in this playground, even if he wasn't a star.

"Would you like to go snowboarding with me tomorrow?" Cameron asked Colt.   "I'm not the best but I'm a fast learner and I already know most of the terrain here. I'd love to show you around. If you get bored, you can leave me in the dust, I'm pretty thick-skinned," he laughed. "I'm considered evil by most people, you know. If you're seen with me then people might start asking questions. Actually, that's probably not a good idea," Cameron said, having second thoughts.

"I'd love to," replied Colt. "That's why I came out here. What time do you want to meet? I have to get a rental because my stuff's in transition right now. I'm not sure how long that will take."

"For most people, like myself, renting equipment is a little bit of a pain in the ass but I'm sure they'll slip you right through because you're with her," Cameron nodded towards Brandi. "Even if she wasn't a major player here, they'd slip you through just because she's so beautiful," he said with a smile. "The two of you put most Hollywood couples to shame, you know that?"

"Thanks for the compliment," Colt responded as he looked over at her. "She is very beautiful. But I'm a real nobody so I'll get in line like everybody else." Actually, he wanted to experience renting equipment to see if it was *a pain in the ass. That would need to change.* "Let's meet you at the main lift at ten o'clock. Is that good?"

"Ten o'clock is perfect. See you then," Cameron said as he got up and headed through door number three. He wanted to find out who ordered all that *Cristal* Alex told him about.

"Hey baby, you ready to roll? We need to get up early tomorrow and it's been a long day," Colt said to Brandi while Alex was mixing drinks for some new arrivals. The main part of the bar was getting a little more crowded so Alex was getting busy.

"Sure, one more of these and you'd have to carry me home," Brandi said pointing to her empty glass. I don't know how people can drink this stuff. It's like jet fuel."

"Our friend just told me how beautiful he thought you were,"

"How much jet fuel has he had? This stuff will make anybody look pretty."

"He's invited us to go snowboarding with him in the morning. Are you in?"

"Absolutely"

"You never told me you're a boarder," he said.

"You never asked. Peel the onion and you will be surprised how sweet it is," said the jet fuel.

"I'm going to start peeling that onion in about ten minutes."

"Is this totally insane what we're doing?" She asked, all joking aside.

"You know, I believe everything happens for a reason, good, bad or indifferent. This is a good thing we have, and for the life of me, I love it and wouldn't change a thing. My grandmother used to say *there's always sunshine after the rain.* You are my sunshine. Let's go home," Colt said as he gave her a quick kiss on the lips. Over her shoulder he yelled goodbye to Alex. Alex smiled and blew them a kiss while she was busily making money off *Causes* so she could flip it and make more money later off the *Cures.* It was so diabolical.

When they got back to the cabins they were frozen. Obviously, the *Cause* didn't cure the cold. They entered Brandi's cabin, which was completely different from Colt's, had less room but a bigger stone fireplace and felt more lived in. *This was probably the one Hansen stayed in when he came up*, thought Colt. Brandi couldn't stop shaking while he added more wood to the coals trying to stoke up a good fire. While he was messing with the fire, she brought out several pillows and blankets and laid them down on the floor in front of the hearth. When it was warm enough, she snuggled underneath one of the mohair blankets and anxiously awaited Colt to join her. He watched her through the corner of his eyes and loved everything he saw. She wasn't petite and fragile looking, but at five-feet seven inches tall, she was tight and quite curvy. Her medium-sized breasts weren't perky because they were beautifully real and soft as the moonlight filtering in through the skylight, or so it appeared. He was getting excited thinking about the possibility of making love to her and a little guilty at the same time because they had progressed so quickly, maybe too quickly.

He couldn't help thinking about Annie-Laurie and Cracker for some strange reason. Also, he tried not to think what Hansen would say if he found out Colt was having more than just a business relationship with Brandi. Although, he was justifying it by saying this was a little different. They were grown-ups and could do as they pleased. He was definitely there for business reasons and she knew it, but obviously it didn't matter to her, which was a really good thing because in the next hour he was going to do things with her that had absolutely nothing to do with business. When he finally crawled underneath the covers with her, she was very happy to see him, to say the least. The first thing she did was slide under the blankets and made him even more excited to be there than he already was. One thing naturally led to another and they finished making love about the same time as the last log burned to coals. It was a beautiful way to fall in love.

"Who are you that just walked into my life?' She asked him before they got up to go to bed.

"I don't know," he answered. "Baby, if you're confused, then I'm lost, so it's a wash."

Wintergreen

"Josh speaking"

"Josh, Hansen Giles from California. Sorry to bother you again, but I wanted to let you know I met your boy yesterday."

"Obviously, he didn't have any trouble finding you, I take it," Josh replied.

"None at all," Hansen laughed. "As a matter of fact, we had lunch together."

"So what did you think about him?" asked Josh.

"I'm very impressed. Maybe not as much as my assistant but he seems like a pretty sharp, confident guy," replied Hansen. "I think she fell in love with him at first glance, not that I blame her. He's a good looking guy."

"Yeah, Colt is a ladies man, Hansen, there's no denying that. He's had women handed to him and women have thrown themselves at him left and right. Hell, even guys want him and the fact of the matter is, he's always the perfect Virginia Gentleman. I've never known him to use or abuse anybody. He's not the hurting kind. If your assistant is interested in him, she's not alone. But I can assure you he will respect her and he won't treat her badly."

"Thanks for sharing that with me, Josh. I really appreciate it and it certainly helps put my mind at ease."

"Is that why you called?"

"Well, let's just say I was a little concerned because I've seen her hurt before. She's a beautiful girl and I'm not sure she's comfortable handling her beauty, if you know what I mean," replied Hansen honestly. "There is one other question I wanted to ask you..," Hansen paused.

"Shoot"

"Do you think Colt is smart enough to manage a resort?"

"*Snowball,*" Josh asked.

"Yes."

"Absolutely, there is no doubt. Like I told you before, he could probably buy it from you but he's not that kind of person. He's an honest, hard working man and I might add I think his creativity will surprise you." Josh finished.

"Creativity in a good way I'm guessing?"

"Colt can make a cloudy day seem like pure sunshine," replied Josh. "I think you should give him a shot."

"That's all I need to know," replied Hansen. "Once again, I appreciate your time."

"I'm glad to be of service. Tell Colt I said hello and we miss him."

"Will do, Josh, take care."

Click.

Snowball

It wasn't as cold as Colt thought it was going to be when he first walked outside the next morning after a lovely evening with Brandi. She was in her cabin getting dressed for a day of snowboarding while he went next door to get his snowboarding clothes. He took his time getting to the other cabin so he could fully appreciate where he was. This was a long journey and he didn't want to miss anything. Eventually, he was going to have to make a few phone calls to Virginia, but not today. He was working today and he wanted to focus on the resort and everything about it before he called Hansen to report in. If he just said it was great then he might as well hop in the car and head back to Virginia. He wasn't planning on that happening, so he had to really understand what Hansen had accomplished. Also, he really felt like he had to come up with some ideas to make it even better. *A tall order for a place such as this*, he thought to himself. So far, everything, for the most part, seemed perfect.

Growing up as a kid skiing in various resorts, he was never allowed to bring his own skis because they were too much trouble to travel with, his parents would tell him. Consequently, he had a lot of experience renting equipment and it was never one of his favorite things to do. The experience of renting a snowboard and boots at *Snowball* was no better. It was crowded, hot, noisy and too busy for him. There weren't enough attendants and the ones working were overwhelmed to the point of NMN, *no more nice.* While Colt was waiting, he had plenty of time to notice the people around him and was able to pick out a few people who were somewhat famous for one reason or another. For the life of him, he couldn't imagine why they would put themselves through the rental process when they could easily afford to avoid that scene. *Maybe they just want to be normal sometimes,* he thought to himself, but quickly dismissed that idea because he knew all too well they never wanted to appear normal. Bottom line, renting equipment was a pain in the ass for everyone, no matter who they were. Colt put his mind to work on how to fix the process.

Brandi was waiting for him outside by the big stone outdoor fireplace. She didn't have to rent equipment because her gear was already at the resort kept stored in a private locker.

"Are we having fun yet?" She asked him when he walked up to her looking a little flushed from the experience.

"Not one of my favorite things to do," he replied. "I wish I had my own stuff with me," he replied shaking his head. "Oh well, a bad start makes for a good ending, right?"

"If you say so Mr. Colt Salley," she laughed. "Didn't anybody try to pick you up in there?"

"I have a date for Happy Hour this afternoon," he said as he gave her a quick kiss to let her know he was joking.

"You know Colt that really wouldn't surprise me judging the way people look at you. But that would really not work for me," she said with furrowed brow.

"I totally understand. Ditto," he replied with a smile.

It was a little before ten when they got over to the main chair lift in the village. Cameron was already there snapping a couple of shots of Brandi and Colt walking towards him.

"You shouldn't be wasting your pictures on us," Colt laughed, "save it for somebody famous. I saw a couple of people you might be interested in back at equipment rental."

"Already been there and done that. I got here early," Cameron replied. "Besides, I'm thinking the two of you are going to be famous before I'm done here," he added.

"Really," Brandi piped in with interest. "Please, do tell."

"I'm not posing nude," Colt added. "That will cost you."

Cameron laughed as he smacked Colt on the back and gave Brandi a hug. The three of them got in line to get on the lift. "I'll tell you about my plan on the way up," he said.

"What plan?" Colt became more curious.

"I want to be famous," Brandi joked. "I'll pose naked."

"That's not exactly what I had in mind," Cameron said as they got on the lift and headed up the mountain. "I've been thinking about this all night and I think I've come up with a pretty cool idea. Do you really want to hear it?"

"Do we have a choice?" Colt asked.

"Not really," Cameron said. "But you are either going to love the idea or hate it."

"Whoa, this sounds serious," Brandi cooed.

"I've spent my entire career taking photos of worthless people who happen to be famous. And famous for all the wrong reasons, I might add. I sell these pictures to anybody who'll buy them. Then they run the pictures, which makes these people even more famous. It's crazy and quite frankly, I'm getting a little bored. Most of them don't deserve the fame and notoriety. The other thing is they have way too much money and too few brains. Most of them end up in rehab because they can't resist temptation. Remember, as the Lord said in The Gospel According to Mark, 'it's not what goes into man that defiles him, it's what comes out of man that defiles him'. These idiots think they are above sin. They are completely oblivious. Not that I'm much better mind you; but snapping pictures of them when they are close to a rehab check-in is where the money is and I think it's disgusting. If you don't believe me, hang around *The Cause* for a couple of nights in a row. You'll see what I'm talking about. There is more stuff going on, under the table, than above it. I can assure you."

"Well, they are privileged people," Colt interjected mockingly. "They deserve the best drugs and the best alcohol that money can buy. Or at least they can afford it. The way I understand it is if they get caught doing something, well anything, it helps their bottom-line portfolio even more, right? Is there such a thing as bad publicity for this crowd?"

"Exactly," Cameron was getting excited. *Finally, he had their attention.* "So, I've been doing some writing on the side because one day I want to write and quit hiding behind trash cans, if you know what I mean. My new plan is to combine pictures with articles I write about certain unknown people and actually turn them into stars. Create my own market. If I could successfully pull this off then I could write my own ticket. Do you get where I'm going with this?" He asked as he glanced over at Colt and Brandi who were looking at the boarders ripping up the slopes underneath them.

"It sounds interesting, but what would it take for an unknown person to become a star over night? There's not any demand for that kind of stuff. Quite frankly, I think you would be wasting your time," Colt added. He was a little distracted by the beauty of the place and the fact that for some reason it made him think of Cracker. The image of her lying on the floor dead in that off-the–wall roadside restaurant was as vivid as the moment it happened. He was looking at his dream and she never got to see hers. It never ceased to amaze him how one person can impact another. In the short time he talked with her, she'd had a significant effect on him and he would never forget her. Cameron was interrupting his moment he was having with her.

"Think about it for a second," Cameron continued somewhat relentlessly. Bringing Colt back into the conversation, where he didn't want to be. "It takes looks, timing and location. That's all. And then everything else will fall into place. Let's take the two of you for example. You definitely have the looks and you're in the right location. You're in Lake Tahoe at a hot new snowboard resort in the Sierra Nevada Mountains, in California. All of which happens to be next to Nevada where the rich come to burn-off excess fuel, which is my term for money. The only thing separating you from the famous people is your entourage."

"What? What does that have to do with anything? I thought your entourage was the by-product of being famous, not something to actually make you famous," Colt said trying to be argumentative because Cameron wouldn't let it go.

"You're absolutely right," replied Cameron. "In most cases having an entourage is a by-product of being famous, sort of a perk. But I happen to think there is another angle that nobody has figured out yet, except for me." He could sense he'd already lost Colt's interest so he decided not to push it.

"Don't leave us hanging out here on this lift," Brandi said. "It's cold up here. What are you talking about?"

"I'll tell you what, "Cameron said, "Before I tip my hand

too early, I want you guys to think about what we talked about today while we're boarding. I'll give you more details this afternoon. I think by then you'll get a better understanding on where I'm going with this."

"If you say so," replied Colt, glad Cameron was willing to drop the subject, at least for the time being. "But I'll have to warn you that I will probably be way too sore to do any thinking today. Look around at how steep those slopes are. I'm probably going to kill myself up here!"

"It's not as bad as it looks," Brandi laughed at Colt as they finally got off the lift at the first run, which happened to be named *Killer.*

Killer didn't kill him. In fact, Colt had a tremendous day discovering every nook and cranny of every slope on the entire resort. There were many beautiful slopes, trails and back-hill powder-boarding areas that were absolutely fantastic. The views from the entire resort were amazing, post card level material. The one thing Colt noticed was each slope had every element of difficulty built-in so the boarders could always stay together no matter what their level of boarding was. Usually, most ski resorts separate the skiers by the complexity of the slopes, thereby separating the skiers based on their ability. The problem is that people who go as groups can not always ski together because some are more advanced than others. This wasn't the case at *Snowball.* Everyone could stay together on every slope. *It was a fantastic concept and an unbelievable engineering feat to pull off,* Colt kept telling himself. All of the slopes eventually came together on a long, gradual run into the village which kept the village alive, one hundred percent of the time.

The courtyard in the village was a hub of activity day and night. People could buy their food and cook their own meals on the multiple outdoor hickory wood-fired grills. It was a great place to meet people and develop camaraderie. Also, there were several rainbow colored outdoor *Roo Bar* kiosks, an idea Hansen learned about while he was in St. Moritz, where people could congregate under many open air tents with space heaters to do shots and party. These were very popular and always crowded. Because of the stereo system with outdoor speakers placed strategically throughout the entire resort from the slopes to the courtyard, there was always music playing in the background. The moment you stepped foot out of your car and into the village and onto the slopes you were constantly in a party atmosphere. The entire layout was painstakingly thought out and, obviously, it was quickly becoming a huge money maker.

Colt was surprised at how well Brandi could board. She stayed with him the entire day boarding through moguls, taking small jumps and surfing the fresh powder on the back-hill runs. Cameron would follow them but he stayed on the less difficult part of the slopes and slowed everybody down a little on the powder because he was still unsure of himself. He was still learning and didn't want to kill himself in the process. All three of them would eventually end up at the same spot near the lifts so the day flowed smoothly. Each time they would stop they would high-five each other to remind themselves how much fun they were having and how cool this place really was. Brandi, dressed in a bright purple body suit with light pink mink trim, was a beautiful sight to see coming down the mountain. Her outfit was more typical of skiers, but with a body like hers, snowboarding clothes wouldn't do her any justice. Her rosy cheeks and big smile made Colt feel very lucky to have met her and when she looked at him, she felt the same way. Cameron couldn't help but notice that everyone around them kept staring at the beautiful couple trying to figure out who they were. He was a professional at watching other people and it was so obvious that Colt and Brandi were magnets for attention. *They were becoming celebrities and didn't even know it*, he thought to himself.

Colt and Brandi both liked Cameron and the three of them

had an unbelievable day together. Cameron never mentioned his idea again because he knew he would be walking on thin ice around Colt. There was something bothering Colt that Cameron couldn't quite figure out, but it wasn't something that he carried on his shoulders, it was something far deeper than that. So Cameron did what he did best, he watched and waited and learned as much about this couple as he could without asking a single question. He could clearly see they were falling in love just by the way they looked at each other. It was new to both of them so they seemed to be a little cautious about letting out too much emotion. Hanging around with Colt and Brandi was definitely taking him away from his job, but he felt positive it would pay off in the long run and by a long shot.

"So what'd you think?" he asked them when they stepped up to one of the *Roo Bars* to do a shot after the final run of the day.

"It was everything I thought it would be," replied Colt, "and more."

"I knew you would love it," added Brandi. "I could tell by your excitement when we pulled in. You looked like a kid who just flew over Disney World. You couldn't wait to get here."

"You mean this isn't Disney?" Colt laughed. "I must be at the wrong place then. I guess I'll have to leave."

"Over my dead body," she said as she frowned from the bite of the shot.

"A couple more of those and you won't even know I'm gone," he laughed.

"I'll tell you what," Cameron interjected. "I found this cute little restaurant down by the lake, not too far from here, with a great happy hour and excellent food. I'd love to treat you two to dinner just to say thanks for a great day. Care to join me?"

"Absolutely. And you can finish telling us about your idea during dinner," Brandi said seriously.

"Fine by me," Colt added. "I feel too good to go lay by a fire and feel my body begin to ache from the pounding I just put it through. I was thinking I should have a "Cure before the Cause, if that's possible."

"Funny man, let's take the resort shuttle," Brandi added, ignoring Colt's jab. "It will take us anywhere on the lake and pick us up as well. We don't want anybody to have to drive when they get here because the likelihood of a DUI after a day like today is high and we would like for our people to come back. It makes it easier for everybody."

"Just another fine service provided by Island Time Properties," Colt added. "Do the shuttles go to the casinos as well?"

"Absolutely," Cameron added to the conversation. "And believe me when I say it's a very dangerous shuttle to catch, if you know what I mean. People in my profession would be foolish to gamble when one lives from paycheck to paycheck."

"Do you like chasing people around?" Brandi asked.

"No way, because everybody hates my guts, but I'm good at it and somebody has to do it. I've made a fairly decent living and I get to see some pretty cool places, like here for example," he added. "Unfortunately, my counterparts will be coming once they figure out this is going to be the new winter playground for the *kiddies.* When that happens, I'll have to move on because I can't stand working with the crowd. I prefer to work alone."

"Have you gotten any good pictures here?" Brandi asked.

"Oh yeah, so far, so good and I think it's going to get better. Believe it or not, I took some today. But *Snowball* hasn't really been discovered yet. Trust me it will be soon, I'm sure of it."

"I hope so," Brandi chimed in, "that's part of the plan. The Paparazzi means free advertising for us and as much as they fight it, the stars love having their pictures taken, no matter what they're doing. It keeps them in the limelight. We want to be their new playground," she closed.

"How do you find them up here?" Colt asked out of general interest. "They're covered from head to toe in snow gear. I would think they would be very hard to recognize."

"*The Cause,*" Cameron answered, "because they love to party. All you have to do is locate their entourage and that's where they are. After you figure it out, it makes it easier to spot them on the slopes, in the village or in the casinos. They have a ridiculous amount of money to burn and every one of them is a pyromaniac. Actually, it's a no-brainer."

They checked-in Colt's equipment and went through the lodge and out to the shuttles. Colt was surprised to see the number of people waiting to be transported to the various areas around the lake. It was a festive crowd and the atmosphere was very special. Everyone was smiling and talking about their experiences on the slopes. *Not a place for the miserable people,* Colt thought. Everywhere he looked he was constantly impressed with how well thought-out the resort was. The guests literally didn't have to think for themselves.

The three of them talked little on the shuttle ride to the restaurant. They were more interested in listening to the others and staring out the windows at heaven. Also, the soreness from boarding all day was settling in.

"This is our stop," Cameron broke the silence. "I think you'll like this place."

"*The Flip Flop Inn,*" Colt laughed out loud. "I already like it." Although for some reason, it made him think about Cracker.

They strolled through the dining area towards the room in the back. There was a small crowd gathered at one end of the bar. They looked like rappers judging from the gold chains and jewelry hanging from their necks. All of them were sporting high-dollar sunglasses. And they were having a good time judging by the number of empty shot glasses sitting on the bar top. The loud conversations turned into complete silence when they walked in. Cameron noticed all of them checking out Colt and Brandi. The rap crowd already knew who Cameron was. He had gotten a few choice shots of them earlier in the day and was slightly abused by one of the body guards. Fortunately, the situation had been discreet enough so Colt and Brandi weren't aware of the incident. Now he was worried, judging by the way they were checking out Brandi.

"What you got there photo boy?" asked the main man, Diggy-Boo, as he was giving Brandi the up-down.

"Just some friends of mine," Cameron said across the bar. He was clearly embarrassed.

"No, I mean, who's the babe?"

"Like I said, she's a friend of mine," Cameron repeated.

"Well why don't you bring her over here and introduce her to me. If you can take my picture then I can meet your friend. I think that's fair," Diggy shot back. His entourage all nodded in agreement as every one of them stayed focused on Brandi and ignored making eye contact with Cameron or Colt.

Colt could read the signs and knew trouble was brewing. He could also tell that Cameron wasn't going to be able to ice the situation and in this remote little restaurant there was nowhere else to go. They were going to have to make nice real fast before it escalated. So Colt picked up his glass of wine and walked over to the crowd and straight up to Diggy-Boo. The body guards were ready to pummel him as soon as Diggy gave them the nod. Colt lifted up his wine glass as a toast.

"How about let's all have a drink and make this fun."

"What makes you think we need more drinks?" asked one of Diggy's boys.

"Because we're here at a bar in a great little restaurant and a couple of days ago I saw a beautiful waitress get gunned down at another great little restaurant, and I'm still deeply bothered by that," Colt said staring straight at Diggy-Boo. "Seeing her lying on the floor with blood everywhere, with a blank stare on her pretty little face, made me realize that life is way too short. I decided I better have more fun. What's the point in making it ugly? The girl you are asking about is Brandi. She's my girlfriend and I love her. Would you like to meet her or are you just going to sit there and stare at her?"

"We cool," Diggy-Boo replied looking back at Colt with some respect. "Let's all do a shot on me. Bartender," he nodded as he waived his empty shot glass around. "Didn't mean no disrespect to the lady," he continued. "But she's a fine looking woman."

"Thanks, Colt replied. "I think you're absolutely right and I'm a very lucky guy."

"I'll drink to that," Diggy added.

"And I'm a huge fan of yours," Brandi said to Diggy-Boo as she stepped around from behind Colt to shake his hand. "It is a pleasure to meet you Diggy-Boo," she added completely unfazed by the situation. "I've seen you perform in Los Angeles. You put on a great show."

Diggy stood up and gave her a bow. "The pleasure is all on me, beautiful, I'm glad I could entertain you. That's what I do." Every one around him nodded in support of their man, mainly for fear of being fired if they didn't.

"Well let's do a shot to your continued success," Brandi added smiling. She was taking full control of the situation without anybody realizing it except Colt. He stepped back so she could run with it. The dust settled quickly.

"We need to talk later about what you saw happen the other day," she said to Colt. "I had no idea," she said with a worried look.

"Yeah, I'm real sorry about that," Diggy added. "That's not right."

"It was a very sad situation," Colt said looking down at the floor, ending the discussion.

No one seemed to mind Cameron taking pictures while they were standing at the bar. He was probably stretching his limits with Diggy-Boo, but getting away with it. After a toast out to Brandi and every one downing their shots, followed by some small talk, Diggy-Boo and his entourage went into the dining room to have dinner. Colt, Brandi and Cameron remained at the bar to decompress with another glass of wine before they ate.

"What was that all about?" Colt asked Cameron directly.

"They caught me taking some pictures today on the slopes and weren't real happy about it. Diggy was busting his ass out there. He definitely didn't want that to be seen by the world so he sent one of his boys over to eliminate the problem," he finished with a shrug. "Sometimes you win and sometimes you lose. Today I lost and tonight I won. Business as usual," he finished.

"Well, are you going to send the pictures of him busting his butt off to the tabloids?" Brandi asked.

"No," replied Cameron, "not those pictures. I have the ones I just took that I might send out. I might make you stars," he said somewhat jokingly, looking at both of them carefully to see what their response would be. "I could tell you enjoyed hanging around with them. You know that more will follow?"

"How's that" Colt asked.

"When you're seen with famous people then that can sometimes make you famous too. Other people want to know who you are, especially when you're better looking than the famous ones," Cameron said. "Would that bother you?"

"I think it would be kind of neat," Brandi chimed in before Colt could answer.

"I'd have to think about that," Colt finished because he was unsure where Cameron was going with it.

Cameron decided to keep a low profile during dinner. He figured he'd said enough. There was a time to talk and a time to observe and he was in the observing mode. It wasn't hard to become fascinated by the magnetism Colt and Brandi exuberated to everyone who came into the restaurant. To the person, they would do a one-eighty scanning the room when they walked in the front door and each one of them stopped dead cold when they locked-on to his new friends. The look of adoration in their eyes confirmed that his idea was a good one, yet he was still at odds on how to share it with them so they would understand and accept it. It would involve a great deal of patience to make it work.

When they got back to the cabin, Colt and Brandi thanked Cameron for a wonderful dinner and retired early to her cabin. Cameron still had work to do so he headed over to the *Cause* to see who was hanging out. They had to leave in the morning for

San Francisco so they wanted to have one more special night together. While Brandi was getting some things organized, Colt slipped over to his cabin to call his parents. He decided not to call Annie-Laurie. There was no point in stirring up a hornet's nest. When he walked back in to Brandi's cabin, there were candles burning throughout, leading all the way to the Jacuzzi. She was immersed in bubbles with her eyes closed and two glasses of wine were resting on the edge of the tub. He sat on the edge of the counter and stared at her for the longest time. She was so beautiful in so many ways. She looked like a china doll lying there and he wanted to lock that image of her in his mind forever. Everything was so incredible and he felt very fortunate to have found her in his life. His guilt was rapidly slipping away.

"Are you just going to stare at me all night or are you going to get in while the water is still hot," she asked mischievously without opening her eyes.

"I love you," he said without moving. "I can't believe I'm saying this but it's true. You have stolen my heart and I hardly know you."

Brandi opened her eyes and cut them over towards Colt before she responded. She hesitated only because she was unsure of what to say. Everything was happening so quickly.

"Why do you love me?"

"Because I have always believed in love at first sight, I've just never experienced it until now. I left someone I was very close to back in Virginia in order to come out here and chase this dream," he said spreading his arms out. "The minute I walked into your office, I think I totally forgot what that dream was. I knew instantly that I loved you. Burly knew it too, he told me," he added with a huge smile. "I can't stop thinking about you and I can't take my eyes off of you. The funny part about it is it's not lust. I don't have to jump in that tub to satisfy some underlying urge. I would be just as happy watching you bathe yourself, drying you off, tucking you into bed and telling you stories about my life and how everything has led up to me meeting you."

"Does that mean you're not getting in?"

"Not at all, I'm definitely getting in. I may never get out," he said as he began to undress.

"I love you too," she said as she closed her eyes and smiled in anticipation of him crawling in beside her. "And I knew it the moment I looked up from Burly and saw you standing there. I couldn't even breathe I was so taken back by my emotions," she continued with her eyes still closed.

He sat on the side of the tub with his feet dangling in the scalding water. It was too hot to submerge his whole body at once, so it would have to be gradual. While his feet and calves were adjusting to the hot water, unrepentantly, she leaned over to the edge and took him in her mouth. He pulled her hair to the side so he could see her face and she raised her eyes to meet his, hoping he would approve. She was pleased to see she made him happy.

"Did you like that?" Brandi asked after she was finished.

"Wow," was all he could muster. "If I fell in that water I might drown because I don't have enough energy to stay afloat. That was amazing."

"You better get in here," she said. "I'm not done with you yet."

"You might be for awhile," he laughed. "I think it might take a while to regroup."

"I'm going to bathe you, silly. By the time you get out of here you will be crawling to bed. Trust me. I'm very easy to please and I find great pleasure in pleasing you."

There were two waterlogged, shriveled-up bodies when they finally made it to bed, yet sleep didn't come quickly. They held on to each other tightly and relished the miracle of their new found love as they continued to explore each other through words and touch into the wee hours of the morning. It was a moment in time they wanted to savor forever.

"What are you doing," he asked her with a giggle when she climbed on top of him in bed with a glass of water and a toothbrush with toothpaste on it. She looked so good in the morning with her flannel pajamas on. He was glad to see she was the type of person who was always comfortable with her looks. She, on the other hand, was glad to see he was naked.

"I'm brushing your teeth before I kiss you," she said with a smile. "Because I happen to know you well enough to know you wouldn't want to kiss me until you felt minty-fresh and I can't wait." She could tell he was quickly waking up. "I see you like to wake up happy," she teased. "I like happy."

"I didn't even know I was awake," he said smiling. "I thought I was just dreaming about you. Baby, you make me happy, so very happy. What a wonderful way to wake up."

"What are we going to tell Hansen?" Colt asked as they were pulling out of the resort on their way back to San Francisco. "I mean he's going to suspect something has happened between us."

"Does it bother you what he thinks?" Brandi asked with a worried expression on her face.

"It doesn't bother me," he replied, "I'm more worried about you."

"Mr. Giles knows I'm a big girl. He doesn't interfere with my personal life."

"But this is also business," Colt shot back almost too quickly. "I mean, we could possibly be working together," he paused. "Do you think he'll have a problem with that? You know him better than I do and I would never do anything to jeopardize your career. I'll walk away before that happens."

"You're not going anywhere my love. Trust me, it will be fine. He's a great guy, you'll see."

They spent the next couple of hours ignoring that subject and talked more about themselves and where they grew up. They talked about religion and politics and families. Colt found out that her father had died in a car accident on the LA freeway several years ago and her mother still lives quite comfortably alone in Anaheim. He discovered Brandi has a tremendous love for God. And she was very loyal to family and friends, including her two sisters who also live in Anaheim near their mother. Brandi goes to visit at least once a month and the entire family still enjoys going to Disneyland together. He admitted he also had tremendous faith in God. He told her about growing up in Richmond and shared the deep history of the city and of Virginia. He was very proud to be a Virginian and it showed through his eyes when he talked about it. He told her about college and about Wintergreen. He told her about what happened to Cracker in that restaurant and how badly it affected him. He avoided talking about Annie-Laurie and he also failed to mention the fact that he was extremely wealthy. He never thought of money as an object of affection and he never wanted wealth to be a factor in how people perceived him. He wanted to be liked, or disliked, because of his natural demeanor and not as some false sense of security that people with money sometimes disclose. Only a few of his friends knew he was independently wealthy. As a result, Colt always worked twice as hard as the next person to prove his resolve. None of this, of which, he shared with Brandi. That would come in time.

San Francisco

They called Hansen when they got to the outskirts of San Francisco. He was in town and decided to meet them for lunch at his favorite Italian restaurant.

"You must be pretty special if he wants to take us there to eat," Brandi said. "He is a bit of a gourmand and he only goes there when he's entertaining his favorite clients."

"Maybe it's a farewell lunch," Colt joked.

"I don't think so," she giggled.

"Why?"

"Because he still has your dog," she said matter-of-factly.

"Oh, yeah, I almost forgot about Burly. Do you see what you're doing to me? It used to be just me and Burly," he shook his head. "Actually, now that you mention it, I'm more worried about what Burly's going to say about us than Hansen."

"Don't worry about Burly," she said confidently. "I petted him before I petted you. He knows where he stands in my petting order."

"I always come in a distant second to Burly," he laughed. He was so enthralled by everything that came out of her mouth. She knew how to press all of his buttons, even the ones he didn't know he had. *How long has he known this person,* he asked himself in amazement, *and how was he going to hide his love for her in front of Hansen?*

It didn't take very long for that last question to be answered when they walked in to the restaurant with her arm in his. *Obviously, she wasn't shy around Mr. Giles,* Colt thought to himself.

"Well, what do we have here?" Hansen spoke as he stood up when they approached his table. "Did you have a good time at *Snowball*?"

"You might say that," Brandi offered as she stole a glance at Colt who was still trying to figure out what to say.

"Let me guess," Hansen bought Colt some time, "It took you guys about two seconds to realize you were meant to be together. Am I right?"

Colt was relieved Hansen was smiling instead of frowning, not that it would change anything, but it sure helped to have it out in the open. Otherwise, a lot of unnecessary time would be wasted in the cover-up process.

"How's Burly doing?" Colt asked.

"Changing the subject already? I love it," Hansen exclaimed. "I knew you two were meant to be together before you did," he laughed. "Burly is having the time of his life. I think he's lost about ten pounds just running through the fields with my dogs. He doesn't even ask about you anymore."

"Thanks for taking good care of him," Colt replied somewhat sheepishly.

"Thanks for taking good care of her," Hansen responded as he nodded approval at Brandi. "She's a great girl and all I want is for her to be happy."

"Will do," Colt smiled as he looked at her. "I give you my word. Though, I'll have to admit I never saw it coming. She ran over me like a train."

"I'm glad everybody is worried about me," Brandi jumped in. "I'm a big girl and can take care of myself if I want to. I just don't want to anymore," she said as she squeezed Colt's hand under the table.

"Josh told me I would like you," Hansen laughed as he changed the subject.

"So you called my old boss?" Colt was surprised.

"Of course," Hansen responded, "I always like to know who I'm dealing with. It eliminates a lot of unnecessary surprises. He said you were the real deal. Why do you think I invited you out to my house? After talking to Josh, I got the impression that the people you left back in Virginia weren't too happy to see you leave. Their loss is our gain," he said as he smiled to Brandi. "Am I right?"

"Indeed," she said.

"So what did you think about our little project? I'm anxious to hear what you have to say. Or did you get to see it?" He joked as he smiled back at Brandi.

"Oh, I had a chance to see it,' replied Colt who was finally beginning to feel comfortable with the situation. "It is absolutely, without question, pure genius. I don't know what prompted you to even think about such a concept, but it is amazing. I think you could open a *Snowball* in every known ski area in the entire world. I wouldn't be surprised if the other ski resorts didn't ask you to do it just to bring in more people. I'm jealous I didn't think of it first," Colt finished.

"So what did you really think?" Hansen laughed out of satisfaction. "You're not just telling me this to make me feel good are you? I'm very proud of what we've accomplished but what do you think we can improve on?"

"Well, let's start with the things that impressed me the most and then I have a few ideas you might like. Is that okay?"

"Fine by me," Hansen replied with interest.

"First of all I thought the giant snowballs on each side of the entrance were amazing. They say everything about the resort without saying anything at all. I think that first impressions really set the tone when you pull in to *Snowball.* A snowboard-only resort has to be different in every way in order to develop a following. I think you captured it right there at the beginning."

"Thanks, that was actually Brandi's idea," Hansen confided as he smiled at her.

"I had no idea," Colt said as he looked at her with pride. "I want to talk about the snowballs some more after I'm finished, so remind me in case I forget. Anyway, the winding road down towards the village is fantastic and the views are breathtaking. You get the whole postcard at first glance so the excitement of pulling into the resort is unbelievable. Being met at the car by a shuttle as soon as you park is an awesome perk and an excellent way to welcome guests to the resort. I think check-in is perfect and I love the lodging that I have seen. Unfortunately, I didn't get to see all of it since I was only there two nights. But from what I've seen everything looks extremely well thought out. I love the courtyard concept and the fact that all the slopes converge into the main courtyard and that everywhere you go on the slopes you have a phenomenal view of both the village and the lake down below. It gives you that homey feeling like you belong there. I also admire how you designed the slopes so people with different skill levels can still board together the entire day. Nothing is worse than not being able to hang with your friends because you're not as good as them. So, in my opinion, that is a huge, huge plus. The colorful *Roo Bars* in the courtyard seem to provide a great deal of entertainment for when you're not boarding. The outdoor hickory wood-fired grills add a nice touch because it allows the guests to not only get involved, but to also get to know one another while they're cooking their own meals. And the smells are fantastic. The piped in music throughout the entire compound gives the resort a unique quality that I think people really enjoy. *The Cause* is awesome and I like the fact that it is a virtual city underground, below the village proper, and gives you a totally different dimension without leaving the compound. The restaurants and shops cater to the boarders and they have the money to be catered to so it's a perfect match. The bottom line is from beginning to end, *Snowball* is extremely well thought out and the setting is second to none. I foresee the potential of developing a complete line of exclusive *Snowball* clothing and accessories as well. Also, I love the location. California is great and Lake Tahoe is even better. I think both of you," he paused while he looked at Hansen and Brandi, "should be so proud of what you've created. It's already a big hit and I can only assume it's going to be a smashing success."

"Thanks for your evaluation," Hansen replied. "That was impressive. Everything you just said was exactly the way we envisioned it would be for the guests. We want every one of them to feel the same way. That way they will keep coming back. Long term is the key to success. We don't want to be just a fad."

"Without a doubt, I think you've already accomplished that," Colt replied nodding his head. "To be honest, I'm honored sitting here talking to you about it. *Snowball* completely blows me away."

"So what do you think we can improve on?" Brandi joined in.

"Let me ask you this first, how do you keep all those giant snowballs intact throughout the season? I mean, how do you keep them from melting?"

"It's funny you asked," Brandi replied. "That turned out

to be a real technical obstacle. It started out as a great idea but quickly turned into a formidable task to actually pull off. What we ultimately did was build the snowballs out of wire mesh and aluminum framing. They have a small trap door which allows us to service the internal cooling units that are inside each one. This keeps them from melting, along with some daily external patch work with actual snow. They constantly have to be maintained, so they're not completely foolproof."

"Interesting," Colt said. "What are you going to do with them in the off-season? You're not going to leave them there without the snow are you?"

Hansen smiled and contemplated Colt's question. "We really haven't decided on that. Maybe we will move them to an obscure place behind the resort and bring them out next season. We definitely will not leave them sitting there when the snow is gone. They would be too much of an eyesore."

"Okay, how are you going to market the resort in the off-season?" Colt asked.

"We will market it as your typical summer retreat. Tahoe offers a lot of diversity year round and we thought we could easily capture a percentage of the business in the off-season as well. The shuttle service will play a more important role because that's when people will really venture out to see all that the area has to offer. We will do multiple excursions and tour packages to support that link," replied Hansen as Brandi nodded at everything he was saying.

"Okay, that's what I thought, I just wanted to make sure so I don't put my foot in my mouth," Colt smiled. "I have some ideas that might make the resort even more unique and special than it already is. First of all, I must say these are merely ideas and if you don't buy into them it will not hurt my feelings. I'm a firm believer in *making a better mousetrap* and constantly look for ways to improve what's already proven. I'm not big into fixing broken things because you end up chasing your tail and losing sight of the path."

"Agreed," Hansen said.

"Anyway, my ideas are strictly complimentary. Start with the snowballs, I figured they had a cooling system inside them which means they have electricity. Why not take it a step further and put some sort of lighting system inside to illuminate the outside. I'm sure the snow would provide an excellent medium for the lights and would make for an interesting creation of a cosmic light show on the external skin of the snowballs. This would be particularly attractive at night and take the snowballs into another dimension. Also, I would expand on your logo and have a life-like replica of a snowboarder on top of each snowball boarding the ball. It carries your logo to the front door of the resort in bigger than life proportions," Colt paused to give them time to absorb the image he was trying to get across.

"What about in the summer?" Brandi asked.

"I'll get to that in a second," Colt said. "Next I want to talk about the staff. I think you need to set up a reward system, maybe on a daily basis, to encourage a greater sense of hospitality from them. They seem to like working at the resort but they need to love working there. What I noticed, for the most part, is they seem to simply be going through the motions. Granted, the attitude picks up a notch in the restaurants and bars, but I think that has everything to do with the higher level of contact the waiters, bartenders and servers have with the guests. That needs to happen the minute the shuttle pulls up to your car and it needs to be consistent throughout the entire resort. In my humble opinion, a happy house is a successful house. Rewarding them in some way will help encourage them to step out of the box a little more. Your staff can easily make or break you." Once again, Colt paused to see if they liked what he was saying or insulted. He didn't want to burn any bridges but he also truly believed in what he was saying.

"How would you recognize them and how would you reward them?" Hansen asked.

"Maybe have them vote on each other, or maybe call a meeting and lay it out to them what you're trying to accomplish and have them help figure out the recognition and rewards program. The more you have them involved the more they will care. Trust me."

"Okay, I'll think about that," Hansen said. " But I like what you are suggesting."

"When I talked about lightscaping the snowballs, I also would like to expand a little more on that topic. You have a world-class snowboard resort, one of a kind. Snowboarders are a little more eclectic, or I should say wired, than the average skier. They certainly have their own type of clothing and a unique type of persona. I would light up the courtyard and the slopes with a Disney level lightscaping system which would be second to none. Make the entire resort turn into something very cosmic at night, where it can be seen from just about every-where around the lake. I'm talking lasers and colorful lighting systems that shoot up trees, the whole nine yards, almost turn-ing the resort into some sort of fantasy land."

"That could be very costly," Brandi chimed in. "I see what you're saying but that's a lot of money."

"Agreed," replied Colt, nodding his head. "Something I would like to discuss after we finish this conversation."

"Okay, go on," Hansen said. He was clearly interested in what Colt was saying and wanted to hear the entire pitch.

"Next," Colt said. "The process for checking out rental equipment sucks. It is a system that quite frankly, has never been perfected. One that I think we, you, can finally fix."

"How so" Hansen asked.

"Simple, you have each person who needs rental equip-ment fill out an on-line post card, checking the boxes of the equipment they need from boots to boards. They step on an electronic pad which analyzes the correct size boot they will require along with their weight so the tension of the bindings can be adjusted. This goes to the equipment room which as-sembles the package and then the boots and boards will be de-livered to each person's room as soon as they unpack their lug-gage. Or, if they are just up for the day, figure out a way they can pay, step on the scale, and their equipment will be handed to them before they walk out to the slopes. But it has to be a very smooth transition. Also, the day they are scheduled to check out, their equipment will be picked up at their rooms so they don't have to lug it back over to check it in. It's a simple process that will take your service to a completely different level."

"I like it," Hansen said. "I agree that the whole rental process is a complete pain in the ass." Brandi nodded approval at the idea. She kept staring at Colt in wonder and amazement. Everything that came out of his mouth was like a beautiful love song. His southern accent was very sophisticated and his animation was contagious. *No wonder I love him,* she thought to herself. Occasionally, Hansen would steal a glance at her and see she was mesmerized by Colt. He wasn't convinced that was a bad thing, because he too, was finding himself wholly immersed in this guy and what he was saying.

"I love the *Roo Bars* in the courtyard and think that type of theme or a variation there of, can be carried out on the slopes. You need some small Chalet-like stops where people can congregate, eat and drink on the mountain itself. Sometimes, after a long ride up, it would be nice to take a break and have a drink or something quick to eat before heading back down. You could call them *Energy Stops* or something like that, or simply expand the Roo-theme up on the mountain. The boarders are all about energy drinks and high-powered caffeine. They like to turn it on when they want to and shut it down when they need to. When you turn them on they make noise and in my opinion, noise is money in the bank." Colt was on a roll so he decided to keep pressing forward. "I would cut out the existing perks to the stars. They have enough money, they don't need any freebies. Instead, pick the top ten or twenty each year and give them a year-long membership to the resort. I would make it such an honor to get one that the stars would wear them like a badge of honor. Maybe put their pictures on a wall where everybody can see them. Obviously, it goes without saying, the membership should come with a lot of perks. But I think they should be invited and it should never be expected. Everybody likes to feel special, only some of them deserve it. Recognize the ones who deserve it and the others will try very hard to follow. This leads me to music," Colt said with a smile. "You had the foresight to put in an awesome sound system throughout the entire resort. The problem is you have obviously purchased a music agreement where there is nothing but continuous music which is great. I think it could be a lot better if you made some basic changes."

"What type of changes?" Hansen asked.

"Hire great DJ's to make the sound system live instead of simulated. They could play great music but they could also talk to the people. You could use that medium to advertise specials, from happy hour drinks to dance contests, whatever. Make it extremely interactive with the guests. Also, a perk to the select stars for being given a membership would be having the opportunity to be a guest DJ. The stars would love it and the guests would really love it. I think it would tie everything into a nice little package. Signed, sealed and delivered," Colt stopped. He was satisfied he held their attention but was a little worried he might have insulted them. It was, after all, their idea he was messing with. "And," he hesitated, "I wouldn't turn away skiers if they show up. I think we make it clear it is a snowboard resort but to totally cut them out may hurt you a little bit. If a group of five comes up and only one of them is a skier, would you really turn him away? I don't think being a little flexible will kill the concept."

"Well, you're probably right. I never wanted to exclude them. But I definitely want it to primarily be a snowboard resort. We can work that out. I tell you what, I'm impressed," replied Hansen. "Brandi, what did you think?" He asked looking over to her.

"I like everything Colt said. I'm a little concerned about putting in a Disney level lightscaping system only because of the costs, but I'll have to admit it would be awesome."

"We'll get to that in a second," Hansen said still digesting everything Colt had said. "What else have you got?"

"Commando Point," Colt responded.

"Commando Point, what is that?" asked Hansen.

"That is what the resort turns into in the off-season," Colt said.

"Well, this ought to be good," Brandi said. "I can't wait to hear this."

"I'm all ears myself," Hansen piped in.

"Let me ask both of you a simple business question," Colt said. "Would you rather have the resort be used by families, say a mother, father and a couple of kids, or would you rather it be used by corporations holding seminars and annual meetings? Who would you expect would spend more money?"

"I know the answer to that one," Hansen said, "but don't stop now, you're on a roll," he laughed.

"Corporations look for ways to train their employees that are unique and different. Commando Point will offer them the most unique and satisfying training exercise that will, quite frankly, redefine teamwork," Colt paused. "Here's how it works. In the off season we turn the lodging into military barracks, in name only. We hire two retired generals, maybe one from the Marines and one from the Army, to be our in-house consultants. Commando Point will feature corporate war games. They could either be for one company or you could have companies compete against each other. The generals serve as consultants to the teams. Weapon of choice would be paint ball guns. Strategy would be to capture or defend a certain target."

"What does that have to do with training?" Brandi asked. "I'm not sure I get it."

"What it does," Hansen interjected, "is it provides a means for employees to develop teamwork in a non-office environment. Almost like a life/death survival situation."

"Exactly," Colt said, pleased that Hansen was paying attention. "The employees learn to work together for the common goal and after fighting a good battle, they have drinks to celebrate their victories or even head to the local casinos to spend even more money. They will go back to their normal lives with a renewed sense of vigor. Commando Point will deliver an end result that is second to none. Think about all the diversity classes that mean nothing or roundtable discussions where you cut down your counterparts in order to make them better people. In my humble opinion, that type of training is outdated, doesn't work and never will. But think about dressing out in fatigues and meeting in a war room to strategize your battle plan and then getting out in the bush and pulling it off. Actually strategizing and taking on other people who'd met in their war room to strategize on how they were going to defend against you. And at the end of the day, everybody gets together to share their emotions and experiences. It is the ultimate team building experience that has absolutely nothing to do with their ordinary work lives. Companies will pay a fortune to send their employees through our boot camp. I guarantee it. And we'll make a lot more money renting out paint ball guns, goggles, and helmets and selling paintballs instead of just housing people who come to hike and spend their money elsewhere. The companies don't mind spending their money and realistically speaking, you don't make a lot of money off families with children," Colt finished.

"I absolutely love it," Hansen said. "I thought my idea was good, but this might even be better. The possibilities seem endless. Figure out how to make it work and let's do it."

"You are going to love this," Colt said to Brandi in particular. "When the snow melts off the snowballs, we cover them with a rubber overlay to make them look like giant paintballs." Colt was bubbling with excitement. "Do you think that's possible?"

"I think anything is possible," she said, already thinking about who she needed to call to set it up.

"I think your ideas are absolutely fantastic," Hansen said slapping his knee. "Now let's talk business. Why exactly are you here? What do you want?"

"I'm here because I believe in your vision," Colt responded. "I'm here because I really want to be a part of it all. And I think it is going to be big, really big. It could be the crown jewel of Tahoe," Colt added, "although, I'm not quite done yet. If money is a problem, I would be more than willing to chip in if you will let me join the team" he smiled at both of them.

"Everything you mention will cost a lot of money," Hansen said. "How much would you be willing to chip in?"

"Ten million, and one will go towards lightscaping the slopes," Colt replied without blinking. Brandi's eyes bulged and her jaw dropped. Obviously, she had no idea.

"Do you think that will cover everything you just mentioned? Because I'm tapped out," Hansen said matter-of-factly.

"If it doesn't, I'll throw in more," Colt said calmly. "I want in and I am willing to do anything from washing dishes to waiting tables to pay my dues."

"Would you be willing to manage the resort until we work out all the bugs" Hansen asked while keeping his fingers crossed under the table.

"Absolutely," Colt said. "When do I start?"

"How about right after lunch," Hansen joked as he stood up to shake Colt's hand. "I had a really good feeling about you from the beginning and I've heard nothing here to change my mind. We can iron out the details where I think you'll be happy. But I need you to get started ASAP. I like everything you said. I'm absolutely amazed you brought this much to the table after only being here a day and a half." Hansen looked over at Brandi and said "So what do you think, is he a keeper?"

"Oh, he's a keeper alright. I'm pretty much speechless right now. I think we need to make a toast," she said as she raised her wine glass. "Welcome aboard, Mr. Salley, welcome aboard."

"Thanks, I'm honored and can't wait to get started," Colt raised his glass.

"Now I want to show you something," Hansen said after they toasted. He reached down beside him and pulled out his laptop computer. "I think you'll find this very interesting. But first, let's order while this thing boots up." The waiter came over to the table when Hansen raised his menu and the three of them ordered.

"Finally," Hansen said after the laptop came to life. "Here, check this out," as he flipped the screen so Colt and Brandi could see it.

"What's that?" Colt said in amazement as he looked at a picture of him and Brandi doing shooters with Diggy-Boo at the bar in *The Flip Flop Inn* in Lake Tahoe. "How did you get that?"

"I have my sources," Hansen smiled.

"*Oh, my....God*," was all Brandi could say as she pointed at the screen with a very flushed look on her face.

"I have the staff give members of the media my business card with their room key, with instructions to call me anytime day or night. It's my way of keeping my finger on the pulse. Looks like that picture will be in all the tabloids next week," Hansen said with a smile as he leaned back in his chair, "that is, according to Cameron."

"Do you know him?" Colt asked in shock.

"I do now," Hansen responded. "He called me this morning and sent the email."

"I'm so sorry Mr..."

"Brandi," Hansen interrupted, "you can stop calling me Mr. Giles. You work with me not just for me. Please, for the last time, call me Hansen. Okay?"

"Yes," she replied apologetically, "I keep forgetting."

"As far as the picture is concerned, trust me, this is fantastic and I'm not mad about it. This is exactly the kind of publicity I want. Take a close look at that picture and tell me what you see?"

"I'm not sure what you mean, Hansen," Brandi responded somewhat confused.

"Then I'll tell you," Hansen said. "On the surface, what you see is two of the best looking people in the world doing shooters with a rap star. The subliminal view shows that he is happier to be with you then you are with him. Just look at his eyes. He's the one checking you out, not the other way around.

It's a great picture. The up side is now everybody is going to want to know more about the two of you. You are on your way to becoming celebrities so you better buckle up. Your boy Cameron has it all figured out."

"Is this the idea Cameron never finished telling us about?" Colt asked Brandi.

"Maybe," she said throwing her hands up in the air.

"From what he told me, he wants to make the two of you the hottest couple since the last one. He plans on making you stars and keeping himself gainfully employed in the process. I think he's on to something. And in my opinion, if you play the game, it will be very good for the resort."

"So you're really okay with this?" Colt asked as he pointed to the screen.

"Absolutely, I think its fantastic PR. People love to be seen with the right people and if you two happen to be the right people, and I think you are, then people are going to come to *Snowball* in droves. When they come, so will the Paparazzi. Then our advertising market goes worldwide and we haven't spent a dime. Quite frankly, I'm tickled pink," he laughed.

"Now how is that going to work with me managing the resort and Brandi in San Fran?" Colt asked.

"Yeah, how's that going to work?" Brandi added.

"Think about it, Colt, when you're managing the resort you will probably meet everyone who checks in, especially if they're important. The photo opportunities will be many. Take advantage of it. I mean really, what could be worse?"

"What about Brandi?" Colt was still confused.

"I see no reason why we have to have an office in San Francisco. We can move it up to Tahoe. It would work out better anyway because I can't stand driving into the city. That way you two can be together if you want and we can all make some money. I want you to know I told Cameron to run the picture and also gave him carte-blanche to the resort. I think his idea of making you stars is brilliant for him and for us," Hansen said as he raised his glass for another toast.

All Colt could think about was how this was going to hurt Annie-Laurie when she saw the picture. She would be devastated and she would also be pissed. Even though it was over between them it would still be a slap in her face and it was certainly not his intention when he left for California. This wasn't part of chasing his dream but she would never buy that explanation. He made a mental note to call her this afternoon when he could be alone and have some time to talk. Meanwhile, they had a wonderful lunch and the karma around the three of them seemed to be unbelievable. Colt felt like he'd known both of them for years and felt extremely comfortable in their company. Working with them was going to be interesting, especially if he drops in a substantial investment in the process.

"Do you have any idea where I can look for housing in Tahoe? That would surely save me some time," he asked them.

"Well, I think for the time being you continue to stay in one of my cabins. That way you can be close and get a better feel for the place. Brandi can move into the other one or however you guys work it out. We'll move the office to one of the offices in the Conference Center and then you can get to work on how to make these new ideas of Colt's happen. I'm open to all of them. I just want you to exercise good business judgment to make sure each one of them is feasible and will work. Colt, if you need a lawyer to represent you in the paper work, let me know. I have several in mind that I think would be a good match for you."

"Works for me," Colt said. "And thanks for the use of the cabin. That will make it a lot easier to get my feet wet, so to speak."

"When do you want us to go up?" Brandi asked.

"As soon as you can work it out," Hansen replied. "Colt might want to go up even as early as tomorrow. You can follow when you get everything taken care of in San Francisco. You have a nice place, so I would suggest subletting for a year. By then we'll know if we're completely crazy or not."

"Where are you going to stay when you come up? I certainly don't want to take over your home," Colt said.

"I'm going to build another cabin. I already have a spot in mind. The only reason I didn't build there in the first place is because I wanted two cabins and I could only fit one in there. But it's an awesome location and believe it or not, I already have the plans drawn up. I'll stay at the lodge in the meantime. With you guys up there, I won't have to come up as much."

"Okay, we have a deal then," said Colt shaking his hand. "I'll stop by and pick up Burly in the morning before I head up."

"He's not going to want to leave the farm," Hansen laughed. "He's having a ball just being a dog."

"I'm sure. He definitely didn't like the long ride across country and he hates the cold. He's probably not going to speak to me for awhile, or at least until she shows up," he said pointing to Brandi. "I think they hit it off better than we did," pointing back to himself.

"I'm not so sure about that," Hansen finished.

"**W**ow," Brandi said as they were pulling away from the restaurant. "My life seems to have changed completely overnight. Do you think we're moving too fast? I'm beginning to feel like I'm in the middle of a hurricane. First I meet you and now I'm moving to Tahoe. What's happening to me? I'm single and twenty-six years and I think I'm way too young to be making these quick decisions."

"You told me the other day when we were riding up to the lake that life is quick, remember?"

"Yeah, but that was when I was worried about you. Now it's me I'm worried about. I'm scared I'm dreaming and wonder if all this is real," she said looking around. "When I look at you, I know I love you. Is that a good thing or a bad thing?"

"Are you asking me if I love you?"

"First of all you I want you to know that money means nothing to me. I believe quality of life is worth so much more than money. And, I had absolutely no idea you were well...rich.

So, I guess I'm not sure what I'm asking. We've been together and I've done some things to you that I don't normally do. What does it mean? What does it mean to you?"

"Brandi, I didn't tell you about the money because it doesn't define who I am. I'm different from most guys. I love the fact that we have developed these feelings for each other so fast. Please believe me. I wasn't looking for this to happen, not in my wildest dreams. But you stole my heart immediately. I can't deny that. I have no plans to change it either unless you feel this is wrong. I can't take my eyes off of you and I hang on to every word that comes out of your mouth. In case you haven't noticed, we've been making love, not having sex. To me, having sex means I want to leave when it's over. I don't ever want to leave you because I'm deeply in love with you."

"Are you sure?"

"No, I'm kidding. Come here," he said as he kissed her lips softly. "Of course I'm sure. I knew it from the minute I first saw you."

"I'm going to hold you to that," she said as she wrapped her arms around him and slid her tongue sweetly into his mouth. "Please don't hurt me, Colt, okay?"

"I will never hurt you. Ever."

Wintergreen

"**W**hat do you mean you're not coming back?" Annie shrieked over the phone. "I thought this was your home. I guess you lied to me then," she finished with lost thoughts of what could have been.

"Annie, I never lied to you and you know it," Colt replied as he was talking to her on his cell phone while he was following Brandi from the office to her home somewhere down near the warehouses in San Francisco. "We had this wonderful thing and I will never forget that, but both of us had to move on and find our passion. I think I have found mine and I sincerely hope you will find yours. You're the one that told me it was over first, remember?"

"But I didn't mean it. I thought it would make you come home. I've been taking care of your home, your truck and that stupid dog, waiting for you to come back. I almost got in the truck and drove out there to get you. You're such a liar!"

"You don't mean that and you know it, Annie," he responded somewhat hurt she felt that way. "You can sell the truck, you can have the cabin and you can send me the dog if that would make you feel any better, but I'm not coming home. I want you to move on with your life like you said you were going to do."

"It's not that easy, Colt. I'm a girl and I'm a girl who happens to be thought of as your girlfriend. I thought I was doing the right thing by supporting you when you decided to *chase your dream*," she said sarcastically. "But I thought I was in that dream somewhere." She tried to hold back the tears that were flowing freely down her cheeks. "It's not that easy for me to move on. I love you and we had so much fun together. What happened?" She was desperate to save what she knew she had already lost.

"Annie, we were best friends and we had an easy affair. It worked well for both of us because neither one of us wanted to be committed at that stage of our lives. We loved each other because it worked at the time, but not for any other reason. I know it and you know it. If it was any more than that, you wouldn't have let me go and I wouldn't have left," Colt said in a defiant tone to keep her from breaking into the sympathy act. She was a good person, she was a very smart person and she was also a vindictive person if she didn't get what she wanted, which was a flaw in her personality he could never accept.

"Have you already met someone else?"

"Yes, but…"

Click

San Francisco

He stared at his phone after it went dead and almost ran into the back of Brandi's car because he'd taken his eyes off the road. He was getting ready to call Annie-Laurie back when he realized Brandi was turning into a parking lot between two warehouses. Reluctantly, he would have to wait to make the call and that meant Annie would be stewing, which wasn't a good thing. He threw the phone on the passenger-side floorboard and contemplated what he was going to say to Brandi when she realized something was wrong. She would come to that realization the minute he got out of the car because there was no way he could hide his mood. To his surprise she didn't say a word. This gave him enough time to calm down and concentrate on the future and not the past.

"It might seem a little rustic on the outside," she said somewhat embarrassed, "but it's a really cool place inside and a great location. And there is every kind of restaurant and bar you can think of within walking distance."

"I didn't picture you as a retro girl," he said trying to smile. He could tell she knew something was wrong by the concerned look on her face but she still didn't ask any questions to pin him down and he really appreciated the space she was giving him.

"To be honest, I didn't like living here at first. My boyfriend for two years and I had just broken up and my father died, so as you can imagine, I wasn't in the best of spirits when I moved in. Hansen really took good care of me and kept me extremely busy so I didn't have a whole lot of time to think. You don't know this, but Hansen and my father were really good friends even though there was a huge age difference between them. That's why I have a hard time calling him by his first name."

"I had no idea," was all Colt could think to say as he was still somewhat distracted by the conversation he'd just had with Annie-Laurie. "Sorry," he began again, "I just got off the phone with someone back in Virginia and the conversation didn't go as well as I had hoped. Excuse me for being a little distant at the moment." He figured he owed her some sort of apology at this point. "I made a mistake and it didn't work out like I thought it would." He could see her concern deepen as her mind tried to comprehend who he had been talking to. "Believe me," he said reassuringly, "this has absolutely nothing to do with you." He wrapped his arms around her and hugged her like there was no tomorrow. *How could he ever hurt this beautiful brown-eyed girl? She has the glisten of life in her eyes and also a sweet vulnerability of innocence.*

Tahoe

Cameron was sitting in the passenger side of his car, parked facing the lake and talking on his cell phone. His feet were propped up on the dashboard with the seat reclined as far back as it could go. The window was cracked to let the crisp cool air seep in which helped keep him from getting too comfortable. Oblivious to the beauty around him, he was deep into the conversation trying to sell his idea to one of his main contacts on the other end of the conference call. He needed to be sharp because the resistance on the other end of the line was stiff. She wasn't buying in and he'd already told Hansen it was a go. He desperately needed Hansen's support so he had to throw him the bone early. Running the picture was his only shot because she wouldn't consider it again. If he could get her tabloid to start the ball rolling, then all the others would follow. That's the way the business worked. She was the best in this monkey-see, monkey-do business. Cameron had a reputation for being a loner and taking unnecessary chances and in the past it had always paid off. But walking a tight edge meant it was as easy to fall off one side as it was the other. If he could get her to bite on his idea then he would be in a position to completely control his future. The problem was she knew it and quite frankly, she had his nuts in a vice.

"We like Diggy-Boo, but we don't see the point of focusing our resources on two people nobody knows or cares about. That's a tough sell, Cameron," said Deanna McBride from *Starbright Magazine.* "We focus on the tabloid crashers."

"I agree with what you're saying", Cameron replied in earnest. "But if you saw what I saw then you would think differently. Take a closer look at that picture and tell me what jumps out at you first?"

"I'm looking at z," she answered candidly. "So what if he's looking at the couple?"

"That's what I mean," Cameron said as he took his feet off the dashboard and sat up in his seat to emphasize his point. "Diggy-Boo is staring at them because they are beautiful people. I've taken twenty to thirty pictures of him and until I captured that one picture, he was only focused on himself, like he's looking in a mirror. And, he demands that everybody around him look up to him. You know how they are. Their egos won't let them look at anybody else but themselves. This couple broke him down. I saw it happen with my own two eyes. And it's not just z. When they walk into a room, people freak out. I'm telling you, I've never seen anything like it in my entire career."

"What you're proposing will take too much time and energy. For the life of me, I can't see the long term investment paying off," Deanna replied.

Cameron was crushed but not defeated. He decided to pause and let Deanna think about it for awhile without his badgering. Clearly, she was on the defensive to everything he was saying so it was useless to keep the conversation moving in the wrong direction.

"Deanna, how long have you worked with me?"

"Don't go down that road Cameron," she cut him off. "I work with a lot of people and no offense but you're nothing special. Anybody can take a picture. Your only saving grace is some of your pictures are unique because you don't run with the rest of the herd, but unfortunately, that's where it ends."

"Have I ever steered you wrong?"

"That's not the point," she responded coldly, "and you know it."

"Have you ever made a star? Have you ever really turned a normal person into an icon?" He pleaded.

"Have you?" She shot back.

"Nobody has, that's my point. If we can pull this off then we could own tabloids for a long, long time. It would be an unbelievable success story. That's all I'm saying," he pleaded. "I would have never thought of it had I not seen the effect these two have on people. It's absolutely unbelievable."

"Cameron," she sighed, "what do you want me to do?"

He was on the edge of his seat now. "Run the picture on the cover full page. Title it *"Who is this couple and where are they"* Put it in huge font."

"You're kidding right?"

"Deanna, I'm dead serious. If we're going to do this, let's do it big time. *Sink little doggy or swim.* If you don't splash it, the readers will simply turn the page. If you splash it across the face then you will dig into their psyche, setting the wheels in motion. Pardon the pun, but it would be like a snowball rolling down the hill, getting bigger and faster as the story progresses. I'll be the one to find them first and my comrades in the Paparazzi will come running. All hell will break loose and I have the inside track. It's a perfect setup," he finished as he crossed his fingers and rolled his eyes to the sky.

"Okay," Deanna finally said with little emotion. "If this fails, I give you my word, I will bury you," she added. "So you better make it work."

"Thank you, Deanna," he replied with confidence. "Run the picture," he demanded politely. He couldn't give her an out because she'd probably get cold feet at the last second. "I'll be back in touch," Cameron finished as he hung up, hopped out of his car and started dancing in the parking lot of the scenic overlook. If anyone saw him, they would have thought he was crazy. He was crazy but now it was time to *swim*. He hopped back in his car and headed back to the resort.

San Francisco

Hansen smiled to himself as he picked up the tabloid, *Starbright Magazine,* at a corner kiosk in downtown San Fran. The picture on the cover jumped off the page to capture his attention while he was more than twenty feet away. He was so excited he had to buy every copy the kiosk had. It was an amazing picture of Brandi and Colt, but not so much so for Diggy-Boo. The picture was extremely well done with all three of them facing towards the camera. Hansen admired the angle with which Cameron was able to capture the moment. Brandi and Colt came across as this amazingly beautiful couple and Diggy-Boo looked like he was idolizing them by the way the shot captured him staring at them. Hansen knew Diggy-Boo was going to be really pissed when he saw his picture on the cover of the tabloid because it's not the pose he would have wanted.

It was perfect, not only for the resort, but for Brandi as well. She was like a younger sister to him and he felt so sorry for her because she was such a sweet, innocent person and she always seemed to get the short end of the stick. When her father died and her boyfriend left her simultaneously, he thought she was going to have a complete breakdown. But to his surprise, she held her own. She kept her chin up and kept a smile on her face even though her eyes clearly showed the pain she was in. If Colt was for real, and he seemed to be, then maybe her luck has changed. Being on the cover of *Starbright* would also help. She was such a beautiful woman and she deserved to become a star. She had more going for her than every woman in Hollywood combined. *There is always sunshine after the rain,* he thought to himself after the attendant gave him change for the twenty-two issues of *Starbright* he purchased. His plan was to mail them to his famous friends in hopes they would find it in themselves to pursue meeting the couple up at the resort.

Los Angeles

"**S**o what do you think?" Deanna asked her team at the weekly staff meeting on Monday morning, which serves as a follow-up to the last week's publication. The staff meeting also serves as a sounding board for the kick-off of the current week's publication.

"I think it's the *shot heard around the world* judging by the amount of hits on our website," Liam, her chief administrative assistant responded with excitement. "They've more than tripled any other publication to date." Liam was an animated little fellow whom some thought was gay while others thought he was just a passionate country bumpkin. "The hits went from the cover of the tabloid directly to the inside story. I've never seen anything like it. I'm not sure we printed enough copies. The calls from our contacts with the other tabloids have more than doubled as well and the Paparazzi seem to be foaming at the mouth," he added. "Either we're on to something big or we've made an unbelievable mistake of massive proportions. Personally, I can't wait to run another picture to see if it's for real. But the numbers speak for themselves. Or should I say scream?"

"We're working on that right now," Deanna piped in. "I have Cameron doing a solo shot of the couple for the feature article we're doing on *Snowball* that will run in the next pub. Let's hope this is the real deal, because if it is, we just created two stars." She paused and scanned the faces around the conference table. It was obvious every one of them was on board with taking the risk.

"I'd sleep with either one of them," another member of her staff joked. "This is hilarious and I'm sure the real stars are going to hate their guts. I love it. Those spoiled little pricks and prickettes don't deserve what they have anyway. For most of them, it's all about timing and a lot of luck."

"Don't bite the hands that feed us just yet," Deanna said, "the little pricks and prickettes, as you so kindly refer to them, pay our salary. No matter what we do with the wonder couple, we still need everyone else so we can stay in the game. This is really just a blip, but hopefully, we can get plenty of mileage out of it before it fades into something else," she finished as the meeting was adjourned.

Charlottesville, Virginia

Annie-Laurie had to drive her younger brother in to Charlottesville for a doctor's appointment and decided to go to the outside mall to exercise her only love, Salley the puppy, while Kenny was getting his physical. The sun was shining and the weather was comfortably warm for that time of year which made for a refreshing break from the cold weather on the mountain at Wintergreen. In no particular hurry, she was simply killing time by strolling down the brick covered sidewalk and window shopping. The University of Virginia had a home basketball game that day so the mall was basically deserted.

Straining to enjoy the day, she was in another world when out of the corner of her eye, she saw it! The tabloid *Starbright Magazine* was sitting next to the other popular tabloids on a stand at the entrance to the only bookstore on the abandoned mall. She immediately knew it was a picture of Colt on the cover before she looked directly at it. She could tell it was him because of the cold chill that ran up her spine. Frozen in time, she remained standing there, unable to move. Finally, as she regained her senses, she turned and stared at the picture for what seemed like an eternity. Salley sat beside her feet wagging his tail and just kept looking up with a perpetual look of confusion on his face. As hard as she tried, she couldn't bring herself to move closer to confirm her worst nightmare. Inevitably, the tears started rolling down her face before her feet started moving. Slowly, one step at a time, she approached the stand displaying the tabloids like it was an activated atomic bomb and if she touched it, it would blow. Instantly, the inhumanity of the tabloids became all too real. Typically, jealousy comes early in a crumbling relationship, but this time, jealousy reared its ugly head after the relationship was over. As she stood there staring at the tabloid, she realized how lonely she was and how she never had any luck. Colt was the best thing that ever happened to her but she was never going to be good enough for him. He was born with a silver spoon in his mouth so no matter where he went, or what he did, he would always come out on top. And even though she loved him, she also hated his guts because he was the lucky one. She couldn't bring herself together enough to look at the girl he was with in the picture and she couldn't bring herself to read the headlines, although they were already engrained in her mind and heart. Subliminally, she took everything in before it totally registered. And finally, when it did register, the bomb went off. She snapped like a twig. She wanted to kill him.

It didn't take long before the owner of the bookstore came out to see if she was okay. The anonymous girl looked lost and forlorn and he could tell by the tears and the look of total devastation on the young woman's face that something was horribly wrong. It was the sad, evil look that bothered him as she turned and walked away with the puppy wagging his tail, trotting happily beside her. Instinctively, he looked down at the tabloids where she had frozen her stare to see if he could figure out what caused this beautiful girl so much pain. Shaking his head, he walked back in to the bookstore to finish reading the story in *Starbright Magazine* about the beautiful couple that nobody knows in Lake Tahoe.

"So what's your problem" asked Annie-Laurie's nineteen year-old brother Kenny when she picked him up. Kenny was full of vim and vigor and had a youthful innocence that often came out in a sarcastic way. "You look like you just had an accident in your pants," he added with a smirk to make his point.

"Thanks," she replied without looking at him. "I really needed to hear that. You have such a way with women. What did the doctor say?"

"Everything looks good, looks like I can play baseball and go off to college and become successful like you," he answered, immediately sorry for what he'd said. "I didn't mean it quite that way," he quickly corrected.

It was too late because Annie-Laurie wasn't listening to him anymore. The extraordinary circumstances of seeing Colt and another girl on the cover of a tabloid magazine exceeded her means of logic regarding life's rules. The contradiction in the fulfillment of Colt's prophecy and the intensity of the moment held grave consequences of terrifying unpredictability for her. It was simply the straw that caused her to snap. And snap she did. She put the truck in drive and floored it out of the parking lot. Her mind was already three thousand miles away.

Tahoe

Colt and Burly rolled into Tahoe from San Francisco on the express train to prosperity. The excitement of a new chapter in his life in the land of make believe was more than he ever imagined. It was almost like he'd forgotten his past life in Virginia, totally. He was seeing nothing but the future and he couldn't wait to get there. The level of profitability of *Snowball* had huge potential but the investment in lifestyle went through the roof. If he looked deeper at his new situation, he would have felt overwhelmed. Yet meeting Brandi and Hansen led him up the mountain. Introduced to a new love and a new ambition, he put his blinders on and tried very hard not to look back.

As they were cruising through the snow covered mountains, he couldn't help but think about Cameron and the tabloids and the forbidden feelings surging deep inside his gut. He knew his parents and Annie-Laurie, in particular, would be crushed if his picture ever came out in the tabloids. It wasn't his intention to purposely hurt anyone, yet he felt somewhat justified in chasing his dream and reaping the benefits that come along with the chase. His parents would rein in his responsibilities to the family and what was expected of him. Annie would never forgive him for leaving in the first place, which all added up to the fact that he was going to have some serious explaining to do.

He'd already made the call to his storage company to have the rest of his belongings shipped to the cabin in Tahoe so his commitment to being there long term was solid. That would totally freak his parents out. Annie, on the other hand, already knew he wasn't coming home. They were compatible in convenience but not in life and that was the deciding factor which made it easier for him to cut the string. He knew she'd understood why he was leaving but he couldn't understand that peculiar look in her eyes. A look that expressed a complex and difficult set of emotions that he wasn't able to process. There was a slight hint of meanness he'd never seen before that compounded the situation beyond what he'd expected. He had hoped to talk to her before any picture came out just to provide some sort of buffer, but he was too chicken to make the call. As he and Burly drove through the beautiful mountains towards Lake Tahoe, he couldn't help but feel the storm clouds brewing their ugly heads above him. *Nothing is ever easy,* he said to himself. Burly just took a deep breath and sighed like he understood.

The feeling of euphoria pulling into *Snowball* overwhelmed him, which he took as a good sign. This time, he slowed the car down to a crawl and scoped out everything from the quality of the road to the number of mountain peaks dotting the beautiful skyline above the village. Through his early research, he knew the area was known historically for the Donner Party catastrophe. In 1846, a group of emigrants got caught in a blistering series of snowstorms and avalanches while trying to cross through the Sierra Nevada's and lost roughly half of their party due to the horrific conditions they encountered. Colt knew this area was sometimes referred to as the *Storm King* because of its high peaks, steep terrain and thunderous snowfalls that could often cause catastrophic conditions which would never to be tamed by mankind. This was part of the allure of the Sierra Nevada's and Lake Tahoe because beauty and hell were forever exposed together.

The village appeared magically as he rounded the bend and brought his thoughts back to the present. He couldn't believe his luck in crossing the country and landing in this fabulous playground for the rich and famous. When he pulled into a parking spot he was surprised that Cameron was there to meet him on the shuttle.

"How'd you know I was here?" Colt asked.

"A little bird told me you were coming up," Cameron was proud to say.

"Would that little bird be Hansen?"

"That would be a pretty good guess. So how's my new rock star?" Cameron asked as they shook hands.

"That's not funny," Colt responded. "You have no idea how much explaining I'm going to have to do if that picture ever comes out."

"Too late my friend, it's already on the stands," Cameron said in defiance as he threw his hands in the air as a gesture of apology. "That's what I do. I make things happen very fast before the next mosquito comes in and steals my blood."

"But why me? Why Brandi? What in the hell could possibly be so interesting about us that would warrant being on the cover of a gossip magazine? I don't understand," Colt said as he was already calculating in his mind what Annie-Laurie would be feeling when she sees the picture. "What tabloid is it?"

"*Starbright*," Cameron said as he picked up a copy lying on the seat next to him and handed it to Colt.

"This is so not good," was all Colt could say as he stared blankly at the picture. "And I don't think Diggy-Boo is going to be too thrilled about this either."

"You got that right," Cameron laughed. "Pardon my language, but he ain't going to be real happy about not being the center of attention. That picture of you and Brandi completely blows him off the page and the headline doesn't help him either," he smiled. "Sometimes you are the cookie and sometimes you are the crumbs. I can assure you, he's feeling kind of crumby and not too happy right now. I've already gotten the expected nasty email from his so-called agent."

"How long will this take to die down?" Colt innocently asked.

"I'm thinking it might never go away," Cameron laughed. "Judging by the hits *Starbright* has been getting ever since that picture hit the stands. I'm afraid you and Brandi have become quite popular."

"What does that mean?" Colt asked as the shuttle started moving towards the lodge.

"It means that you two have instantly become sensations. The rest of my lovely counterparts have already checked into the resort and will probably offer you quite a reception in about, let me think," he paused and put his finger to his temple, "one minute."

"You're kidding me, right?. No way..."

"Yes way..."

"Whaaaaat?" Colts eyes bulged. "It's absolutely absurd. I don't get it," he said confused.

"You don't understand the game my friend," Cameron said with confidence. "The media, especially the tabloids, are constantly in need of the next big thing. Look at all the other stars on the market today. They're old news. They're all burnt out and their stories have been told a gazillion times to the point that nobody cares anymore. Quite frankly, they're idiots for the most part and they're just filling the blanks until someone like you and Brandi erupt onto the scene. I'll be willing to bet you some of my counterparts have already rooted her out and are snapping pics as we speak."

"No way..."

"Again, yes way," Cameron nodded his head emphatically. "I have no doubt because I know how the system works and I know how they operate. That's what we do."

"Well, what in the world am I supposed to do now?"

"Enjoy the ride, my friend. Enjoy the ride."

"Don't get me wrong Cameron, I'm flattered. I mean, it's pretty cool. But I don't know how to act. When I see the younger stars in the spotlight, they seem to hate everything and everybody. I can't live my life like that. That's not my personality."

"Then don't," Cameron responded.

"What do you mean?"

"Don't fight it. Embrace it with your own style. Sell yourself the best way you know how. Instead of becoming popular because you've become public enemy number one, make the public want to be you. This is not just what I want, Hansen wants this too because it's good public relations for *Snowball*.

He's no fool. Just be you and everything will be just fine. Okay?"

"I really think you're just pulling my leg," Colt said brushing off the conversation. "Hansen wouldn't really..," Colt stopped in mid-sentence as the bus pulled into the circle at the lodge.

"Think again my friend," Cameron said as he pointed to the herd of Paparazzi surrounding the entrance to the main lodge. "The mosquitoes have landed. All I'm asking is that you give me the exclusive. I think I've earned that."

"What is that?" Colt asked as he pointed towards them. "Are they here for me?"

"Bingo."

"What am I supposed to do?" Colt asked while he was feeling the beginnings of a panic attack.

"Buckle up and enjoy the ride because it's show time. And by the way, you can thank me later."

"How am I supposed to do that?"

"Like I said, I want it. I want to be in on everything that happens up here. I want the lion's share of the pictures in the tabloids to be taken by me and I want the stories. I can only do that if I'm the first to know. Mr. Giles has already agreed. Eventually, they will start dogging me," he said nodding outside at the gathering. "But I've been down that road before so I can deal with it."

"I think you're blowing smoke," Colt said still flushed. He was basically attacked when he stepped down from the shuttle. So many questions were coming at him he couldn't understand what anybody was asking. Video cameras, microphones and wires were all over the place, with flashes going off and people blocking his path. Colt was at a total loss on how to deal with the situation. Finally, he made it to the top of the steps and he turned around so they could all see him. He quickly counted at least fifteen freezing bodies. He paused to take everything in.

"Drinks are on me at *The Cause* at four o'clock. I'll answer all of your questions then." He turned and was ushered in by the staff. Thinking he was going to find relief when he walked into the lodge, he quickly realized he was wrong. The staff surrounded him as quickly as the Paparazzi outside. Instantly, Colt had about twenty new best friends. The funny thing was he ate it up. Cameron sat back and watched his little project begin to light up. It reminded him of adding a new extension to the space station and finally powering it up. It was a beautiful sight. *He knew he was right*, he smiled to himself. *Deanna was going to be kissing his butt.* He'd granted her first dibbs in return for taking a chance and running the picture. If this really took off, then *Starbright Magazine* could jump to number one in the tabloids. *It's all good,* he smiled to himself.

San Francisco

What in the world were all these reporters doing outside of my building? Did someone get killed or something, Brandi thought to herself as she emerged from the front door dragging one of her suitcases. She was halfway down the sidewalk before she realized that for some unbelievably strange reason, all these people are here for her. It took her a few moments to get her sea legs and recover from the embarrassment of instantly being the center of attention. *You would think someone would at least offer to help me with the suitcase,* she recovered.

The swarm erupted into bedlam when they realized it was her and started buzzing all over the place. She'd been busy packing for Tahoe and closing down her apartment so she hadn't seen the tabloid and had no idea why they were there. Consequently, the barrage of questions weren't making any sense as she continued to pull her suitcase through the crowd and put it in the trunk of her car. Finally, someone realized her innocence to the situation and handed her a copy of *Starbright*. Brandi stopped in her tracks and just stared at the picture. Immediately, a million thoughts ripped through her head and absolutely none of them made any sense. The flashes were like questions and the questions were like flashes and they both kept barraging her like dodge balls.

"Where are you from?"

Flash, flash

"Are you going to do any acting?"

Flash, flash

"Who does your make up?"

Flash, flash

"Did you sleep with Diggy-Boo?"

Flash, flash

"Are you going to see Colt Salley?"

Flash, flash

"Can you do lunch?"

Flash, flash

"Can you do dinner?"

Flash, flash

"Can I sleep with you?"

Flash, flash

After multiple flashes, finally, Brandi Steele regained her composure. She leaned against the back of her car and held her hand up until the crowd became silent and the last picture was taken. But instead of speaking right away, she slowly scanned the faces of each and every one of the Paparazzi and smiled at each one them in the process. The prospects of a very lucrative lifestyle and the opportunity to promote *Snowball* did not escape her in the moment. In her silence, her underlying beauty was beginning to emerge from the lack of make-up and the somewhat ratty clothes she was wearing while cleaning her apartment for hopefully, the last time. Every one of them immediately fell in love with her. Obviously, this perfectly built brunette, with dark brown eyes that dazzled without the paint, had the inner workings of someone able to reach beyond her simple beauty and envelope the people she came in contact with and take them to a level of adolescent lust. The fact that she was actually a real person with real feelings and this beautiful innocence actually silenced the Paparazzi like they had never been silenced before. Their addiction to her was set in stone and they were more than interested to hear what she has to say.

"I am honored you have taken time out of your day to come down here to meet me. I feel like Cinderella and I sincerely appreciate the attention," she smiled as they melted. "I'm going to answer a couple of the questions I was able to decipher. First of all, I'm not an actress, I'm a business person who happens to work for Mr. Hansen Giles and we have developed the hottest new resort in the Sierra Nevada Mountains called *Snowball*. Actually, I'm packing as we speak. I will be moving there indefinitely to work with my very good friend and counterpart, Mr. Colt Salley. We will be launching this resort to a level that has yet to be seen. If you haven't been there, you should come. You are more than welcome. I think you will be pleasantly surprised at what you discover. Mr. Salley is already there and I'm sure he would love to meet and talk to each and every one of you. Please don't think of me as rude, but I have several suit-cases to bring down to the car and would sincerely appreciate some help," she finished as she turned and headed back up the sidewalk with more volunteers following her than she could ever imagine. "Oh," she turned and said as an afterthought, "no, you cannot sleep with me. I already have someone in my life but I'm flattered," She seductively smiled as she flipped her hair out of her face, turned and headed up the sidewalk.

As she was walking back into her building, being followed by *God knows who*, she rolled her eyes and wondered if she'd said too much or not enough. Obviously, they were all willing to help her pack so it must have been okay. Brandi decided at that point to get to know each one of them on a first name basis and treat them with a hospitality they'd never seen before. She realized this was her moment and she was more than prepared to take advantage of it.

By the end of the morning, her apartment was spit-polished and shined, bags were successfully loaded in the trunk of her car and she had fifteen new best friends. She absolutely killed them with kindness and treated them like human beings. No one had ever done that before. To close the deal and make them completely humbled, she took all of them out to lunch to show her appreciation for their help. After lunch, she blew them kisses, hopped in her loaded-up car and pointed it east, towards Tahoe. What she didn't realize was that every one of them fell in love with her, each for different reasons. And they were going to follow Cameron's example and help make her a star. She just hoped Hansen and Colt would approve on the way she handled the situation.

Wintergreen

Small communities make fine wine from the grapevine of gossip. The news of Annie-Laurie and Colt's breakup had spread like wildfire after he left for California. Some people were happy and some were sad. The happy ones were the jealous ones and the sad ones were their true friends. The fact that Annie-Laurie and Colt were so well liked made it difficult for anyone to take sides, consequently, no one said anything and that was the worst thing they could ever do to her. Her sensitivities were at DEFCON 1, the most dangerous level, and she felt totally alone. By the time she got back up on the mountain after having seen the tabloid it was too late for her to recover from the shock. It also didn't take long for *Starbright Magazine* to get up the mountain behind her. It ripped through *Wintergreen* like a 10.5 earthquake. And the aftershocks didn't let up. There wasn't one person who didn't know about the picture so the balance of power between loyalty to both her and Colt had shifted towards him and the silence around her was deafening. Annie-Laurie went from being totally devastated to completely lost and irrational. Her world was crashing like a spent satellite falling through space towards earth at an ungodly speed and totally out of control; getting ready to burn.

When she dropped her brother off at her parents' house in the valley she'd convinced him to take the puppy for a while. That was the only smart thing she had done. She drove up to the cabin because she needed to be completely alone and unhampered by responsibilities. Acting blindly, she went about packing her luggage with the bare essentials and closing up the cabin with methodical precision. Tears were flowing freely and her anger evaporated them on the cheeks of her face. Every time she revisited the picture of Colt and that girl, she shuddered at the realization that she'd lost the battle. She was alone in one of the most beautiful, scenic places in the world and to her it seemed all too much like a living hell. She had to get out. She had to meet the devil in his own backyard.

When she finished packing, Annie-Laurie drove back down the mountain, went to the bank and withdrew all of her savings, which amounted to roughly seven thousand dollars. She called her parents and told them she was moving to California. She told her brother she loved him and asked him to please take extra special care of the puppy. She filled her truck up with gas, bought some bottled water, a map and a couple packs of cigarettes, a habit she'd given up long ago. She drove over to the Interstate and pointed her direction west, towards the sun, towards Tahoe. She'd have plenty of time on the road to actually figure out what she was going to say and do when she got there. But she had to get there and she had to settle the score. It was, in fact, her nature.

The Cause

He was true to his word and Cameron really appreciated that. Colt walked into the bar at exactly three-thirty just like he said he would. Holding his cell phone to one ear, he quickly scanned the afternoon crowd of partying snowboarders until he spotted Cameron and walked over and sat down in the booth across from him. He held one finger up to his lips, indicating he would be off the phone in a second. While he was talking on the phone, Cameron took time to scan the room and noticed just about every one in the bar was checking Colt out. Cameron wasn't sure whether it was because the picture on *Starbright* or just the fact they were intrigued with him as a person. Either way, it really didn't matter because Colt was well on his way to becoming rather famous, and in time, everybody would know who he was. Cameron sat back in the booth, extremely pleased with himself. He knew this was going to be good.

"Do you know what you've done?" Colt asked as he laid his cell phone on the table. "Your pals were outside Brandi's building this morning waiting for her to come out. How did all this happen so quickly?"

"First of all they're not my pals, we just happen to be in the same business. I operate alone. That's why I'm here talking to you and not over at that table across the room staring at you," Cameron said as he nodded for Colt to check it out. "Those guys are showing you the courtesy of waiting until four o'clock before they come at you, but believe me, they're coming. Secondly, I told you this was for real. I think in the end, it's going to work out well for both you and *Snowball* and it's going to be a great ride. To be honest, I would have been extremely disappointed if they hadn't camped outside of her house this morning."

"Yeah, I know what you told me, but I really didn't believe you. It seemed too far fetched. I mean, we're not important, we're just ordinary people."

"Not anymore my friend. Your normal days have gone bye-bye," Cameron said as he pumped his fist in the air. "Both of you have something very special. Something so special you don't even know it. You're not ordinary by any stretch of the imagination. Extraordinary might be a better description. Look, I know it's hard for you to see what I see. But I get paid to see. It's my job and I'm good at it. And what I see is people melting at your feet when they're around you and that, my friend, is not ordinary. The same goes for Brandi. She's got that thing too. The two of you together make famous Hollywood couples look like a 70's re-run. Trust me, I know what I'm talking about," Cameron finished, satisfied with his sales pitch. "So how did she handle the mosquitoes?"

"Apparently, she handled the situation like a pro because they helped her finish cleaning her apartment and packed her car. Then she took them all to lunch. So I'm guessing each and every one of them fell in love with her, just like I did," Colt laughed as he shook his head. "She's something else, that girl."

"That's better than a star would handle it. Who has ever taken them to lunch? This is fantastic!" Cameron was on the edge of his seat bubbling with excitement. "I'm telling you, she has them worshiping the ground she walks on. I knew I was right about you two. You guys are going to re-write the book on how to deal with the Paparazzi. All you have to do is make us adore you and you'll be set for life. For some reason, everybody treats us like roaches, so we ultimately derive a great deal of pleasure out of hounding them. Now if we become friends, then it turns into the barter system. Do you understand what I'm saying?"

"I scratch your back and you scratch mine?" Colt said.

"Exactly, it's that simple. It's not rocket science. Give the mosquitoes blood and they will show you respect and give you fame. That way, everybody is happy," Cameron said enthusiastically. "Evidently, she gets it. That's awesome."

"When I talked to her, she sounded so excited. She was made for fame," Colt said with pride. "You know when she looks at people, they melt like butter. It's the strangest thing. I think my role will be more of a support role to her," he said seriously.

"Don't kid yourself, my friend. Your game is as good as hers. The two of you are a fantastic team."

"Hello, boys," the cute little waitress with the snowboard tan kindly interrupted. "My name is Lenna. Alex thought you might be thirsty so she made you a couple of house specials. I hope you like them."

"Thanks, Lenna," Colt said. "Hey, would you mind getting Alex to mix up another batch and take a round to that table over there," he said as he pointed to the table of Paparazzi. "I'll take care of everything. Just make sure they're happy."

"Absolutely, Mr. Salley, glad to do it," the star-struck waitress said as she spun around and mouthed the words *oh my God!*

"How did she know my name?" Colt said to Cameron.

"Everybody's going to know who you are. It comes with the territory. I hope you enjoy getting hit on because they're going to come after you like there is no tomorrow."

"That sounds painful," Colt laughed.

"No pain, no gain," Cameron said with a laugh. "Speaking of pain, here come the mosquitoes, right on time."

"Is this the way it's always going to be?" Colt asked before they got to the table.

"Pretty much," replied Cameron. "It's life in the fast lane."

"You know what I need? I need to go fishing. That's what I do to get away. I haven't even really started this job yet and I already need to go fishing," Colt laughed.

"We can take care of that," Cameron said. "There's a pretty big fishing hole at the bottom of the hill, in case you've forgotten."

"Had my eye on it the second I rolled into town. Do me a favor and set it up. I think I need that. But give me some time to get settled in my new job. I still need to iron out a few wrinkles."

"Don't you think it is a little cold to go fishing?"

"It's never too cold to fish."

"If you say so, I'll set it up. I love pulling the wool over these guys' heads anyway. They've gotta hate my guts."

Colt looked up at the Paparazzi as they approached the table. He put his best game face on and welcomed them again to *Snowball*. After they took a couple of pictures of him sitting at the table, Lenna showed up with drinks for everybody.

"Do you have a private area where we can all sit?" Colt asked her. "There's not enough room here."

"Sure do," she happily replied. "It's already set up and waiting for you. If you will follow me, we have you in the Board Room, get it?" She laughed.

"They thought of everything didn't they?" Colt asked out to no one in particular.

They all picked up their drinks and followed her into the Board Room. Colt made a mental note to start focusing on getting to know all the staff. He'd really wanted that to be his first priority, however, for whatever reason, the Paparazzi came first. He knew he was going to have to make the next couple of hours count because it was his first opportunity to sell himself and *Snowball*. They, meaning the twelve who showed up, were unusually quiet based on what Colt expected. Maybe they were just getting the lay of the land and would launch into their notorious nasty behavior once they felt more comfortable. Or maybe they were really going to be cooperative. It was anybody's guess.

"I will start by welcoming all of you, including myself, to *Snowball*. This is as new to me as it is to you. My name is Colt Salley and I'm from Virginia. When I first read about this resort I knew I had to come out and be a part of it. Mr. Giles has been kind enough to give me a shot at managing the resort. My experience is somewhat limited but my enthusiasm is second to none so I think it'll work. Brandi Steele, Mr. Hansen's assistant will be joining me. Together, we will make *Snowball* one of the best resorts in America. Also, I think you will be interested to hear this, our first priority is to make *Snowball* the playground for the rich and famous," he paused to watch the expressions of everyone around the table. Still, to his surprise, there was total silence. He stole a quick glance at Cameron who only responded by raising his eyebrows.

"Anyway," he continued, "with that being said, we also welcome each and every one of you to be a part of this interesting journey. We realize that in order to reach millions of people, and the right people, you represent the best medium to bring *who's who* to Lake Tahoe and specifically to *Snowball*. The public will see the top stars boarding down our slopes, drinking shots at our *Roo Bars* and partying all night here at *The Cause*. They, meaning everybody who's anybody, will want to be a part of this experience. In order for this to happen we need you and welcome you and will do everything in our power to make your stay here as comfortable as possible. I have to be honest and tell you that you are our advertising medium. You scratch our backs and we scratch yours," he smiled at Cameron. "The stars who visit us will have to understand how we work together and not fight your interest in them. On the reverse side, if you show them some respect then I think everything will work out just fine. However, if you beat them up and don't give them some space, then you might as well go back to Hollywood, or wherever, and camp outside their gates because that won't work here. This is going to be a wonderful place where everybody gets along." Once again, Colt paused, this time to take a sip of his drink. "Are there any questions?"

"I have one," one of the Paparazzi said. "What's so special about one or two pictures of someone special boarding the slopes in her pajamas? After that, we are out of here. I mean, it should get old pretty quick."

"You bring up a good point," Colt responded. "And what

you just said represents the absolute worst case scenario. We feel it is important to work together. Everybody, including myself," once again he smiled at Cameron, "likes to be on the covers of the tabloids. Who wouldn't? What we would like to do is help bring you together with the people you are interested in, and do it in a very amicable way. I think in a way that you are totally unaccustomed to. We think it is extremely important to brag about who comes to visit us. We also want to have big parties where everybody is invited. We want to have the stars serve as guest DJ's with each and every one of you spending time in the booth with them. We will work very hard so everyone gets to know each other and I guarantee you that you will get unlimited material to work with and unlimited resources to help you," he smiled as he looked around the table. "All we ask is that you keep us in the tabloids. Quite honestly, we need the publicity,"

"Where do you fit in?" asked another member of the Paparazzi.

"What do you mean?"

"Well. What if we want to take pictures of you and Brandi Steele? Is that going to be okay?"

"Of course it will be okay. But to be honest, I have no idea why you would want to do that," Colt kidded as he noticed Cameron cringe at his response. "In closing, I want to say that I would like to get to know all of you and if you ever have any questions, I will give you my cell phone number so you can reach me any time, day or night. Now, would you like to join me for dinner over at *Burton's*? It's on me." Colt noticed Cameron relaxed a little when he said that.

Without hesitation, everybody got up and shook hands with Colt. Cameron was pleased the way Colt handled himself around his fellow comrades. On the way out of *The Cause,* Colt thanked Lenna and Alex, the bartender, and told them he would be back after dinner to settle up. Clearly, it was a bold move to get on the good side of Paparazzi. They seemed to let their guard down a little and by the end of dinner Colt had them laughing, joking and literally eating out of the palms of his hands. Cameron hoped Brandi had accomplished as much with her followers. Their first impressions were going to make or break his plan. He had no doubt that everything was moving in the right direction.

After dinner, they went back to *The Cause* for after dinner drinks. Colt was very happy to see Brandi sitting at the bar talking to Alex along with their new Paparazzi friends. He was relieved to see she'd made it safely up from San Francisco. He snuck up behind her and gave her a surprise hug. Then he whispered something in her ear that made her smile before she turned around and gave him a quick kiss in front of the flashing cameras. For the next hour, they were the target of affection from the staff and the Paparazzi. By the end of the evening the party had gone nuclear. Everyone was dancing with each other and doing shots like there was no tomorrow. And if there was a tomorrow, they would have to return to *The Cause* to find *The Cure.*

Cameron calculated at least three more tabloids would be featuring Colt Salley and Brandi Steele and of course, *Snowball,* based on the success of the evening. His comrades had never been treated so well and really seemed to appreciate the warm reception. He could tell they loved being there and absolutely adored their new targets. Surprisingly, their new targets adored them as well. Plans were being made for a large group to get together and snowboard the next day. Colt told his new entourage they would all meet at noon and make a few runs followed by a round of drinks at one of the *Roo Bars.* He and Brandi quietly slipped away when the party reached peak level so no one really noticed, or cared, that they'd left.

When they got back to his cabin, Colt noticed Brandi's bags weren't there. He wasn't sure whether to ask her about it or simply let it play out. He couldn't stand the thought of her staying in the cabin next to his without them being together night and day. That fictitious arrangement was not going to work for him. Instinctively, Brandi noticed Colt scan the room when they walked in. Her motives were genuine in trying not to be too presumptuous about their relationship. Certain expectations would become more natural the more they got to know each other. But they were still early in their relationship, although they've already covered some major ground. She was a very smart woman.

"Let's talk about today," Colt said as he placed a couple of logs on the crumpled paper in the fireplace while she poured them a glass of Merlot. "We haven't discussed our new-found fame," he said as he gave her a quick glance.

"Are you comfortable with it?" Brandi asked as she walked over to hand him his wine.

"I guess so, although it seems somewhat remarkable because everything has happened so fast. This is like the craziest thing I have ever experienced in my life."

"Think about the young stars in Hollywood and how quickly things happen to them. They don't even realize what hit them," she justified.

"I'm not sure I realize what's hit me," Colt responded as he stared into the beginnings of a nice fire. "I mean if you compare my lifestyle three weeks ago to now, it's like night and day. The distinctive contrast is spectacular on one hand," he held out one hand. "And mind boggling on the other," he extended the other hand. "The interesting thing is I love every second of it."

"Me too," she said as she wrapped her arms around him from behind and lay her head on his shoulder to stare at the fire.

"Are we really allowed to have all this? I mean, is this fair? If I think about it too hard I start to feel guilty."

"I think that's normal. I feel a little guilty myself but I'm happy. I know from past experiences that happiness doesn't come easily."

Colt turned to her and stared deep into her eyes. He could see hints of pain from her past as well as the gleam of happiness about her present situation. He knew she was a strong woman with strong convictions. He also knew she was fragile. She was not the type of person who would dedicate her future on a mindless flirtatious endeavor. She needed something more out of life and was willing to endure the pain, if that's what it took, to get what she wanted. *I'm going to be your sunshine,* he thought to himself.

"What do you think about Cameron?" She broke the spell.

"I like him," he said. "Cameron's a really nice guy in a cut-throat business. He's smart and he knows how to operate, that's for sure. He's a schemer, I know that."

"What do you mean?"

"Think about it, Brandi. He dreamed all of this up for us, the attention, the pictures, the whole nine yards. Quite frankly, I think his plan was sophisticated and remarkable. He's seems to be making something out of nothing and that's not an easy thing to do. I'm not belittling our unique situation, but look at what he's done in a very narrow window of time. It's amazing and I have to give him a lot of credit for pulling this off. One day, I'm going to get him to explain it to me in complete detail."

"I know," Brandi said, "it's almost like he invented a new drug."

"Exactly"

"Do you like being the new drug?"

"Somebody's got to do it," he laughed. "It might as well be us. I tried to eschew my public responsibility as far as my family was concerned but this is different. I like the limelight and I'm thinking you do too. Or maybe it's just California. I'm not sure."

"I love it," she said seriously. "I've never wanted to be just anybody. My whole life I've dreamed of being somebody special. I just never knew how to get there. Maybe, Cameron came along at the right time for both of us."

"Absolutely," Colt said. "And I think you came along at the right time for me."

"Ditto to that," she said as she slid her tongue softly into his mouth. "It would be a lonely ride without you."

"By the way," he backed away for a second.

"What?"

"I'll slip next door and get your luggage before you wake up in the morning."

"Thanks," she pouted, "I didn't know what to do."

"Let's go to bed."

"I thought you'd never ask."

Nowhere

Annie was completely highway hypnotized. The passenger floorboard of her truck was littered with candy wrappers, empty potato chip bags and empty bottles of water. If she didn't have to stop and go to the bathroom she probably never would have gotten out of the truck. When she did stop, it seemed like every gas station had that damned tabloid on the front rack. Each time she saw it the more it hurt and the madder she got. It was like rubbing sea salt on an open wound, causing it to rip a little more. To make matters worse, the copy she purchased was sitting on the front seat beside her. Colt's picture was glowing with pure delight, which caused her mood to tumble deeper into despair with each mile that passed. At longer rest stops she would entertain herself by pulling out her laptop and researching her destination. She also learned a great deal about the photographer, Cameron Toscanini, as well as the resort *Snowball*. She figured by the time she landed in Tahoe, she would know as much about the place as if she'd lived there her entire life. That would give her a start.

Her cell phone rang about twenty times. She didn't even flinch or give answering it a second thought. She was worried someone might talk her into turning around, or worse, it could be Colt calling. She wanted to see him face to face so turning back wasn't an option. Feeling completely isolated in her thoughts and struggling with the physical, as well as mental aspects of the long trip across country, she kept moving into the void. She had no expectations regarding the outcome of the journey.

Being an outdoors person, she kept herself entertained looking at the interesting changes in landscape as she drove west. At one point in her journey, she noticed a beautiful arrangement of flowers in the shape of a cross beneath the window of a roadside diner, smack dab in the middle of *nowhere*. For some reason, she thought about the significance of that flower arrangement until she was at least *two miles west of nowhere*. There was a strange personal connection that weighed on her mind until the hypnosis kicked back in. And beyond lays Kansas. *Oh my.*

The complexity of her emotions conflicted with the physical and mental side of her being. She had absolutely no idea what she was doing or was about to do. She shuddered at the thought of seeing Colt and wondered what would go through his mind upon seeing her. Judging by the smile on his face in the picture, he was not going to be pleased. Much later, she finally made it into Kansas, the state that never ends. Much, much later she decided to stop at a restaurant in Burlington, Colorado and have a decent meal, a cold beer and some real coffee. Also, it was a good time to check her email. She did a quick make-over in the rearview mirror before she went inside. Avoiding some interested stares from the local boys, she parked herself in a booth in the corner so she could concentrate on her computer and not be bothered. After ordering a modest meal of meat loaf, mashed potatoes with gravy, a side of string beans and an Amstel Light in the bottle, she booted up her laptop.

Oblivious to her surroundings, she sipped on her beer and navigated through to her inbox while waiting for the waitress to bring her dinner. Scanning her emails with passive interest, her heart nearly stopped when she saw an email from Cameron

Toscanini. When all this began, she was diligent about finding out everything she could about the resort, its owner Hansen Giles, *Starbright Magazine* and of course, Cameron Toscanini, the notorious photographer. She never thought she'd actually be able to get to him, but that's the wonder of electronic communication. If you're persistent enough you can at least make contact, however, the person on the other end might not reply. In this case, he did. She was so engrossed in reading his email that she hardly noticed her dinner had been placed on the table. Evidently, he'd bought her story about being one of Colt's best friends since childhood and the fact that she was on her way to Hollywood to become an actress and wanted to surprise him in Tahoe as she was blowing through town. She'd figured the Hollywood thing would get Cameron's interest and not the fact that she was a friend of Colt's. She'd also included some rather provocative innuendos about wondering whether to become a model or an actress to hopefully appeal to the manly ego side of Mr. Toscanini in her email without being too presumptuous. She also emphatically implied that she wanted her visit to be a complete surprise to Colt. Annie-Laurie knew what lit men up and she also knew how to strike the match and not claim responsibility. When she sent the email to him, she wanted to make sure he would respond if he actually got it and it worked. Obviously, she ignited Cameron's predictable weaknesses.

Dear Annie,
(Or should I call you, Annie-Laurie)

I think it is so exciting you're an old friend of Colt's and want to surprise him. I must advise against going all the way to Hollywood, though, because it's such a depressing place for ninety-nine percent of the people who live there. Meaning, only a few of the rich and famous are actually truly happy and most of them aren't actors or models. Even if you make it as an actress, I'm sure you'll find life here in Tahoe much more interesting. Please don't get me wrong, I'm not trying to rain on your parade but it really is a shitty town. I would love to play a part in the surprise. Colt has become a good friend and I think it would be awesome if one of his old friends showed up from his past to pay him a visit. I'm not exactly sure when you're coming into town but I've planned, believe it or not, a fishing trip on the lake for him this coming Sunday morning with some of my colleagues. He's become quite popular with the people in my profession so I thought it would be fun to make a day trip out of it. Apparently, he really likes to fish because he wants to go fishing up here in this frigid weather, which is why I rented a rather large boat with a heated cabin (for me). Ha! If you could make it in time, maybe you could be on the boat before he arrives and surprise him there. Might make for an-other good photo op. Sorry, I still have a little business in me. Let me know what you think. Included is my cell phone number. Why don't you give me a call and we can talk live. Cameo

Immediately, her mind started racing. Her first response was to laugh mockingly out loud. Colt wasn't a real fisherman. He liked to sit beside the mountain stream and trout fish with an occasional joint or two. It was his way of escaping reality when he felt he needed some quiet time to reload. She doubted he actually ever fished on a large body of water in his life. And she wasn't naïve enough to think this was going to be any sort of a homecoming. Her expectations were only limited to find-ing some sort of closure to a bewildering situation. Reviving his love for her was probably not an option, which over time had left a very bad taste in her mouth. It was Thursday evening and she was two-thirds of the way there. She could make it there by Saturday, but it would be exhausting. Reluctantly, she shoveled her food down and gulped down two cups of coffee before she paid the tab and left without acknowledging the stares from the boys as she trotted out to her truck. Confused and upset, she had to plug in her cell phone to the charger before she could make the call to *Cameo.*

San Francisco

Hansen couldn't be more pleased and he wasn't blind to the fact that timing and luck has everything to do with success. *Snowball,* after only being opened a short while, is now a hot new player in the world of resorts and his understudy, Brandi, appears to have found happiness and fame. The word from his contacts in Tahoe is that Colt is extremely well liked and re-spected and the media adores the hospitality of their new *Power Couple.* Hansen was skeptical when he was first approached by Cameron with his imaginative plan, yet his skepticism was quickly squashed when *Starbright* bought into the story. Now everything is moving forward with astonishing speed. *Cameron wasn't so stupid after all.* The congratulatory calls from Hansen's influential friends around the country overwhelmed him with a sense of pleasure and accomplishment. Amazingly, potential investors were also calling, encouraging Hansen to reproduce *Snowball* in other areas around the world. Something Colt had mentioned when they first met.

"Hello," Hansen said after the ringing of the telephone startled him back to reality.

"Mr. Giles, I hope I didn't call at a bad time," Cameron said on the other end of the line.

"Not at all, Cameron," Hansen replied. "I was just think-ing about you and your hair-brained scheme anyway. Your tim-ing is excellent. What can I do for you?"

"I thought I should check in and see if you are happy with the progress so far?"

"I'm ecstatic. I would never have believed something like this would evolve into something so big. *Snowball* is getting a huge amount of national and international publicity, mostly because of you. I owe you for that."

"You don't owe me anything, Mr. Giles. I should be thanking you for having enough faith in me to give me the green light. But there are a couple of things I wanted to run by you."

"Absolutely, I'm all ears," Hansen replied.

"Well, to start with...," Cameron replied with some hesitation, "I feel like my plan is starting to fizzle a little bit."

"What do you mean?"

"I'm worried my counterparts are getting a little bored and are feeling the need to move on. Don't get me wrong, they adore Colt and Brandi. They love the amenities of the resort and the many opportunities to grab some good pictures of the stars. But by nature, our living is not easy and we're not used to the red carpet treatment. They're no scandals up here and I think some of the tabloids want more as well."

"So what do you want me to do?" Hansen asked with a concerned yet somewhat annoyed manner.

"Give me the green light on my new plan."

"Which is?"

"I recently received an email from an old friend of Colt's who is in route to Tahoe as we speak. She says she's a life-long friend and wants to surprise him before she heads on to Hollywood to become an actress. Chasing her dreams like everybody else, I guess. Anyway, I responded by inviting her to join us on a little fishing expedition I've arranged for Colt."

"Fishing," Hansen spat. "It's cold as hell up there. Are you crazy?"

"Not me, but Colt is. He asked for me to arrange it so that's what I did. I rented a forty-five foot fishing boat, big enough for ten to twelve people, and the captain. We're going out on Sunday. Obviously, it has a nice heated cabin because I don't fish and I'm not freezing my ass off. But anyway, I've invited several of my counterparts to join us, trying to keep up their interest for a little longer. I figure a day of drinking beer and fishing would make for a better bonding situation. Now, having his friend showing up to surprise him would make for an excellent photo opportunity. If you know what I mean?"

"No, I don't know what you mean. What about Brandi? She's not going to like this even if this girl is just an old friend. Are you trying to create a scandal for the tabloids?"

"Yes. I know it sounds cold but the Paparazzi need a scandal. I figure if this girl is really just an old friend then Brandi will be able to deal with it. Actually, I'm going to ask her to join us so she doesn't feel left out. If this thing goes off like I think it will, no one, is going to get hurt just because the tabloids are bending the truth a little bit. It might make for a good party by the end of the day."

"Are you sure this girl is just a friend, because I don't want Brandi to get hurt. That's just not going to happen. I don't care about *Snowball* that much. Do you understand?"

"That's what she said in her email. She's an old friend and just wants to surprise him and say hello before she continues on to Hollywood to become a star. That's all I know but it sounds legit to me. I'm going to make arrangements for her to stay at the resort. She will go over to the marina with me early in the morning to load the boat up with the supplies we'll need. She'll sit in the cabin until Colt and Brandi come on board. Then she will come out and surprise him. It should work out great. Besides, Brandi's on the fence anyway because she's not into fishing. She probably won't come along on the trip. When Colt's friend comes out of the cabin to surprise him, my boys will get plenty of pictures, for all the wrong reasons I might add. Then we all go fishing and have a great day. They send their pictures in, the tabloids print the scandal, though there isn't really one, and everyone is happy. Plus, you get more free publicity. Trust me on this one because I would never ever do anything to hurt Brandi. I give you my word. She's one of the sweetest people I've ever known and she's become a really good friend."

"You better be right. That's all I have to say," replied Hansen, still not totally sold on the idea.

"There's more," Cameron.

"I figured that. What else?"

"I need you to pay for the rental because I can't afford it."

"Why do I get the feeling I'm being railroaded? So how much is it going to cost me?" Hansen laughed at the absurdity of the request.

"It's going to cost fifteen hundred dollars for the day, which includes the tip for the captain. Remember, you're getting free publicity."

"Touché... Okay, but this better not go down the wrong way."

"There's one more thing," Cameron added.

"Really, I can't imagine."

"I think you should have a Boardwalk of Fame at *Snowball*."

"And what is that?"

"An area where pictures of the rich and famous are posted in really nice frames to be seen by whoever visits the resort. Get it, board, as in snowboard and walk of fame as in famous people who have been captured enjoying your great resort. Sort of like a knock-off of the stars on Hollywood Boulevard. I think everybody who is anybody would love to have their picture hanging in the Boardwalk of Fame at *Snowball*. To see and be seen is the name of the game and any opportunity to be seen is about the most important thing they do. I want to be your resident photographer. I've been on the run my whole life and I need to stop before it kills me. I could do my other thing on the side and hopefully the million dollars a year you're going to pay me would make up the difference," Cameron finished with the joke.

"Why don't we make it an even two million," Hansen shot back. "I hate odd numbers."

"Works for me. Seriously, I think I could prove my worth."

"Have you run this by Colt and Brandi?"

"Not yet, I thought I'd get your blessing first."

"If they buy in then I'm good too. We'll come up with something that will work for the both of us."

"Thanks."

"On a trial basis for a couple of months just to make sure I'm not getting in over my head. I don't want to see you drown in your own bullshit."

"You are way too funny. Thanks for giving me a chance."

"You just watch out for Brandi."

"Trust me, I will."

Snowball

After he finished talking with Hansen, Cameron leaned back in his chair and rolled his eyes. He was so tired of being a hustler. *How much longer could he do this* he wondered to himself. He tossed his cell phone on the bed and it started ringing the minute it hit the mattress. Giving it a nervous glance, his first reaction was to cuss because he actually had to get up and walk two-feet over to pick it up. His second thought was that Mr. Giles suddenly got cold feet. Cameron actually considered not answering it but knew Mr. Giles would be mad. When he picked it up and looked at caller ID, he was surprised he didn't recognize the number. "Nothing good ever comes out of an unknown number," he said out loud. Reluctantly, he hit the answer button.

"Hello?"

"Is this Cameo?" said a very seductive, husky, feminine voice which had slight hint of a sophisticated southern accent.

"Cameo the shark, as my friends often call me," he said jokingly. His senses were immediately turned on by this voice without a face. His guess is she has to be a knockout. There is no way a voice like that could come out of an ugly face. No way.

"My name is Annie-Laurie and I'm the friend of Colt's from Virginia. You know," she paused, "from my email."

"Of course," Cameron checked himself. He should have

figured that out immediately. "Are you still planning on coming through Tahoe on your way to becoming a famous actress," he joked.

"I sure am," she said strangely seriously. "I'm a little burned-out from driving so much, but I plan on getting to Tahoe Saturday afternoon. Do you think I will be able to surprise Colt?" She cut right to the chase.

Cameron started seeing red flags go up. "So you're really just an old friend of his from the past?"

She immediately sensed his hesitation. "Oh yeah, we go way back. He was my boyfriend when we were neighbors. I think I was at probably six at the time. We broke up when I was six and a half because I couldn't deal with his fits of jealously over Ty Bridges. Ty and I dated at least for a couple of weeks before my family moved to a nicer neighborhood which had nicer boys. So I moved on as well. But Colt's parents and mine remain great friends and so do we." She figured that was enough to settle him down. "You didn't tell him I was coming did you, Mr. Shark?" she flirted.

"Actually, it's Toscanini. And no, I didn't tell him." Cameron was struggling to regain his composure over the phone because her voice was sucking out any reason he had left in his jumbled mind. "I'm trying to work everything out so it will be a surprise."

"Thank you so much," she said in the sweetest voice she could imitate, while she rolled her eyes. If he could see the vindictive look on her face then he would have been totally confused at the sweetness coming out of the meanness. "I think he will be really excited to see me. We haven't seen each other in about twelve years. I've grown up quite a bit since then."

"Annie,"

"That's Annie-Laurie," she corrected him.

"I'm sorry, Annie-Laurie, I absolutely love your name. Sounds like your voice," he flirted. "I need to tell you something so we're on the same page about the surprise."

"Okay," she replied uncaringly.

"Colt has a girlfriend and I think they're very serious."

"I could tell he was in love by the look on his face in the picture in *Starbright*," she said as nicely as she could without totally throwing up all over the inside of her truck. "Mr. Shark, I mean Toscanini, I'm just a friend and I'm very happy for him. I don't plan on sleeping with him. I plan on sleeping with you," she added to throw him a curve ball.

"Great!" was all he could say, clearly flustered by her directness. He couldn't tell if she was serious or simply teasing him. He was kind of hoping she was serious, judging her by the sound of her voice. "I'm going to book you a room at the resort, but call me when you get here and I will meet you at your car. We'll get you checked in and I'll take you out to dinner, away from the resort of course, so he won't see you before the big surprise." Cameron had wanted to go back to *The Flip Flop Inn* anyway. It was off the beaten path so he felt confident Colt wouldn't run into them. Suddenly, he was getting excited about meeting the face behind the voice.

"Thank you so much," Annie-Laurie said in her ditziest voice. "I'll call you Saturday afternoon. I wasn't kidding about what I said about sleeping with you," she added before she clicked off the phone.

Cameron stared at his cell phone with his mouth open in awe like someone on the other end told him he'd just won the lottery. He slowly shut it, gave it a quick kiss and tossed it back on the bed, satisfied everything was going to work just fine. He came to the realization his world was definitely doing a complete one-eighty too. He sat back down at his desk to finish the list of items he needed to purchase for the fishing trip. Tequila shooters was an add-on to help fight off the cold. He was evidently distracted after his conversation with Annie-Laurie. Her comment, not once, but twice, about sleeping with him totally bewildered him and filled him with unusual expectations about meeting this perfect stranger for the first time. Blood started circulating through his body in a way it hadn't circulated in a long time. He shuddered at the thought of having sex because he found it never really lived up to his expectations. He was going to have to stifle his runaway imagination and concentrate on the plan, simple as that. However, no matter how hard he tried to concentrate, all he could think about was this strange girl who just waltzed into his life. All of a sudden, he didn't care about the surprise party.

Colt stared at Brandi from a distance as she was drying off from her shower. She was so peaceful and graceful in her movements and her soft expression of contentment radiated from her like light from the sun. Each brief glimpse of her nudity as her towel caressed over her body was like a brushstroke of beauty, only to be matched by another brushstroke. He should have gotten up and helped her dry off but he was too mesmerized to move. He sat there like an adolescent in class staring at his beautiful French teacher, daydreaming about what it would be like to touch her in places he'd only seen in the pictures from the magazine hidden in his tree fort. She had amazing hair, brown that was naturally straight and soft brown eyes that glistened with the golden highlights and an intoxicating sparkle in her smile. She would tease him with her look of sensuality when she would occasionally glance over to him and catch him staring. Finally, when she was totally dry, she walked towards him and dropped the towel to the floor and just stood there in front of him totally naked and unmoving. She would stand there as long as he wanted her to. Occasionally, she would slowly turn around so he could enjoy another angle and slowly turn back to face him. She was so beautiful, he wanted to cry.

"Do you like?" Brandi said in a very soft voice.

"Yes I like. But I would be just as happy if you were fully dressed. What did I do to deserve you in my life?"

"You walked into my office and I fell in love with Burly," she said, still in a very soft voice. "Then I looked up and fell in love with you."

Burly trotted into the room when he heard his name mentioned. Once he scoped out the situation, as if on cue, he turned around and went back into the other room to lie by the fire. He was very happy with his new surroundings and his new mom. She let him sleep with them.

"I hate to beat a dead horse, but do you really believe in love at first sight?" Colt asked her. "I can see it happening to one person, but can it happen to two people at the same time? Is that really possible or am I just being too romantic?"

"I don't know about you, but I've been in love with you my whole life, only I just found you," she said as she slowly walked towards him still naked. "So whatever you say will complete the answer to your question."

"Then I guess it can happen," he smiled with satisfaction.

Brandi bent down, put her arms on his shoulders and looked deep into his eyes, searching for the truth. What she saw was a beautiful man who loved her.

"You are my life," she whispered into his ear.

"I came out here to chase my dream," he confessed. "I saw something happen on the journey that I know was a message to me. It was a message telling me how fragile life can be. It was a message telling me not to walk through life alone anymore. It was a message telling me that the dream I was chasing was the dream of finding you. I want to take care of you for the rest your life," he whispered back to her. "Will you marry me?"

"What did you say?"

"Brandi, I want to spend the rest of my life with you. I want to have a son and I want to have a daughter who looks just like her mother. I want to be your husband. I want you to be my wife and live together happily ever after." He reached around behind his back, pulled out this small black box, got down on his knee and lifted the box up to her and repeated what he'd said earlier. "I love you more than anything. You are my world and you are my life. Will you marry me?"

Brandi looked at Colt in total disbelief. She looked at

each strand of his sandy blond hair that hung loosely almost to his shoulders. She softly stroked the bristle of hair on his two-day old unshaven face and she gazed deep into his deep blue eyes. As the tears of joy began to overwhelm her, she began to shudder with happiness. She nervously caressed the box as if she was afraid to open it because, if she opened it, it would be her eyes opening after a beautiful dream and it would all be just a dream.

"Where did you get this? Is this for real? Is there really something in this box?"

"Why don't you think about my question before you open it? Do you think you love me enough to be my wife and share our lives together forever? If you think yes, then open the box. If you think no, just shoot me dead because I couldn't stand the thought of living the rest of my life without you. I'm not kidding. I love you more than I've ever loved anything. Brandi, will you marry me?"

"Yes! Yes! Yes!" she said as she wrapped her arms around him and kissed him. "I love you. I need you and I want to have your beautiful children and I want to spend the rest of my life with you. You are my life. I think about you every waking moment. I dream about you when I'm sleeping. I try to picture your boyish smile and it makes me smile when I'm alone. I never want you to hurt, or feel sad or feel lonely. That would break my heart. I can't live without you, Colt Salley. I just can't live without you." She sat down on the bed beside him, laid her head on his shoulder so they both could see her open the box. When she opened it, she immediately gasped, followed by convulsions of tears and smiles and sobs of happiness. What she saw was the most beautiful diamond ring she had ever seen in her entire life. It wasn't the size, because it was small by certain standards, but it was sophisticated and extraordinary and very, very old. She saw lifetimes of happiness passed down from generation to generation in this ring. She wanted to stare at it forever.

"I had it brought out by courier from Richmond earlier this week. It has been in my family forever. I know this is quick and some people will say it's insane but I know this is meant to be." He reached over, lifted the ring out of the box and slid it on to her finger. It was a perfect fit. She sat there, completely overrun with emotion. Colt picked up her towel and wrapped it around her so she wouldn't get chilled and let her enjoy the moment for as long as her heart desired.

"It's the most beautiful thing I have ever seen in my life," she said as she forced herself to look away from it to stare into his eyes, "except for you."

On instinct, Colt gave a quick whistle and within two seconds, Burly flew into the room and jumped on the bed, almost knocking them down. He started licking both of them like there was no tomorrow.

"She said yes, Burly. She said yes! We're going to be a family," Colt said hugging him. It looked like Colt and Burly were both crying. Brandi wrapped her arms around both of them and they had a major, major group hug. All three of them snuggled throughout the entire evening, each in their own world of happiness. It was the most beautiful moment there ever was.

The next morning Colt woke up alone in bed. Confused, he wrapped himself in a blanket and shuffled to the kitchen. He stopped at the door and was overwhelmed at what he saw. Brandi was standing at the sink in front of the window with the sunrise illuminating her like an angel. She was holding up her hand and staring at the ring, watching the cascade of light burning through the prism and sobbing. Burly was lying at her feet protecting her. He turned his head to face Colt, blinked and turned his head back to her. He wasn't leaving her side for anything. It reminded Colt of his favorite song *Angel* by *Jack Johnson*, he knew it by heart:

I've got an angel
She doesn't wear any wings
She wears a heart that can melt my own
She wears a smile that can make me want to sing...

"Good morning," he said when she turned around. "Are you okay?"

She immediately ran into his arms and hugged him like she would never let go.

"There is one thing you have to understand about me," she choked out. "I cry when I'm happy. I may never stop crying. I love you so much! I love you so much!"

Nevada

Annie-Laurie was probably forty-five minutes outside of Lake Tahoe. She was worn out and fit to be tied. Throughout the entire trip she refused to think about what she was doing. She blinded herself enough to get there without having fits of regrets. It was an internal protective mechanism which allowed her to push on. However, the closer she got, the more her heart started to pound. The frustration of the unknown was working its ugly head to the surface. Her self-imposed therapy was having a lot of trouble suppressing those negative thoughts. She was dazed and she knew it. If she didn't pull herself together soon then no telling what would happen. At that point, she made a command decision and pulled into a Holiday Inn Express, grabbed her bag from the passenger seat and checked in.

She walked into her room, cut the shower on and let the steam envelop the bathroom before she stepped in to wash away the road. She stood in the shower forever, unmoving, just letting the water beat the tar out of her. It was a horrible feeling to be frightened and alone. The more she stood there the better she began to feel and she could feel her confidence slowly returning. She had to have a clear head when she got to the resort. She reached down between her legs to guide the cascade of hot water to her place of comfort. She always found solace in making herself have an orgasm in the shower. It was the ultimate cleansing. The warm sensation began to envelop her and her legs became weak and her body heaved at the spasms of her release. She had to put her other hand on the wall to prevent herself from falling altogether. She could feel her wetness being diluted by the hot water washing away her doubt. Still trembling, she dried herself off and proceeded to make herself look absolutely stunning. Satisfied with her work, she quickly repacked her bag and headed out the door. The attendant was dumbfounded when she walked silently by him out to her truck and drove off, one hour after she checked in. The thoughts of her beautiful transformation stayed with him the rest of the afternoon.

Once she was back on the road, with renewed confidence, she picked up her cell phone and made the call. She rehearsed what she was going to say enough to pull it off without a hitch.

"Hello?"

"Hello, Mr. Shark, this is your friendly cross-country traveler calling to check in."

"Annie-Laurie, see, I remembered," Cameron said with a hint of excitement in his voice. "I've been waiting for you to call. I thought you got lost out there somewhere."

"It's kind of hard to get lost when you've been on the same road for about a million miles," she joked halfheartedly. "It has been one hell of a ride and I think I need a drink."

"Works for me," Cameron said. "Do you want to come here and dump your stuff or do you want to meet me somewhere?"

"Let's meet," she replied. "I'm too exhausted to check in and go back out. I figure since I'm finally here, I might as well enjoy myself."

"I like the way you think. Where exactly are you right now?"

After she told him, it was easy for him to give her directions to *The Flip Flop Inn*. She was actually closer to it than he was so he grabbed his coat and bolted out the door. He scanned the parking lot when he pulled in at five fifteen on that Saturday afternoon. It was still early, so there were only a few cars in the lot. He spotted her truck with the Virginia license plates. Surprised, and maybe a little disappointed she was driving a truck, he parked beside her and glanced inside the cab before joining her in the restaurant. He was even more disappointed when he saw that the inside of her truck was a train wreck. Trash was everywhere. At that point he almost got back in his car and drove away. His first impression convinced him her looks would be similar to the way she kept her vehicle. However, curiosity still had the best of him and he gallantly went inside. He hung his coat on the rack and scanned the dining room and didn't see anyone that could be her. *She must be at the bar*, he thought to himself. Somewhat reluctantly, he headed into the bar. She was the only person in there, seated at the end, nursing what looked like a cosmo, giving him a chance to check her out before she turned to greet him.

She sensed it when Mr. Shark walked in. Before she turned her head, she closed her eyes, took a deep breath and put herself into the zone. She really wasn't headed to Hollywood to become an actress, but she would have to put on the performance of a lifetime and she knew it. He was her conduit from her past to her future. Granted, there were probably other ways, but this was her best opportunity and she wasn't going to miss the boat. She turned and smiled.

"Mr. Shark I presume"

"Actually, it's Toscanini," he said while regaining his composure. "But you can call me whatever you want." Clearly, he was pleasantly surprised at this pretty little southern gal from Virginia. She wasn't the least bit intimidated at meeting a stranger. Her green eyes and freckles accentuated her personality and her wavy brown hair framed what turned out to be a very beautiful woman. Immediately, he was jealous she was here to surprise Colt. He didn't want to share. She stood up to give him a complimentary hug when he approached the bar. Every nerve ending in his body was on alert and felt every part of her body touching him in the hug. She was tight, fit and extremely well proportioned for a woman with approximately five-feet, three inches in height. *She was a good six inches shorter than him which made for an excellent fit for sex*, he selfishly thought.

"I took a chance and ordered you a straight-up martini with olives," she said. "If you don't want it then I guess I'll have to drink it. In a way, I'm kind of hoping you don't want it," she said as the green in her eyes danced across the gloss of the bar top. She lightly flipped her head back down to take another sip of her cosmo.

"Shaken, not stirred, I hope," as he sat on the stool next to her.

"Clever," she said as she smiled and patted him on the shoulder. "You should become an actor instead of me. With a name like Toscanini, I think it's a no-brainer, Mr. Shark. You're clearly a man of many options. Kind of makes a girl like me want to drink myself silly."

"Don't be silly," he chided. "I wouldn't be an actor if you transformed me into Brad Pitt. I know enough about the profession to not want in. But don't let me discourage you though, to each his own," he finished as the bartender handed him his martini.

"Here's to a successful journey," he toasted to her.

"Thank you," she tapped his glass and took another sip. "If I don't get something to eat then this drink might cause my clothes to fall off."

He almost sprayed his sip across the bar and all over the bartender. Looking at her before he spoke, he was totally blown away by her confidence and directness. Clearly, she was more woman than he was man. *Are all southern women like this? If so, then I'm going to have to put in for a relocation package.* "Well," he recovered. "We can go grab a table or we can order here. What's your fancy?"

"You," she looked him straight in the eyes, "but let's just eat dinner here at the bar. I'm not in the mood to move right now. I will be later."

"Wow, you don't beat around the bush do you?"

"Not really, my daddy taught me to say what I mean and to mean what I say. What's the point in playing games?"

"Good question. I never thought about it quite that way. Maybe we should order."

They spent the entire time talking about where she came from and why she was moving to California. Annie-Laurie made up so much stuff even she was beginning to believe it. She was somewhat regretful because she knew the time would come when he would see the real story and it probably wasn't going to be pretty. But she had to play the game all the way through to achieve the desired results, which also meant fucking him to get back at Colt. Somewhere, along the course of her travels she'd lost all sense of direction.

Having breakfast for dinner is always a treat. Having breakfast for dinner with martinis is insane. By the time they wolfed down eggs, bacon, pancakes, biscuits, gravy and four drinks each, including two body hugs, Cameron, alias Mr. Shark, was downright giddy over his luck. It was simply way too good to try to understand what was happening. He anxiously and intoxicatingly walked through the pearly gates and entered into the land of the second brain in a big-way. She graciously held his hand and guided him down the yellow brick road of no return. He had no idea he was being used like a condom. With each new drink the mirage became clearer. He was in. He recited to her a poem he'd written called *Season of Love*. He told her he hopes have it published one day when he hangs up his Paparazzo hat and becomes a writer.

Walking with my head down on
*   this cold dark lonely road*
Listening to the silence of
*   the beauty of the snow*
The winter wind is swirling through
*   the emptiness of the night*

And I know everything would be alright
if I could fall in love tonight

The warmth of the sunshine does little
to ease the pain
From the coldness in my heart and
the beauty of the spring
I'm searching for you like
a flower for the light
And I know everything would be alright
if I could fall in love tonight

The sweat rolls down my face and
hides my tears of loneliness
I can see you in my dreams on
these long hot summer nights
I hear your voice between my ears and
I can touch you with my mind
And I know everything would be alright
if I could fall in love tonight

The radiance of the fall is here and
I finally found my love so dear
Happiness now controls my soul and
shines the light like leaves of gold
Seasons will change and so will I and
I will feel their beauty with you by my side
Everything is going to be alright
because I fell in love tonight
I found the season of love

She wasn't impressed. He was too tipsy to notice. After dinner, he thought it would be a good idea to leave her truck at the Inn and pick it up after the fishing trip. That way he could drive her over to *Snowball* and sneak her in without the risk of bumping into Colt and ruining the surprise. Plus his trunk was

SCOTT PETTIT

loaded with stuff to take on the boat. He wasn't planning on worrying about it in the morning. The ride over was somewhat eventful with her playing with him and kissing him while he was driving. He was worried he would get pulled, and worse, that he wouldn't make it to the resort and satisfy the urges she'd created by spoon feeding him. The thought of getting on a boat on a cold lake in the morning was about the furthest thing from his mind. Thankfully, he'd already organized everything down to Brandi and Colt arriving just before lift-off. Brandi didn't really want to join them until Cameron assured her it was a really nice boat with a really nice, warm cabin. For the life of him, he couldn't imagine that Colt would be upset when he saw Annie-Laurie and hopefully, he wouldn't be upset that she was with him. He'd become such a good friend, he'd probably be happy about the connection.

It was about eight o'clock when they got to *Snowball* and they went directly to his place, which by now was a small one-room bungalow on the edge of the village. Her mood seemed to change as they walked through the snow that was painting a fresh coat on the courtyard. She seemed somewhat distant and much less playful, much more somber than he anticipated. He was surprised she wasn't impressed with the resort but he at-tributed it to her long drive and lots of alcohol. However, he had every intention of not letting her sleep, at least for awhile. He was too far down the path for that.

The sex was wild, at the same time nice and ugly and had absolutely no meaning. It was the passion of two lost souls meeting in the darkness of the night. It was obvious they would part ways in the morning, at least mentally. There was no talking, or laughing or appreciation, just two lonely people screaming in the forest for attention and nobody hearing them. He woke up in the morning to the noise of her crying in the bathroom. He lightly tapped on the door to let her know he was coming in.

"What's wrong?" he asked. "Did I do something wrong?"

"No," she mumbled through her sobs. "You did exactly

172

what you were supposed to do."

"What does that mean?"

"Nothing, absolutely nothing," she replied despondently. "What time do we need to leave?"

"Are you sure you want to do this? You really don't seem like you're in the mood to pull off a surprise."

"Trust me," she said coldly. "I'll get myself there. That's what I do. That's me. Haven't you figured that out?"

"I didn't know I was supposed to," he said as he shut the door. "We need to leave within the hour. Just let me know when you're done so I can grab a shower."

They walked through the village and out to her truck without taking the shuttle. He wanted to clear his head and she wasn't talking. He felt lucky they didn't bump into Colt before they made it out of the resort. The silence on the ride to the marina was deafening. He was surprised at her change in personality. She was satisfied to finally be there.

Wintergreen

Josh was sitting at his desk reading *Starbright Magazine* when Annie-Laurie's brother, Kenny walked in.

"Hey Kenny, how are you doing?"

"Okay, I guess," Kenny responded somewhat gloomily.

"Look at this," Josh said as he flipped the tabloid around. "Colt's on the cover. Can you believe that?"

"I know," Kenny looked down. "That's why I'm here."

"What do you mean, Kenny?"

"My sister left a couple of days ago."

"Where did she go?"

"I think she went to California," he said pointing at Colt's picture so Josh could make the connection.

"Why would she do that? I heard they broke up."

"He broke up with her but I don't think she took it that

well."

"What does she hope to accomplish by chasing him all the way across the country?"

"You tell me," Kenny looked at him directly. "I'm just a kid, but I'm worried. She wasn't herself the last time I saw her and now she's gone. Mom and Dad don't seem to care all that much, but I miss her and want her to come back home."

"I'm sure there is nothing to worry about, Kenny. I'll tell you what, I'll track her down and call you when I find her."

"That would be great, Mr. Witherspoon. Here is my number. I really appreciate you looking into this. You were the only one I could think to turn to," he said as he turned and walked out of the office.

Josh stared at the picture and started to put two and two together. He looked at his watch and it was eleven-thirty east coast time, which meant it was eight-thirty in San Francisco. So he picked up the phone and made the call.

"Hello, Hansen Giles speaking."

"Hansen, Josh Witherspoon from Wintergreen, Virginia."

"Of course, Josh," Hansen said. "I'd recognize that accent anywhere. What can I do for you? Please don't tell me you're calling to get Colt to come back home. I don't think that's going to happen," he joked.

"Well, that's not exactly why I called. This is probably nothing, but there's this girl Colt used to have a thing with and they broke up before he left to go out there. Her brother just stopped by and asked me if I could track her down."

"I'm not really following you, Josh. Why are you calling me?"

"He thinks his sister is on her way to California. Since Colt's picture with another woman is on the cover of *Starbright*, I think he might be right. She very well could be going out there to confront him. She's a great person but I wouldn't put it past her."

"I smell a rat," was all Hansen could say. *He knew it. Nothing is as it seems*. Hansen was already cussing himself for agreeing to Cameron's hair-brained scheme. "I think she's already here."

"How do you know?"

"Because a girl called the other day and talked to someone who works for me. She told him she was an old family friend of Colt's and wanted to stop by to surprise him before she went on to Hollywood. He invited her to join them on a little fishing excursion up at Lake Tahoe so she could surprise Colt. He seemed convinced she wasn't making it up. It has to be the same girl."

"I'd be willing to bet my life on it, Hansen," Josh said in earnest. "Annie-Laurie is a pretty sharp girl and I've heard rumors she hasn't been real happy since Colt left. It might be worth checking out. Can you call Colt and at least warn him? I'm not sure she would do anything crazy, but you never know what love, or lack of, can do to a person. Especially, a jealous person," Josh added as he looked at the photograph.

"I'll do my best, but it might already be too late. I'll make a few calls, and if I can't reach them, I'll call a friend of mine on the local police force up there and ask him to at least check it out just to be on the safe side. I'll call you when I find out something."

"Thanks, Hansen, I really appreciate it."

After placing two calls, one to Cameron and the other to Colt, Hansen realized they probably didn't have their cell phones with them while they were out on the water, although for the life of him, he couldn't figure out why. He knew Brandi didn't fish so he doubted seriously that she would tag along. However, if the Paparazzi had their way, she'd be there. He sat there contemplating whether or not he should make the next call. If it turned out to be nothing, he would look like an idiot.

Oh well, he said to himself. *It's always better to be safe than sorry.* He opened his cell phone and looked up the number to the South Lake Tahoe Police Department, the law enforcement organization that patrols the southern end of the lake. Reluctantly, he dialed the number.

"South Lake Tahoe Police Department, how may I direct your call?" said the voice on the other end of the line.

"May I speak to Leroy Washington?"

"Let me check to see if he's in. He normally doesn't work on Sundays. Is this an emergency?"

"I don't think so but I have a situation I'm worried about and I wanted to run it by Leroy to see what he thinks. He and I are good friends," Hansen added hoping that would be the magic to get Leroy on the phone.

"He's not picking up the phone at his desk, sir. If you give me your number, I'll have him paged and he should call you momentarily. He's pretty good about that," said the sympathetic voice.

"Thank you so much. Just tell him Hansen Giles needs to speak to him ASAP. He has my number."

"Are you the gentleman that opened *Snowball*?"

"One and the same," Hansen replied.

"It is a beautiful place, Mr. Giles. I'll personally page Leroy."

"I really appreciate your help," Hansen finished. While he was waiting for Leroy to call he paced around his office like a caged lion. The more he thought about it the more worried he became. It was a very long twenty minutes before his phone rang.

"Is that you, Leroy?"

"Mr. Giles," said Leroy, "sorry it took me so long to get back to you. I was in church giving communion. I couldn't just pour the juice down my neighbor's throat," Leroy laughed. "Is there a problem?"

"Sorry to bother you while you're in church, Leroy," Hansen said, embarrassed he wasn't in church himself. "Something has come up that is probably nothing but I have some red flags going up and I was wondering if you could do me a favor and check it out. I'll make a nice donation to the department for your time."

"You don't have to do that, Mr. Giles," which meant he

did. "What's the problem?"

After Hansen gave him the rundown, Leroy agreed to at least patrol the water and check it out. He doubted there would be any problems, but he wanted to keep Mr. Giles happy. The donations really help the department. "I'll be back in touch."

"Thanks, Leroy, you're an officer and a gentleman," Hansen said appreciatively.

Leroy went over and whispered something in his wife's ear and she nodded like she's probably done a thousand times. He slipped out, hopped in his car and headed to the marina. It was a twenty minute drive so he played some gospel to keep him in that church mode.

South Lake Marina,
Lake Tahoe

The day started out strange and it just got stranger. By nine-o'clock in the morning the sun was shining, it was snowing and there wasn't a soul in sight around the marina. Annie-Laurie was either extremely hung-over or about to commit suicide, at this point Cameron couldn't care less. He knew the boat at the end of the dock was his rental, so he loaded everything onto the deck beside it. On his last trip to the car he politely suggested to her that if she was still in the mood to surprise Colt, she better go sit in the cabin of the boat. She rolled her eyes at him, painstakingly got out and trudged down to the dock, climbed on to the boat, walked into the cabin and slammed the door.

"I thought I was pretty good last night, even if I do say so myself," he mumbled towards the boat.

"Mr. Toscanini?"

"That would be me," Cameron replied as he turned around. *Thank God someone around here talks.*

"I'm Captain Ron and I'll be your guide today. And you don't have to tell me you've heard the name before. I'm well aware it's a popular movie," he smiled. "Most people just call me

Ron. I see you've already started loading the boat," he continued as he nodded towards the cabin. "Let me give you a hand with the rest of your gear, I mean beer."

"Some of us are just along for the ride," Cameron threw his hands up in confession. "Only three or four will actually be fishing. Do you think they will catch anything? It's really cold today."

"Oh, I'm sure we can find one or two notorious Tahoe Mackinaw Lake Trout that are willing to make our guests happy."

"Great. That's a big boat," Cameron said while giving it the once over.

"It's a forty-five foot Delta. It's the biggest one we have in our fleet."

"What's her name?"

"*Easy Living.* When will the others get here?"

"They should be here by now. The guests of honor should be here by nine-thirty. I would like to get going as soon as they hop on the boat. I have a surprise for one of them and it might be pretty cool if we were under way when I bring her out," Cameron said as he nodded towards the cabin.

"No problem sir, we're ready to shove-off as soon as you give me the word. Just make sure everyone gets their life vests on."

Cameron heard doors shut on the van and looked around to see his counterparts were right on schedule. He noticed they had more camera gear than they had sense. He counted six of them which worked out perfectly because the boat could only carry twelve. He ran up to help them so everything would be done before Colt and Brandi showed up. After the equipment was loaded and the first beer was popped, he walked into the cabin to finally check on Annie-Laurie. She was slouched in the chair staring at nothing.

"What is wrong?" Cameron had to ask her. He couldn't take it anymore. If she didn't get happy, he was going to plant her dockside. He wasn't going to let her ruin the trip. "Was it that bad last night? I mean, I had fun and I thought you did. Was it something I said?"

Annie-Laurie looked at him and almost burst into tears. She thought she'd be able to control her emotions but she couldn't seem to get it together. She was so worried about seeing Colt she couldn't even focus on Cameron. She was smart enough to notice his apprehension about having her on board and knew if she didn't get it together, he might ruin her surprise and totally destroy her entire reason for coming to California. The only thing she could do to buy some time was to walk over and hug him. He would have to show her compassion, whether he wanted to or not.

"I'm sorry," she said. "I'm just a little emotional from the long drive and the time change. And I'm also a little hung-over. I'm a woman, what can I say," as she slapped her hands on her hips in hopes of getting herself in gear. "I think the wrong time of the month just hit me."

"Do you still want to go through this surprise thing? I mean, is it that big of a deal?" Cameron asked.

Short of having a complete panic attack, she recognized the fact that she was totally at his mercy. If he had any inkling of the damage she could inflict, he would run for shore to get help. Colt was not going to be happy to see her and she knew it. All she wanted to do was call his bluff to remind him that everything he said to her before he left was only lies. Once that was done, she would quietly get back in her truck and go find a cliff. She only wanted five minutes to get closure. Of course, there was the outside chance he would be happy to see her and that would be awesome, even though she would still be mad at him. She wasn't banking on that outcome, but she was banking on having her act together when she confronted him. The last thing she wanted him to see was her weak side.

"I'm sorry, Cameron," she opened. "I think if I can just lie down for a little bit, I'll feel better. Go back out and have a beer. Just tap on the door when you think I should come out. It'll be fun, I promise, and I'll make it up to you later, okay?"

The sex is damned good, he thought to himself. "All right," he conceded. "I hope you'll begin to feel better and I'll come get you when it's time for the big surprise."

"You're a doll," she mustered as she rubbed his cheek. "Now go have fun."

"**Y**our phone's ringing," Brandi said as she reached for his coat in the back seat.

"I have a rule," he said as he held her arm from pulling it out of the pocket. "No phones when I'm fishing. It disturbs the fish."

"But we're in the car," she giggled.

"That's not the point. If I'm on my way to go fishing, then theoretically, I'm already fishing. The fish can sense bad vibes and they go hide. It's all very technical," he winked at her. "Besides, if I'm going to have a family, I better get serious about being an outdoorsman. I need to be able to put meat on the table."

"Yeah," she laughed, "I've already seen the meat. You have a lot of work to do."

"What? You're kidding, right? It was cold last night."

She rested her head on his shoulder and rubbed his leg like she was petting Burly. "It's all good, Mr. Salley. It's all good."

"Did I ever tell you about my favorite TV commercial? The one where you see the backs of this couple facing the ocean and his cell phone, which is sitting beside two Coronas, starts ringing and he tosses it into the ocean. I love that," he said with so much enthusiasm. "I want to do it one time. I think it would be great."

"I can already see I'm going to have to be the practical one in the relationship. Me and Burly," she added.

"I love hearing you talk, you know that?" Colt looked at her. "I'll never have to say another word for the rest of my life. I'm just going to sit there and listen to you and stare."

"You're going to get bored pretty fast," she laughed.

"I will never get bored with you. I promise. Hey, is that the marina?" Colt asked, bringing himself back to reality as he pulled into the parking lot. "We have to be quiet, remember, the fish?"

"All right, I'm bringing the cell phone," she joked.

"Wow, look at the size of that boat!" Colt was like a kid in a candy store, he was so excited. "I could live on that. This is going to be great!"

"Do you fish a lot?"

"No, I just like to talk about it, sounds cool. I'm from the mountains of Virginia. Mainly, I fish in the Rockfish River which is about ten feet wide and maybe two feet deep. Not real rocket science. I do like to fish, especially, when I feel the need to just slip away for awhile. There's something about it that's very relaxing and peaceful. Unfortunately," Colt added when he looked at all the people already on the boat, "this is going to be more like work."

"Yeah, I see what you mean," Brandi said. "I knew Cameron wanted this to be some kind of big deal, that's why I almost bailed, except, I want to watch you work your magic, both with the fish and the Paparazzi," she tapped him on the shoulder and stole a quick kiss. "Besides, I want to see their faces when they see we're engaged. That should be interesting," she finished by touching her ring to make sure it's real.

"That's probably going to change everything. I love you, baby, and that's all that matters to me. Everything else is just not that important."

"Should we do this or should we go back home to our son and lay by the fire and have wild and crazy sex when Burly's asleep? It's snowing out here," she added for effect.

"Oh, you make it sound so good. Let's go home," he said seriously.

"Are you serious? We can't, I mean I guess we can if you want to." She would love that option.

"I'm kidding. I have to put meat on the table. I have responsibilities now," Colt boasted. "Besides, we're going to have to be more careful what we do in front of Burly, I noticed he's been checking you out a lot lately. I'm starting to get a little jealous."

"As you should, I love that mutt."

They got out of the car and put their coats on. Colt tossed his cell on the front seat before he shut the door and locked the car. He opened the trunk, pulled out a cooler and hoisted over his right shoulder carrying it like a waiter carrying a tray of food. He paused to look at her. He couldn't believe his destiny. He came all the way to California to find the girl he was going to spend the rest of his life with. By the time they got to the boat he was panting from the weight of the cooler.

"That was too heavy for you to carry alone," Brandi said. "I could have helped you."

"I'm good," he said between gasps. "Besides, it's a surprise,"

"Hey, guys," Cameron jumped on to the dock to give Colt a hand with the cooler. He gave Brandi a quick peck on the cheek. "Are you guys ready for an awesome day?"

"Absolutely," Colt replied. "But can we really catch fish while it's snowing? You'd think they would avoid the surface like the plague."

"Captain Ron says they're waiting for you to come out and play," Cameron laughed. "Besides, the snow supposed to stop any minute. They have to come up for air sometime, don't they?"

"To be honest, Cameron, I'm too happy to care," Colt said with a big smile as they hoisted the cooler over to the boys on the boat.

"Well, I can guarantee you one thing," Cameron said. "Even if the fish aren't biting, it's still going to be an interesting day, hopefully, a great day," Cameron said with a small degree of hesitation.

"I'm with you brother," Colt replied as he helped Brandi climb on board.

As soon as they were boarded, Cameron gave thumbs up

to the captain in the window of the cabin. The ropes were pulled and the boat slightly rose from the power of the engines as it pulled away from the dock. The water was smooth as glass so they didn't immediately put on their life vests. It was such a smooth ride, like riding in a car. The captain was too pre-occupied to notice. Even the snow disappeared on the surface without causing ripples. Except for the sounds of the mighty engines, muffled by the water, it was an amazing feeling for all of them. The pleasantries of handshakes and hugs were exchanged so they could get the formalities over with early. The guys, still not used to being treated like human beings, kept casual conversation to a minimum. Everybody liked each other but it still wasn't a homogeneous crowd. Conversation on a first name basis was still pretty far into the trip. Sharing his engagement story with the Paparazzi wasn't high on Colt's list. Regardless, he reached down and opened the cooler. There were eight bot-tles of *Cristal* champagne packed in ice. He handed plastic cups to Brandi to pass around and gave Cameron a bottle to open as he began to open another.

"Wow," Cameron said. "*Cristal*, that's pretty special. I guess I'll be able to take my Budweiser home."

"Oh, you have no idea," Colt said. "Let's fill'em up, I want to make a toast."

"Maybe this is going to be the fish's lucky day," Cameron said as the cameras started flashing all around them. "Why fish when you can drink *Cristal*? We only get to take pictures of people drinking this stuff," he said to no one in particular. He figured they'd loosen up after a couple gulps of some of the best champagne money can buy.

"May I have your attention for a second?" Colt said as he topped off the last cup. "I promise you, I'll try to be brief. First of all I would like to thank Cameron for arranging all of this and I hope we have an awesome day out here in paradise," he raised his cup and swooped it around for all to take in the view, "So here's to you, Cameron," as he raised his cup. "Thanks, my friend." Everybody raised their glasses and took sips with one hand and tried to snap pictures with the other to capture the moment. "Brandi," Colt motioned for her to stand beside him. He put his arm around her and whispered something to her. She smiled and whispered *thank you*. Once again, the cameras went ballistic. "I would like to share something very special with you today. I have experienced a wonderful journey in my transition from Virginia to California. Along the way I learned the meaning of enjoying life every day. I have seen the beauty this world has to offer and I have fallen in love," he said as he began to tear up as he looked at her.

Cameron immediately noticed the ring. This pleased him because he knew this was truly going to be a great day. It was an excellent time to bring out Annie-Laurie so she could be a part of this.

About the same time as these thoughts were going through his head, a police car pulled into the parking lot back at the marina. Leroy could still see the wake pattern from the boat leaving the dock. Everything looked normal to him, but he decided to hop on the police department's boat and follow them out of respect for Mr. Giles. He'd radioed ahead to make sure it was ready so in no time he was freezing his butt off on the water with his overcoat and suit on.

"Colt," Cameron interrupted. "I'm sorry, but before you continue, I think there is somebody here who would enjoy this moment too," Cameron started walking towards the cabin. The boys all got into position to photograph whoever was going to come out. Colt was a little upset. He stopped his toast but quickly recovered thinking that Hansen was on the boat. It would be awesome for him to be a part of this moment, so he quickly got over being mad.

The silhouette of Annie-Laurie's blurred frame through the glass as she walked towards the door in the cabin to the boat deck was unmistakable. Colt almost dropped his cup and within a nano-second, his world crashed like the stock market during the depression. There was no place to hide and there was absolutely no time to recover from the shock before their eyes would meet. As the door opened, she was illuminated with flashes from the cameras and enveloped by the falling snow. She had been watching the events through the window and had already seen the ring. The tears were out of control but it was too late for her to care. She was as much in shock as he was. Everybody froze when they saw her expression and for a second the flashes stopped because they sensed something was terribly wrong. Only the two of them knew what the hell it was. Brandi was the first one to do the math and her knees almost buckled when she figured it out. She knew her good fortune was too good to be true. Silence surrounded them, even the muffle of the engines seemed to silence themselves during the moment. The sun's rays shone through the falling snow and it all made for a very surreal, eerie situation. Cameron immediately knew he'd been used. It didn't take much to figure that out. His comrades quickly recovered and went back to work because they were trained to take advantage of these rare moments.

Their eyes were frozen in time, not even blinking when an occasional snowflake interrupted their vision. Slowly, one step at a time, she walked towards him. Tears were flowing off her face like water off Niagara Falls. He couldn't believe Annie-Laurie was actually here. His cup was still halfway up in toast mode. Suddenly, which seemed like a lifetime, they were face to face staring at each other and letting all their emotions flow out of their eyes. His was sadness and hers was madness. Given time, there was so much Colt wanted to say but nothing came out of his mouth. He was paralyzed. It was so unreal that he'd even forgotten Brandi was standing beside him. *What could he say?* In a word, he was a deer caught in the headlights. The silence lasted an eternity and then suddenly, she snapped.

"You're such a liar," she shrieked as she shoved him with both hands in the chest. They were on a boat, moving across a rather large body of water. The force of her push along with the forward momentum of the boat was too much for him to overcome and he went flying. His body hit the back wall of the boat and the momentum caused him to do a complete flip, before he made a splash. The wake of the boat swallowed him like a whale does plankton. The cup landed on top of where he went in and served as the only marker, because he was gone. Within seconds, the boat seemed like it was miles away from where he went in. Then all hell broke loose on board. Cameron screamed for someone to get the captain to turn the boat around while he focused on the cup, trying desperately not to lose the spot. Annie-Laurie gasped. It wasn't what she wanted to do and within seconds, the horror of what she had done caused her to fall flat out on the deck, unconscious. Brandi was at the edge of the boat screaming for Colt.

Leroy was about a half-mile behind them and saw it go down. He pushed the throttles to the max while he reached for the radio to summon the Emergency Response Team. He knew this was a very bad situation with probably no chance of a positive outcome. After he made the desperate call for help, he immediately started to recite the Lord's Prayer, over and over. Again, he estimated he would get there about the same time as the captain could get the boat turned around. He could tell from that distance that the body that went overboard wasn't wearing a life vest and without it, from his experience, there was no way it could survive in that water. The only saving grace was that the water was cold.

Colt didn't feel the push and he didn't feel hitting the back of the boat, but he did feel his body flipping in mid air. In that instant he knew he was in big trouble and the only thing that went through his mind was the verse:

I've got an angel
She doesn't wear any wings…

When his body hit the water, the combination of the impact with the cold was instantaneous and totally shocking. And it only lasted a second. The minute his face felt the rush of cold, it triggered what they call a Mammalian Diving Reflex, which causes the body to totally shut down. This reflex causes the body to lapse into an oxygen-saving mode which allows for maximum time under water. It causes three things to happen to the body simultaneously, which may help to prevent immediate death. The first is an immediate reduction in heart rate called bradycardia. The second is a decrease in blood flow to the extremities which increases the supply of blood and oxygen to the brain and other vital organs, called peripheral vasoconstriction. Thirdly, it causes tremendous shift in blood plasma to the thoracic cavity which ultimately helps to prevent the lungs from collapsing under pressure. All of these actions represent the medical reasons for possible survival in cold water. The theoretical reason is *you ain't dead until you're warm dead.*

In a situation like this it doesn't matter if you're conscious or unconscious when you go in. It would help, however, if you were a kid because their chances of survival are infinitely greater. This autonomic nervous system mechanism pulls oxygenated blood away from the limbs back to the heart and brain which creates the necessary circuitry between the heart and brain to conserve oxygen in a very cold state. The one thing Colt had going for him was instinctively, he held his breath on impact, which gave his body added amounts of oxygen to store. Potentially, he could remain submerged for up to twenty minutes and still survive without causing any brain damage. By preventing the water from interrupting the body's absorption of oxygen, it was possible his body could avoid hypoxia and acidosis, which lead to death by cardiac arrest. Of course, the only two people who knew all this were Captain Ron and Leroy. The downside is the body has a greater likelihood of sinking in this lake because of fewer bacteria from the constant coldness. The upside is Leroy and Ron knew there might be a possibility the person could still be alive even after forty-five minutes after being pulled out, even if there were no visible signs of life. This knowledge wasn't passed on to the passengers who were hysterically tripping all over themselves. The only saving grace was the cup remained visible and represented the only lifeline for Colt.

As both boats converged, Leroy had to slow down because he didn't see the clear plastic cup and had no bearing on the proximity of the body. The last thing he wanted to do was run over it with his boat. He was able to see the captain pointing so he knew something was in the water nearby. Slowing down to an almost idle position, he could hear in the background the welcoming sound of an approaching helicopter. He knew its birds-eye view was critical in spotting the body and would guide them in from above. So he picked up the mike and made contact as the helicopter drew closer. Clearly, somebody was going to have to risk going in to get the body and he was pretty sure he was the likely candidate. He began preparing himself by putting his mind in the zone and constantly repeating the Lord's Prayer, something he'd continued to do almost unconsciously since he saw the body go in.

Back on the deck of the fishing boat was another story altogether. There were a host of issues unfolding, all of which were not good. Brandi was still leaning over the back of the boat screaming Colt's name hysterically, to no avail. Annie-Laure had regained some sort of consciousness, although the shock at what she'd just done completely paralyzed her. Cameron was totally focusing on the cup, in desperate hopes of saving his friend, while simultaneously cursing himself for his sheer stupidity. Plastic cups were rolling around on the deck and the pungent smell of champagne added to the nausea of fear. Some of the boys continued their job, on point, snapping pictures of the entire scene of pure bedlam. It was just plain sick.

Having successfully turned the large boat around, Captain Ron stopped way short of the cup, much to the disbelief of Cameron, even though he was sure the cup had moved quite a bit on the surface. Cameron kept pointing towards it trying to get the captain's attention above the screams from Brandi. What Cameron didn't understand, however, was the body was in forward motion when it hit the water, and the under-current from the boat's forward motion would continue to propel the heavier body in the direction of the boat faster than the cup floating on the surface. The only hope of saving him at this point was to stay as calm as possible and exercise extreme patience. Theoretically, they still had time. The captain was now scanning for the body under the surface at a better angle than Leroy, because he was higher, but was hoping the helicopter would spot it immediately. The water was calm which allowed for much greater visibility from higher up. The captain could also see Leroy was in communication with the helicopter, so he switched channels to get in on the conversation. The best case scenario was for Leroy to go in and get the body with the captain using his boat as a rescue vehicle for both of them. The helicopter pilot and crew could direct the operation from above. So as much as he could see the panic in his passenger's eyes, because of his apparent lack of action, he was really putting his boat in the best position possible for the ultimate rescue. Both the pilot of the helicopter and Leroy knew this as well, even before the three-way conversation began. Leroy finally saw the cup the captain had been pointing towards and, he too, did the math and angled his boat closer towards the fishing boat than the cup. The whole time Cameron was screaming that they were totally missing the spot. And, by this time, Colt had been under for at least five minutes, if not much, much longer. Leroy cussed himself for not first checking his watch when the body went in. That was a crucial error on his part and he would never forgive himself for it as long as he lived.

The pilot swung the helicopter around so he could face the water in the same direction as the sun peaking through the clouds so they wouldn't be blinded by the glare shimmering across the water. This is why they constantly went through relentless training. Everything has to operate on knowledge and natural instinct verses painting by numbers in a real-life situation.

His copilot spotted the body. Immediately the three-way communications began to coordinate the rescue. The body was submerged approximately four feet under the surface in a face down position and obviously, not moving. The need to get it out of the water precluded any attempt to get it on board the helicopter. The helicopter lifted straight up and slightly off to the side for better visibility during the rescue, less blade turbulence on the water and to be in the right position to lower the life-line for Leroy once he got it to the surface. The plan was to help Leroy get the body on the boat before he went into the dive reflex himself, or worse, drown. The pilot also radioed Ron instructions about what to do with them when both people were finally on board. Of course the body would have to air-lifted to the hospital immediately.

On the boat deck, Cameron noticed the operator of the other boat stripping down to the bare minimum, all the while inching his boat closer and closer to a certain point in the water. He could also feel a slight thrust from their boat as it turned slightly to get closer to his boat. He knew by the slowness of the operation they'd given up hope on Colt being alive. He sunk to his knees and began to cry while he watched the whole thing unfold. Brandi finally took her eyes off the cup and quit screaming Colt's name. She realized he was gone from her life forever. It was devastating. She too, immediately went into shock. Finally, after being directed by the pilot into the perfect position, Leroy crossed his heart, threw a couple of life preservers in the water above the body and strapped on his inflatable preserver. Hopefully, he would be able to inflate it once he got to the body and both of them would be pulled back up to the surface. The last thing he did before he went overboard was splash the ice cold water on his face several times to get used to the shock he would feel when he went in. When he hit the water, the only thing his body wanted to do, instinctively, was to get back to the surface immediately. He had to fight with everything in his soul to push himself down under. He grabbed the body tightly by the collar, calculating that was the best vantage point to prevent the coat from coming off during the rescue and causing the body to sink away before they could rise to the surface. Leroy knew he had precious little time himself. He was already feeling multiple things changing in his own body. But the inflatable did is job. When they reached the surface, true to form and many, many hours of practice, the life-line from the helicopter was directly where he could reach out and hook his arm into it so the helicopter could drag them ever so slowly to the edge of the fishing boat. He was already frozen but his adrenalin kept him in the moment.

Within seconds many hands were pulling them out of the water on to the deck of the fishing boat. Leroy figured he was in *stage one* of hypothermia based on the fact he was experiencing severe trembling and his extremities were numb. The emerging goose bumps were rapidly forming an insulating layer which hopefully would help him from entering *stage two* hypothermia where his muscles would quit working altogether. Based on instructions from the pilot of the helicopter, Captain Ron knew they had to perform a gradual warming exercise on Leroy. Colt was a whole different problem. Fortunately, the pilot was getting ready to lower the basket so they could med-vac him to Barton Memorial Hospital in South Lake Tahoe. He stole a quick second to scan the faces of the passengers and knew there would be many more problems to deal with before this day was over. First things first, every one of them needed to get inside and begin helping each other, specifically the two women, and pray.

"Cameron! Cameron!" The captain yelled as loud as he could. "Get them all inside the cabin! We need to make way for the basket! Make sure everybody understands they need to help these women too! Do it now! " A couple of the guys were still taking pictures of everything around them, including Colt lying face-up on the deck. He wasn't moving and he wasn't breathing. They were convinced he was dead and even though they were working, they were totally devastated. A true photographer feels the need to capture the picture. The grieving process can come at a later time. They were interrupted back to reality when Cameron started corralling them into the cabin. In earnest, he grabbed two of the ones snapping pictures to help him get the women inside. Both women were dead weight for different reasons. Then he went back out to help Captain Ron get Colt in the basket, which was the most difficult thing he'd ever done in his life.

After they loaded Colt, the captain went to work on Leroy. He had brought down from the bridge a thermos of hot coffee to start getting warm liquid in him. They had to get some blankets around him and he made two of the guys wrap their arms around him and hug him to warm his body with close body contact. And they had to keep him still. After the captain finally gained control over the chaotic situation, he went over to Brandi and whispered something into her ear. Her eyes flickered as if he'd said something that sparked a tiny, remote sense of hope. Still, she, along with everyone else on the boat, knew Colt was dead. The captain said to have faith.

The task of attaching Leroy's boat to the tow-line went without a hitch and the fishing boat headed back towards the marina, about the same time the helicopter landed at Barton Memorial. The atmosphere in the cabin was catastrophic. Brandi attacked Annie-Laurie and she was just letting her pummel away. She was cognizant enough to know what she had done and she wanted to die. No amount of pain could justify her actions. She felt pure rage when she pushed Colt but she didn't mean to kill him. She didn't even put her hands up to block Brandi's assault. A couple of the boys tried to break it up while the others kept taking pictures. Cameron, for the first time in his life, vowed he would never take another picture again, as long as he lived. He started crying uncontrollably and blamed himself for everything and was convinced he was never going to survive this feeling of being responsible for Colt's death.

It seemed like an eternity before they reached the marina. Police cars were already there when they got to the dock. By the time they disembarked, Leroy had significantly improved to the point that he was fully in charge if the situation. He had no choice but to place Annie-Laurie under arrest for attempted murder. It took a while to get statements from everyone, except

Brandi, because she couldn't talk. When they finished, Leroy joined Annie-Laurie in the patrol car and took her to the police station.

As Brandi and Cameron were walking by Colt's car in the parking lot, Brandi came back to life when she heard Colt's cell phone ringing from the front seat. She was beginning to show signs of denial. Her mind and emotions were playing tricks on her. Cameron basically had to drag her to his car. They sat in the car forever in total silence, not knowing which way to go. Finally, after sitting there for what seemed like eternity, Cameron made the decision they had to be with Colt, no matter what. He started the car, put it in drive and sped towards the hospital. Even when he rounded corners at a higher than normal rate of speed her body didn't waver an inch. If her eyes weren't bulging out of her head, Cameron would have sworn she was dead, because she stared at nothing. Her anger at what happened was becoming apparent. Anger, being such a powerful emotion evolved into bargaining, where she wanted to strike some sort of deal with God in order to bring Colt back. The reality of the situation was spiraling deep into depression and all Cameron could do was sit there and watch all these emotions rip across her face like a nuclear blast. He could tell she would never be able to accept what happened to the one she loved. It was impossible.

When they got to the police station, Leroy helped Annie-Laurie get out of the back seat and two officers, who'd been standing there waiting, escorted her inside. The first thing Leroy had to do was make a call, so he went directly to his office, changed into a set of workout clothes which he never used, and sat down at his desk to contemplate exactly how he was going to tell Mr. Giles what had happened. He knew from experience, this was going to be a very difficult call to make. Reluctantly, he dialed the number. Hansen answered before Leroy even heard it ring.

"Leroy, what's going on? I can't get anybody to answer their phones. I've been calling and…"

"Mr. Giles," Leroy interrupted, "We've had a very unfortunate situation happen on the lake." Leroy paused long enough for Mr. Giles to process what he just said. "You were right about the girl. She was bad news."

"Tell me what happened," Hansen said solemnly as he dropped his head on the desk, knowing he was not going to like what he heard.

He sat there in stone cold silence while Leroy explained everything. Fortunately, Leroy gave him a hint of hope when he explained the mammalian dive reflex in detail. After they hung up, Hansen called his driver. He needed to get to the airport and rent a helicopter to take him to Barton Memorial in Tahoe. Then he picked up the phone to call Josh in Wintergreen.

Leroy walked into the holding room with two cups of coffee. He'd had enough time to digest the situation and realize it wasn't pre-meditated. That usually evokes more rage of emotions in the assailant. This girl pushed herself overboard when she pushed him. Leroy was more concerned about suicide than booking her for attempted murder, although he knew he had certain formalities to follow. She was a total wreck. It would take days, maybe weeks to get the real story out of her. He just wanted to smooth her transition back to reality as best he could under the circumstances.

After they loaded all the equipment in the back of the van, they piled in to head to the hospital. Gordino was the driver and sort of their leader. Being Paparazzi, they'd been around each other for years and worked together on many projects, but they had never witnessed anything like this before. The whole situation was way too surreal to make any sense out of it on an individual basis. Gordino knew there was still work to be done before they let this out of the bag. He was grounded enough to know they had captured an amazing story and he wanted every one to be on the same playing field before they sent the pictures to their prospective clients. The first thing they had to do was confirm Colt was really dead, although there was no doubt. Then they had to organize their thoughts and interpretations of what had just happened in order to accurately re-create the chain of events and sensationalize the story. Unfortunately, they had to make a living and by the nature of their profession, they had to blow it up like a hot air balloon and sell this thing for as long as they could before they moved on to the next big thing. It was complicated but it was that simple. No one in the van questioned where he was going because they knew they had to go to the hospital for confirmation, so they all stared out the windows of the van trying to piece the puzzle together in their own minds.

Gordino pulled into the Emergency Room parking lot and left the van running because he didn't think he'd be too long. The other five sat in silence anticipating the inevitable. Gordino is always groomed to the max. That's his calling card. He knew looking presentable was the key to get through some otherwise closed doors. Walking into the Emergency Room was a perfect example. If the staff realized he represented the media, they would have put up the China Wall. He was in a hurry so he had to think fast on his feet by pretending to be Colt's brother. It was cold but necessary in order to prevent the wall. With each new person he talked to as he went up the chain, he began to come to the realization that Colt might still be alive and when he got to the head nurse in ICU, he knew it. Amazing as it was, Colt being alive was going to drastically change their story. He was shocked to learn that they had revived Colt in the helicopter while it was in route to Barton. It had something to do with him going into a dive reflex when he hit the water, which prevented him from drowning. That was the good news, she said. The bad news is he's in a coma and totally non-responsive and in super-critical condition. The nurse mentioned that he appeared to be in a state of severe traumatic shock. Only God knew for how long, or if, he would survive at all. She said she'd seen cases like this before where people remained in comas for days and even weeks. There was a case she referred to where a man had been in a coma for nineteen years and came out of it. The story is his wife never left his side, rotated him every hour on the hour and never gave up hope. Although, his world had changed dramatically in nineteen years, he did come out of it. So there was hope, albeit very little hope at this stage.

Before he went out to the van, Gordino sat in the lobby of the Emergency Room for a long while to collect his thoughts and to let the staff get familiar with his face. He might need to come back again and he wanted red carpet service. Time is money and so is timing. While he was sitting there he noticed Cameron and Brandi walk in. They didn't see him in the corner because they weren't looking and he wanted to keep it that way. He patiently waited until they were escorted to ICU before he got up to leave.

He couldn't get over the fact that Colt was still alive. It was an absolute miracle and it was the miracle that got his mind to thinking. This guy was dead. He saw it with his own two eyes. There was no doubt about it. By the time he got back to the van he had formulated a plan. It was so out of the box it was almost dangerous, but he couldn't foresee a down-side. Colt was alive at this point so he knew they had to move in an entirely different direction in order to sensationalize the story. The path he'd come up with was going to make a lot of people very uneasy and that's what made him nervous. He was going to have to do some homework to make it sellable but it would make an amazing story if it worked. He had to hurry if they were going to meet next week's deadline.

The ride back to the bunkhouse was uneventful. He didn't tell the boys what he discovered in the hospital. They knew Colt was dead. No one had anything to say because they were way too buried in their own thoughts and mentally exhausted, ready to call it a day and a bad one at that. Gordino was busy running over the possibilities in his mind, so the silence of the ride allowed him time to stay focused. Fortunately, the stage had already been set and it was simply a matter of selling the story based on the information they had, which was considerable. As they drove along one of the most scenic places on the planet, you would have thought every one of them was staring straight into hell judging from their facial expressions. Watching someone die can do that to a person. Gordino knew this and wanted them to think about what they'd witnessed until they were literally nauseated with grief. Consequently, when they learned Colt was still alive, the news would amplify the magnitude of the miracle to seem bigger than life as they know it. Generally, in their line of work, anything that was bigger than life was considered forbidden territory. The prospect of crossing the line in this particular situation could elevate the level of profitability beyond what any of them had ever seen in their entire careers. And that was his hook.

"Guys, pull out your laptops and let's take a look at the pictures," he said to them as they were about to separate to find sanctuary in their individual stalls in the bunkhouse.

"Why? I've seen enough for one day," Leo said. "As a matter of fact I've seen enough to last me a lifetime. I'm going to bed," he finished as he turned and walked away from the group standing there.

"Yeah, me too," echoed one after the other.

Gordino let them get about ten paces away before he said "He's alive." And that's all he needed to say to stop them in their tracks. Leo was the first to turn around.

"What did you say?"

"Colt is alive," Gordino pronounced emphatically.

"No way" Leo said looking around to every one in the room for support. "We were there too, Gordi, we saw him. He's dead."

"Really, is that what you truly believe?"

"Is this some kind of a sick joke?"

"Well let me ask you some questions," Gordino addressed the room. "Hold your hands up if you think he's dead?" All hands went up immediately, without question. "Okay, hold your hand up if you think he could have been revived." No one held up their hand. "Okay," Gordino continued, "Hold your hand up if you would think it would be a miracle if in fact Colt is still alive." Once again, all hands went up.

"You're a sick man, Gordi," Leo said as he turned back around to leave the room.

"Leo," Gordino called out to him. "Do you really think I would make this up? I'm not kidding, Colt is alive!" Gordino yelled out to the entire room. "Why do you think I was in the hospital so long? You guys were so wrapped up in grief you had no idea I was in there for almost an hour. I'm telling you, he's alive."

Now he had everybody's undivided attention. He could see smiles of relief and high fives being passed around. He let the good news settle before he continued. "There's some bad news that goes along with the good news," he added as he noticed the confused and upset looks from the boys. Clearly they were getting tired of the little game he was playing. "He's alive but he's in a coma. There is a really good chance he won't live and there is a huge chance he may never come out of the coma. But, he's definitely alive."

"That's amazing," Leo said as he sat down on the sofa and put his head in his hands, overcome with emotion. "I don't know what to say." Like dominos, the other four guys sat down around the fireplace and tried to come to grips with this new information. Gordino let them sit there for a long time without saying anything. Finally, he figured it was time to ask the million dollar question.

"I think we all know," he continued, "based on what we witnessed, Colt Salley died in that water. No one could have survived that. When they got him back on the boat, he clearly wasn't breathing and he'd been lying there for at least five minutes before they got him into the basket to be air-lifted out.

Surely, he wasn't moving or breathing." Everyone in the room looked dumbfounded. They looked at each other in apprehension that someone else would speak up, but the news was so profound, no one would touch it. It was so far over their heads it was ridiculous.

"My question to you is… what do you think he saw on the other side? Think about it for a minute. What did he see on the other side? I think..," he paused for effect. "We have an amazing story here," he finished as he held his arms up to God.

When she saw the look of total devastation on the beautiful woman's face, she knew she had to take her to a much happier place and she had to get her there quickly. The intensive care nurse had to paint a better picture than ethically she should have, but she had to cross the line to save this woman from spiraling into the land of no return. She would have to second guess her decision at a later time. It was the constant fiddling with the ring that caught her eye. The numbness of seeing someone you love lying there in a coma is more comforting than death, but not much. Especially, with the complexity of medical issues this young man was facing. The woman desperately needed a prayer of hope and she also needed to get busy and help him in order to help herself.

"What is your name," she asked her.

"Excuse me?" Brandi blinked in confusion.

"Young lady, what is your name?" The nurse softly repeated.

"Ah… Brandi. Brandi Steele, with an e," she was used to saying.

"Brandi, my name is Maria and I need your help, okay? I need you to get yourself together. Do you think you can do that? Get yourself together?"

"I don't know. I don't think I ca…"

"Yes you can sweetheart because you have to."

"What do y..."

"He really needs you and he needs you right now," the nurse said to her as she looked down at Colt lying there on the bed looking extremely pale, with his eyes closed and IV's going into him every which way but loose. "Brandi Steele, with an e," Maria said as she pointed to Colt. "He needs to know you're here with him. He needs to hear you talk to him and he needs you to convince him everything is going to be all right. Can you do that for him?"

"Can he hear me?"

"You bet." Maria silently crossed her heart. "He's in a very deep place right now, but he can hear you so don't be alarmed or discouraged if he doesn't let you know it. But I promise you," she said as she stared deep into Brandi's eyes. "He can hear you."

"What do I say?"

"Sweetheart, you tell him everything you've ever wanted to tell him and then some. He needs your love to pull him out of the place he's in right now. He can't do it alone. Trust me, you can do it, I can see it in your eyes. True love is the most powerful medicine there is, after faith and prayer. Use everything you have in your soul. I've seen it work and I have absolutely no doubt both of you are going to be just fine and have a wonderful life together."

Brandi looked at Maria in total disbelief. Maria had tons of experience in these situations and she hit all the right buttons to get Brandi focused. She stared at Maria while her courage returned which gave her a sense of determination to the point where she told herself *she was never going to let him go, never. She would stay with him until hell froze over if she had to. Absolutely, she could do it! But she also needed help.*

"Excuse me for one second," she said with renewed passion. "I'll be right back, there's something I need to do."

"Okay honey, but try to hurry. I'll sit with him and tell him how pretty you are and what a lucky guy he is."

Brandi bolted out of the ICU and ran down the hallway to find Cameron. She found him sitting in the waiting room bawling his eyes out.

"Cameron," she said as she tried to shake some sense into him. "He's going to be all right, I promise because I'm not going to let him die. But you have to do me a huge favor, okay? Can you do something for me?"

Cameron stared at her through a wall of tears and was amazed at the look of strength and determination he saw in her face. "What do you need? Just tell me," he said in earnest.

"I need you to go back to our cabin and get Burly. We need him in a big way. There's a connection Colt has with him and Colt needs him to be with him right now. Can you do that for Colt?"

"Brandi, I'll have Burly here in twenty minutes. I'll get Alex to go get him and bring him here. That'll save some time."

"Hurry up," she said as she spun and ran back down the hallway. "Bring him into the ICU and don't let anybody stop you," she yelled over her shoulder.

In her twenty-six years of nursing, Marie Tinsley had never seen anything like it. There was a huge brown dog in her ICU. She was going to object until she witnessed the love that dog had for his owner. He cautiously jumped up on the bed and, careful to avoid the IV lines, laid down beside his master and softly licked his face and whimpered noises to him. It was the most touching thing she'd ever seen, by a long shot. Brandi was on the other side holding his hand and whispering in his other ear. *He's going to be just fine,* Maria Tinsley said to herself as she stepped out of the room to get a water dish.

The reason that Polish railway worker came out of the coma he'd been in for nineteen years was because his wife performed the job of an entire intensive care team, 24/7, for nineteen years. She did it through love and determination and most of all faith. Maria loved that story and she saw the love and determination and faith in both Brandi and the dog. She was willing to bet she was going witness a miracle and she was going to do everything in her power to allow that dog and that woman to do their magic, rules or no rules. *Lord Christ, please help them.*

Starbright Magazine
New York

"**L**et's put this together and run it," Deanna said to her team sitting around the table in the conference room. "I mean, we built this couple up out of nothing anyway, I don't see a downside except some very high-level people in the government will be enraged. But this won't be the first time we crossed the line."

"I think it's a little premature and real risky," cautioned Liam, her assistant. "I wish we could reach Cameron. I think we need to talk to him before we make a mistake. The guy is in a coma, he's not dead for God's sake!"

"We can't wait forever on him," Deanna said emphatically. "He's still at the hospital with the girl and we don't have the luxury to sit and wait for the right time. The right time is now. Remember, our competition will be all over this. Think about it. What's going on here?" She held her arms out and looked at everyone in the room. "What do we do for a living? I'll tell you what we do. We make money by sensationalizing stories about people who thrive on this. Who do we sell this to? We sell it to the masses who buy into our hogwash. This might be the story of the century and it's for real," she emphasized.

"I don't see it," Liam responded. "A guy drowned and now he's in a coma. This stuff happens all the time, believe it or not. It just happens to be someone we put on the cover of *Starbright*. I mean, it's definitely a story, but it's way too early to cross that line."

"On the surface I agree, Liam," Deanna said. "But this goes far deeper than that. How many religions are there in the world?"

"I don't know, several. Maybe ten big ones, I don't know."

"Did you know seventy-eight percent of the people in the United States alone consider themselves Christians? I'm no mathematical wizard, but that represents a whole lot of people who believe in life after death. Those same people have absolutely no idea what that means. Think about the numbers worldwide. It's staggering."

"I don't know," Liam piped in while he started running the numbers. "Probably seventy to eighty percent of the world's population,"

"Okay, let's just say there are ten different religions, just to work with a round figure," Deanna added to make her point. "If someone dies, do you think they all agree on the same direction that person will take in the afterlife?"

"That's a definite no," Liam laughed nervously as he looked around the table.

"Exactly my point," Deanna exploded. "No one really knows what's on the other side. Some religions have credible answers and some are beyond belief and somewhat contradictory. Are we born with immortal souls? Do our souls transform to a place of bliss upon death, or is all this just a greater consciousness? What's our reward or punishment? What about reincarnation? The short of it is that we have never been able to answer the billion dollar question. And this is not the question of the century my friends. This is the question of our human existence," Deanna stopped to see their reactions. "The Lord said 'Eye hath not seen, nor ear heard, neither hath entered into the heart of man those things which the Lord hath prepared for them that love him.' Let that sink in for a minute."

She continued, "Nothing has been sold more aggressively, or for that matter, more successfully in the entire world than religion, of all kinds. And they still don't have the answer to the big question. What do we think is on the other side," she mouthed slowly. "They can tell you what to expect and what you need to do to get there, but that's it. Nobody knows," she held up her hands. "This means nobody has snuck back over to this side to give us the news we'd love to hear. I'm pretty sure I didn't get the memo," she closed convincingly. "And that my friends would be why we're running the story."

She walked around the entire room and touched everyone once on the shoulder which was her way of establishing that personal connection with each one of them individually. Finally, she got back to her seat, reached down on the table and picked up the remote and pointed it towards the blank screen on the wall behind her. As of yet, she was the only one in the room to see the proof of the next cover page. She wanted to prepare them for what they were about to see. Before she hit the button, she turned back and stared briefly at each and every one of them one more time. Emotionally, at this point, they were on the edge of their seats, anxious to see whatever it was that was going to magically appear on the screen. Then she pressed the button and gasps of horror could be heard around the room.

What illuminated the blank screen was the latest cover design of *Starbright* Magazine for next week's release. The cover showed a crystal clear picture of the deck of the fishing boat on Lake Tahoe. The shot focused on the face of Brandi Steele, who was standing next to where Colt Salley had been standing, with a look of sheer horror on her face. Clearly, she was witnessing the murder of her boyfriend. The picture also showed the back profile of another woman at a slight angle with her arms extended in the direction of Colt Salley, whom she'd just pushed overboard. Also captured in the picture, in an airborne position, was Colt making a deadly splash in the treacherously cold water of Lake Tahoe. The look of absolute panic on his face just before impact with the water said it all. The headline, in bold font, simply read:

Jealous ex-girlfriend travels across country and pushes Colt Salley into the freezing waters of Lake Tahoe. He is pronounced dead at time of rescue and Amazingly... He came back from the dead and is in a coma.

WHAT DID HE SEE ON THE OTHER SIDE?

"I'm going to flip through the pictures and I want every one of you to take notes. Then we are going to write the story of a lifetime. These people want sensationalism and that's exactly what we're going to give them, even if it takes us all night to do it. Remember, when you test their beliefs, you are going to create controversy like you've never seen before. And controversy sells."

Deanna flashed the sequence of pictures across the screen. "Apparently, Colt was in the middle of a toast. It could have something to do with the ring you can clearly see on Brandi Steele's left finger. My guess is they just got engaged. Now another woman enters the picture and she pushes Colt overboard. We are going to flash these pics through the article...in sequence." Everyone around the table stared in horror at the scene that unfolded in front of their eyes. Some people had to fight to hold back their tears. It was clearly evident the water showed no mercy. In the background, the snowed-in landscape surrounding the lake was a strong indication of how bitterly cold the water was. Some pictures even captured the snowflakes falling. That anyone could survive falling in, much less being submerged for many minutes, was beyond all sense of reason. It was the shock and the horror in the eyes of everyone on the boat that amplified the tragedy being played out on the screen. The pictures were extremely vivid and told the entire story as it unfolded. "Clearly," Deanna continued, "the policeman dressed in his Sunday's best is a hero. He risks his own life to get to Colt from several feet under water." Then she cut to the pictures of Colt lying motionless on the deck of the boat, not breathing and dead white in color. The expressions of the people surrounding him had death written all over them as well. It was the chaotic look of not being able to do anything about the situation, the feeling of sheer helplessness that was so gruesome to look at.

"I know this will not have a happy ending and that is extremely unfortunate. We cannot change fate. But what we can do is tell the story and sell this rag for all its worth. That is not negotiable. Remember," Deanna said to her team, "We introduced them to the world. They are not strangers to our readers. That is our hook, line, and pardon the pun, sinker."

She let the rest of the pictures tell the story. Each one had to deal with their feelings of sorrow and grief. She wanted them to feel exactly what the readers would feel when they read the story. Colt and Brandi are adorable and lovable and now they're hurting. She wanted the entire world to feel their pain. "Let's get to work people." Everyone around the table sat there in stunned silence because they knew a story like this would open Pandora's Box. "Now!"

Lake Tahoe
Barton Memorial Hospital

Brandi loved him so much. He was her life and she needed him. She wasn't about to let him slip away. No way. She never left his side for a second. She combed his hair, rubbed his unshaven face and kissed his hands to reassure him she was always there with him. It was sometimes difficult for his nurse, Maria, to turn him because Brandi didn't want to move away from his side for a second. Burly was right there with her as well, on the bed with his master. Colt looked so peaceful, lying there in the middle of the two of them with his eyes closed, neither smiling nor despondent about his predicament. He was lying there motionless, unaware of the constant beep of the machines and the occasional shuffle of activity in the unit.

Miraculously, he was the only patient in the ICU at the time, which was probably the only reason Burly was allowed to stay. Of the three, Burly was the glue that held them together. If he sensed Brandi breaking down he'd lick her hand and Colt's face to keep them hanging on. There were times when Maria would stand off to the side and witness this unbelievable display of love and determination and she would silently slip out of the room to cry her heart out. She doubted Colt would wake up from this ordeal and she also realized, based on her medical knowledge, it was out of the doctor's control. It was clearly in God's hands. His recovery would have to come from a higher place and his girlfriend and his dog had to help him get there. He needed all the help he could get.

Maria was also well aware of the fact that news of the event had reached the media. And for whatever reason, a circus was beginning to develop in the waiting room and points outside the hospital. She'd seen the tabloid picture and knew this was no ordinary couple facing the crisis. Other people were very interested in how all this was going to play out and she had to make sure they were kept at bay because their distraction would do nothing to help the situation in the unit. The administrators at the front desk were getting overwhelmed with questions and requests to gain access. It was beyond absurd how the media was reacting and they were relentless in their quest for information. Cameron remained in the waiting room, silently in the corner by himself. He wouldn't talk to anyone except Maria and Brandi. He was ready to commit suicide.

It wasn't until a couple days later when the tabloids hit the shelves that all hell broke loose. Obviously, they had access to pictures no one else had and their stories around those pictures opened a forum of discussions that would raise the hair on the back of your neck. They took a common love story-turned tragedy and evolved it into the religious question of the century. It was so calculated. Preachers around the world were preparing their sermons based on the questions generated by Colt's plight, surrounding the great beyond. The public was completely in sync with the heartbeat of the story. The magnitude of interest went beyond anything to hit the news wires since the Presidential election. Eventually, the hospital had to hire security just to deal with the satellite trucks and news reporters who swarmed around like bees who couldn't get into the hive. Even the rap star, Diggy-Boo cancelled a performance to return to Tahoe to offer his support. It was amazing and it was sad. The longer Colt remained in a coma the more intense the outside world became. The far-out remote possibility that he actually might have the answer to immortality escalated into the gospel of truth and the people were on pins and needles, waiting to hear what he would say. There were no words to describe what was happening.

Occoquan, Virginia

Four men were sitting around a table in the restaurant facing the river having a nice casual business lunch. At first appearance they looked like pharmaceutical sales reps, with their suit coats hanging on the backs of their chairs. The sun was shining on this unseasonably warm winter's day, and the early birds of spring were chirping in the background of this scenic little town located in the distant suburbs of Washington, D. C. The conversation around the table was light and amicable. It was like they were comparing best practices from successful sales calls. At times, one of the men would slap his knee while in tears from laughing at something one of them said. The waitress enjoyed waiting on them because they were appreciative of her services to the point of being somewhat attracted to her, and she was always looking for an opportunity to better her place in life. Four successful looking gentlemen always brought out the best in her waitressing skills.

After they finished eating, the youngest of the four paid the bill and left her a handsome tip. She was pleased but disappointed they'd left the table and her standing there, waiting once again, for the next opportunity to find her 'Knight in Shining Armor'. They walked out to the parking lot, continuing their jovial conversation. Finally, out of earshot from anybody else, the tone of the conversation became very serious. Obviously, there was some business they needed to clear up before they parted ways.

"This has to stop before it gets out of hand. It goes against God's will," said the younger one, probably in his mid-thirties.

"It's already out of hand," said the most distinguished gentleman in the group. "Have you looked at the news? The whole world is sitting on top of this time bomb. I don't have to tell you what will happen to the government if this guy wakes up."

"What do you mean?"

"What I mean is," replied the distinguished one, "if this Colt fellow wakes up and says there is nothing on the other side, we're going to witness a collapse between Church and State that is unprecedented in the history of mankind. The whole world is on the edge of their seats anxiously waiting for him to wake up and deliver the answer to the one question that has confounded mankind for centuries. *What's on the other side?* The question of not knowing for sure what lies beyond life is kept in tack by beliefs stemming from faith. You allow something or someone to take that away and all hell will break loose. Think about the impact just on religion alone. I'm telling you, this situation could ignite a holy war like no other and it could crush governments, nations and the entire world-wide economy. Yes, it is that bad."

"So what are you saying?"

"Do I really have to say anything at all? Can't you figure it out on your own? We have been given a mission. By whom and from whom I cannot say. This is one of those situations where the *buck stops here*. It can't go any further than the four of us because it's way, way, way too dangerous. We have to put an end to it and we have to do it right now. Trust me that there are many out there who are counting on us to end this right now, if not yesterday. It absolutely has to be put to bed. And, need I have to say that you will carry this secret to your graves? We are running out of time, let's make it happen."

"How do you propose we do that?"

"We call John in Vegas."

"Okay, but how do you propose he'll get in there? The place is surrounded by the media. It's already a circus."

"John does this for a living. He'll have to figure it out on his own. The media can't be allowed to cross a line like this. They've been getting away with murder for too long, and I for one am sick and tired of it. I want to let them know they're not as big as they think they are. Freedom of speech is not free. They absolutely cannot be allowed to attack the very foundation of this world."

"Don't you think that's a bit risky? It could go all the way back to the President."

"So what, the government is on the other side of the fence on this one," the younger man piped in. "Actually, this is so far over the President's head that it's buried inside an agency that doesn't even exist. That's why we do what we do and get paid the big bucks. Enough said, I think we know what we have to do," he held up his hands. "I'll make the call."

Las Vegas, Nevada

John was enjoying a little mid-morning delight with one of his dear friends in the entertainment industry. She had talent. His burner phone couldn't have started ringing at a worse time. Any normal human being would have at least ridden it out before calling in, but John knew better. He didn't get many calls, but when he did, his whole world came to a grinding halt, immediately if not sooner. John, a master of disguise, could alter his appearance to look like anybody in the world, including the President. This was his safety net. No one could ever get to him because they didn't know who he was. All he would give them was the city and the beeper number which changed after every assignment.

Reluctantly, he smacked her on the fanny and told her they'd have to finish later, something had come up. Astounded and completely out of breath, she climbed off the top of him and mumbled her way to the bathroom. She knew from previous experiences with him that it was time to leave. No questions. After she left, John slid out the back door of his townhouse in a jogging suit and ran to an apartment complex a mile and a half down the road where he kept a second car parked just for situations like this one. He drove for an hour before he spotted probably one of the last remaining outside phone booths in the entire city, if not the whole world. He was going to have to change the way he contacted them eventually to catch up with the changing technology, but for now, this was the safest way for him to conduct business. It would be very hard to trace in a timely manner. By then, he would be long gone.

"So what's up?" He asked nonchalantly when someone answered the call.

"Same old, same old," was the reply. "Have you been keeping up with the news lately?"

"Hard not to," John replied. "People are so vulnerable."

"Too vulnerable, if you get my drift."

"Yeah, I get it," John said. "Who?

"Sleeping beauty"

"That's cold!"

"I think he's used to it by now."

"Okay, when?"

"Yesterday"

"Should have been the day before," John made light. "Each day it gets a little more out of control."

"Well," the voice on the other end said. "Some things take time."

"That's one thing I have plenty of," John finished.

"Well make good use of it and oh,"... the voice hesitated, "this time leave a mark."

"What? You're kidding me, right?"

"Wish I was."

"Whatever. Later,"

Click

He got back in his car and drove off in the opposite direction he came from, thinking about his new assignment and how best to go about accomplishing it. An hour later, he was jogging back to his townhouse. He immediately got on line to do some research because he needed to learn more about Barton Memorial Hospital, hypothermia, severe traumatic shock and comas. He hadn't played doctor in a long time so he had bone up on the terminology and pack accordingly. After he showered, he loaded his Toyota *Yaris* and headed west towards Lake Tahoe.

It was a gorgeous day to take a ride and this car gets great gas mileage to boot, he laughed to himself. The thing he enjoyed the most about the car was it made him completely anonymous. He could rob a bank and then go through the drive-thru to get change and wouldn't be recognized by the same teller he'd just robbed. In this car, people wouldn't notice him even if he was a top ten movie star. It's the kind of car the President should be riding around in because it would save a boat-load of money on security, not to mention gas.

Lake Tahoe

When Hansen finally made it to the hospital, he was shocked to see the carnival-like atmosphere of media entrapping the hospital. Obviously, it was a reflection on the weaknesses of the masses allowing them to be exploited by sensationalism of a simple, tragic story. If there was another worldly event happening at the same time, then this place would be a desert. Maybe. Hansen had his driver drop him off at the main entrance and he quickly pushed through the small crowd hanging around, monitoring the comings and goings of anybody who was somebody. To date, Diggy-Boo was the biggest thing to happen at the gate. Hansen was small potatoes, so he got in unscathed. As he worked his way towards the ICU, he was surprised at the normalcy of day-to-day operations inside the hospital itself. The extra security made sure of that.

When he got to the gatekeeper covering the unit, security tightened up a little more. They weren't going to just let anybody in to see Colt, which made sense. His family had just arrived by private jet from Virginia, so they were being very careful to not let things get out of hand. Brandi, after meeting Colt's parents briefly at bedside, had stepped out into the waiting room and was silently staring at the floor when Hansen found her. He went over and sat next to her and both of them hugged and cried. He knew she was hurting but had no idea it was this bad. When they finally came up for air, she shared with Hansen the news of their recent engagement, which made things worse. To Hansen, it seemed like her destiny to get to the good place where she deserved to be was never going to happen. One step forward and two steps backwards, unfortunately, was her mantra.

Cameron walked back in the exit door near the waiting

room. He'd just taken Burly out to get some fresh air and go to the bathroom. He saw Brandi and Mr. Giles. Unsure of what Hansen was going to say to him, he sat down beside them and introduced himself with an apology. There was nothing else left to be said.

"Mr. Giles? I'm Cameron Toscanini, the one who's responsible for this mess."

Hansen stole himself away from Brandi to shake Cameron's hand. "I think you're carrying too much of the blame, Cameron. Things happen all the time that we can't control. You had good intentions and that's all that matters. Wish and hindsight are the two ugliest words in the English language. Don't let it keep you down. Look to the future and decide how you can make the best of this horrible situation."

Cameron was completely at a loss for words. He never expected to receive such worldly support and advice from Mr. Giles. He expected the exact opposite, finger pointing, accusations and complete dismissal. Hansen reached down to play with Burly and said to no one in particular that he felt positive energy and something good was going to come out of this. He'd made a few calls and the best doctors in the country were working together to help Colt come out of this. Brandi was on the edge of her seat listening to him; soaking up everything he said praying these doctors would be able to help Colt. But she knew in her heart it was out of their hands. It was up to God and God only.

"Brandi," Hansen said directly to her. "He's going to be fine. I promise you. Why don't you go to the cabin and get some rest and come back in the morning with a fresh face and a fresh attitude. It will help you and it will certainly help him. I'll have my driver take you. Cameron and I will stay through the night and watch him for you, and of course, Burly," he said as he rubbed his head again. Colt has his parents here and we'll be here when they leave so he'll never be alone."

"Hansen," she said as the tears started flowing again. "I won't be able to sleep. It would be useless for me to leave. I can't leave him. I love him so much!" She put her face in her hands and bawled.

Hansen looked over at Cameron and winked, "I'll make sure you get something to help you sleep and we'll get you right back here at the crack of dawn. He needs you," Hansen emphasized. "But he needs you to be strong and only rest will help you get your strength back. The doctors say it will be a while before he wakes up and you'll be here when that happens. I absolutely guarantee that. Okay?" Hansen said in a fatherly tone to make her give in. He pulled out his cell phone and called his driver to explain the situation. When he hung up, he asked Cameron to step aside for a second so he could talk to Brandi in private. Cameron got up to move to the other side of the waiting room and Burly went over and lay at Brandi's feet.

"Brandi," Hansen spoke in a whisper. "Things got out of hand here and I'm partially to blame for this catastrophe. I had big dreams, like everybody else, and I let them guide my decisions. But that doesn't make it wrong, just unfortunate. Anyway, I knew the minute I saw you walk in with Colt you had fallen in love with him. I also knew he was the perfect person for you in so many ways. The reason I'm telling you this is because I believe in the bottom of my heart that you guys deserve a chance. You deserve to be with each other and you deserve to go through life enjoying the good things life has to offer. This has been a long-standing promise I made to your father that I would make sure you were gong to be all right. I'm a man of my word. Colt will come out of this and you will be fine and you will be married and have beautiful children and you will live a long and happy life together. Go home, get some rest and come back in the morning with your best face on. Let's get the game plan going and get your boy back. Okay?"

"Yes, sir," she couldn't help but say.

Hansen held her hand and they both stood up and started walking down the hallway towards the entrance to the hospital. He stopped, when he heard a whine from Burly, and turned around and winked to Cameron who was holding his leash. His wink gave Cameron renewed strength to help in the fight and forget about the past. *So much for hindsight,* he said to himself.

She was already feeling drowsy effects of the Sonata and the Xanax Hansen's driver had given to her in the car. They shouldn't be mixed, but it was a mild dose of both, enough Xanax to relax and enough Sonata to buy her some serious and much needed deep sleep. It was an excellent call to get her out of the hospital. She would awaken in the morning more refreshed to face the new day. She needed Burly but she knew Colt needed him more. She crawled under the covers and settled in for a good cry before she drifted off to a better place for the night. Her saving grace was Alex was by her bedside.

He rolled into the hospital parking lot about the same time Brandi got back to her lonely cabin. John surveyed the crowd outside the hospital. They had obviously dissipated somewhat because nothing ever happened in a hospital after hours, so there were only a few stakeouts on point. He put his thin mustache on and elongated his sideburns. With a dab of makeup, he totally changed his complexion to a slightly red-faced, older, sophisticated looking doctor. He completed the disguise with a stethoscope hanging around his neck, coming together just below the knot in his loosely tied tie. It was after hours so he had to look like he was working overtime. He added a little mousse and mussed-up his hair enough to finish out that unkempt preppy look so many doctors had.

He'd parked in the lot directly behind the doctor's parking lot. After he felt comfortable in costume, he opened his trunk, grabbed his old doctor bag and headed towards the hospital emergency entrance. He purposefully routed himself through the physician parking lot just in case someone noticed him on camera. He'd look like any normal doctor making late night rounds. He slowed his walk and made himself look as tired as he could when he walked into the hospital. He went directly to the administrative check in counter and magically turned himself into doctor.

"Could you tell me where the ICU is please," he said matter-of-factly and without any emotion whatsoever.

"Third hallway down on the right and go straight to the end. You can't miss it," the attendant said for the millionth time in her career. She'd never seen him before but it didn't matter. Doctors come and go nowadays like the wind.

With each step John took towards the ICU, he was building his confidence and getting himself in the zone. He had to appear overly confident without being insulting in order to get in a late-night visit, unannounced and unknown. When he rounded the corner it was show time. He'd been in situations like this his entire professional career so it was like riding a bicycle. It was natural, he'd just have to make it believable. As his luck would have it, Nurse Maria, the commandant, was at home lying in bed, reading another Sandra Brown novel. Sandra helped her vacate from her job better then anybody.

John, the doctor, approached the counter and asked the nurse on duty if he could see Mr. Salley's chart. "I'm an endocrinologist," he said before she could ask him who he was. "I promised his primary care physician back in Virginia that I would drop in on Mr. Salley and give him a report. Professional courtesy," he confessed. "Here's my card," John handed her his card he'd printed up earlier on his computer, for verification. That was all he had to do. The nurse reached over and handed him Colt's chart. Instead of walking directly into the unit, he went over to a vacant seat at the nurse's station and pretended to read the entire dossier from cover to cover. It was the authentic thing to do. When he finished, he handed her the chart back. She failed to notice the thin coating of glue on each of his fingers to cover his fingerprints.

"Do you mind if I pay Mr. Salley a visit?" John said in his best doctor's voice.

"Not at all, sir," she replied. "Actually, for the first time since he's been here, he's alone. Except for his dog, Burly," she added.

"His dog" John asked, surprised they would allow a dog in ICU.

"Don't ask," the nurse waved her hand and smiled as she went back to work reading the newspaper.

Hansen and Cameron were still in the waiting room discussing the chain of events. Hansen wanted to know everything from beginning to end, so they'd been in the waiting room awhile. Before they got started, however, Cameron walked Burly back into the unit so someone, dog included, would be with Colt at all times. They were in such an overwhelmingly deep discussion about what happened on the water that they didn't even notice the so-called doctor walk in to the ICU.

John scanned the room thoroughly when he went in. Pleasantly surprised to see Mr. Salley, alias Sleeping Beauty, was the only one in the room, except of course, a rather handsome chocolate lab lying on a composite of pillows on the floor beside the bed. The humming of the ventilator and the beeping sound of the pulse-oxinator attached to Colt's finger were the only noises to be heard. The dog was wide awake and staring at John with keen interest with his head still resting on one of the pillows. The dog offered up a low growl as John reached in his bag and pulled out a small canister of dry nitrogen gas, primarily used for flushing telephone lines. He reached over and disabled the low oxygen alarm on the ventilator and took the pulse-oxinator off Colt's finger and placed it on his own. He attached a clear plastic hose to the end of the dry nitrogen canister and inserted it into the ventilator line. All he really had to do was pull out the ventilator far enough so Colt wouldn't get any oxygen in his lungs and he would suffocate. But they had given him instructions to leave a mark. After he finished attaching the hose, he was ready to release one hundred percent nitrogen gas into the ventilator line, in place of the oxygen, feeding

Colt's lungs. It would be a quick, painless death. Afterwards, he would reattach the oxygen line, replace the pulse-oxinator, back on Colt's finger, re-enable the low oxygen alarm on the ventilator and throw the nitrogen canister in his bag. Finally, he would rush out and alarm the nurse reading the paper that Colt was coding. Following the ensuing frenzy, he'd quietly slip out the door and across the physician's parking lot, hop in the *Yaris* and disappear discreetly into the night.

Unfortunately, something unusual happened. Burly growled at him louder this time because he sensed something was terribly wrong. Annoyed by the fact that the dog was in the ICU anyway, John kicked him hard to silence him. Instead of shutting up, Burly did the exact opposite, he attacked him. He lifted up on all fours and leaped towards John's face, all in one fluid, calculated motion. He was vicious and unforgiving. Because John was focused on Colt, he'd totally turned away from the dog and was caught off balance when the dog hit. The bed Colt was lying in was pushed in the melee halfway across the unit, crashing in to the wall. Trays went flying, IV's ripped out and Burly never stopped his assault. For some reason, he sensed what John was up to and he was going to do everything in his power to stop him. The attack was insanely aggressive, relentless, and loud.

When she heard the deafening noise coming from the ICU, the nurse half-way catapulted over the counter and ran in to the unit. Because the curtains were closed, she had absolutely no idea what could have happened. Hansen and Cameron also heard the noise and came running. Inside ICU was total chaos. Burly was on top of the doctor trying to rip his head off by the neck, medical equipment was scattered all the way across the room and the doctor was screaming at the top of his lungs from the pain Burly was inflicting. The nurse tried, unsuccessfully, to pull Burly off of him. Hansen and Cameron had to help her when they arrived. At this point Burly was the guilty one, until the nurse noticed the canister of dry nitrogen, which was attached to a plastic tube lying on the floor next to the doctor. The doctor rolled around on the floor in pain, holding back the blood gushing from his neck.

She knew the canister wasn't part of the many medical devices used to keep people alive. The crooked mustache on the doctor's face sent off alarms in her that scared even Hansen and Cameron.

"Grab him," she screamed at the top of her lungs. "He's a fake and I think he tried to kill my patient," she finished by holding up the canister. "He's a murderer," she shrieked and suddenly rushed to attend to Colt. When she got to him, she jumped back in shock and let out another yell.

"What's all the commotion about," Colt asked with a huge, weak smile on his face. "I'm trying to get some sleep here," he joked.

"Oh! My! God! You're awake," was all she could say as tears erupted down her face in total amazement.

Hansen and Cameron were still holding down the doctor when they looked up at Colt. Both of them were crying with happiness even though they were still in the middle of restraining the doctor.

"I never left," Colt said weakly. "I wasn't dead. I could hear everything from the helicopter ride to now. I was just in too deep to let anyone know. But I was never dead," he smiled weakly. "When I heard Burly growl, I knew something was wrong and it brought me back," he finished as Burly jumped up on the bed and started licking his face. Burly was the hero and he knew it.

When security finally got to the unit, everything was under control. They took the so-called doctor away to another part of the hospital to hold him in a secure place until the police could get there and take over. Hansen, once again, summoned his driver and told him to bring Brandi back to the hospital as soon as possible.

The driver called the bartender from *The Cause* to help

him. He had Alex get her out of a dead sleep and help her get ready to return to the hospital. All she told Brandi was there had been a change in Colt's condition. She knew the change was for the better but she wasn't totally sure what that meant. In any case, it was too special to ruin. By the time they got to the hospital, Brandi was coming out of her sleep-cocktail hangover. Alarm bells were going off all over the place in her mind. She kept asking Alex questions that weren't making any sense. Alex pleaded the fifth and simply said Brandi was needed back immediately. To Brandi, it seemed like it took forever to get there and the longer it took the more worried she became. When they finally walked to the hospital, she knew something was terribly wrong judging by the fact there were two police cars parked in the circle at the entrance.

She was so overwhelmed with fear that Alex had to practically carry her to the ICU. When they rounded the corner, they saw a small crowd of people standing outside the door, including Colt's parents. They were crying, but it was a happy cry which totally confused her. They patted her on the shoulder for support as she walked by them and into the unit. Then her knees buckled. Colt was sitting up in the bed smiling at her with a fresh rose between his teeth. To her it seemed like a mirage, something so surreal it was beyond reality. Finally, after what seemed like eternity, she was able to regain her composure. She ran over to him and buried her head in his chest and sobbed like there was no tomorrow. He gave her the rose. She kissed him and re-buried her face in his chest and sobbed some more.

"Did you miss me", Colt said jokingly, hoping to lighten the look of shock he could still see in her eyes.

"Actually, I was wondering when Burly was coming back home. Now him, I missed", she said while wiping away the tears. "I was getting tired of talking to you and you always ignoring me. If it wasn't for Burly, I would have left you three days ago". She was recovering.

"Brandi, I heard everything you whispered to me and felt every touch. I was screaming trying to let you know, but nothing would come out. It was breaking my heart and killing me in the process. I could tell Burly was helping to keep you grounded. He knew I was going to be okay. But for the life of me, I could not figure out what was wrong. I'm so sorry if I hurt you. Please forgive me. I love you so much".

She knew they'd been given the miracle of a second chance and she was never, ever going to let him go. All she could do was stare at him and touch him, to convince herself this wasn't a lie. Her tears spoke for her heart. That was all she could say. Burly said it all by licking Colt in the face and beating her with his tail. Between the three of them, it was a picture of absolute love and purity.

Hansen stood over in the corner with Cameron and they both cried while witnessing a scene they would never forget as long as they lived. The media was notified by a special news conference set up the next morning at the hospital. They sensationalized Colt's miraculous recovery, sidestepping their sensationalized story about what he may have seen on the other side. Unaware of the attempted murder charge, they quietly went away, disturbed and wondering what was going to be the next big thing.

Leroy came to the hospital and spent over an hour with Colt and Brandi to get the entire sequence of events straight from a legal perspective. After he felt comfortable with the circumstances, he had his deputy bring Annie-Laurie into the room. At first, there was dead silence, except for an occasional sniffle. Reluctantly, Brandi felt she should give them time alone to settle their differences, so she waited outside the unit. That was as far away as she was willing to separate herself from Colt. Annie-Laurie sat down beside his bed and took some time to regain her composure.

"I'm so sorry for what I did Colt. I never meant to hurt you in any way. I would never do that. It's just hard for me to let you go. I thought all along you would come home to me. When I saw the picture, I knew that was never going to happen and I guess I snapped. I know it's not fair to you but it's not fair to me either. You said you'd come back and I believed you. Why can't we…"

"I'm sorry Annie. I'm so, so sorry," he saved her from going down the road of no return. "It's over between us and it's not your fault. I know you didn't mean to hurt me. As a matter of fact, I deserved it," he held up his hands. "I never meant to hurt you either, but I did and I will always be regretful. Something happened to me out here and I never saw it coming. Nor was I looking for it," he emphasized. "But it happened and I'm going to stay. This is where I belong. I hope you find your place because I'll always love you and always wish you great happiness. I found my dream and I hope you find yours." She stood up, leaned over and gave him a long kiss on the forehead before she turned and walked out. As she passed Brandi standing outside the doorway, she stopped and looked at her for a second before she spoke.

"I'm sorry for what I did. I didn't mean to hurt him. I just never wanted to let him go. Please take care of him for me. He's so very special," she finished as she gave her a hug. Leroy witnessed all this and finally made his decision to drop the charges of attempted murder. This was truly an accident of misguided love and this young girl deserved a chance to find her own life back home, in Virginia.

Nurse Maria came bounding around the corner and passed the two women at the door. She stopped when she saw Colt sitting up in his bed, and gave him the meanest look. "I've been waiting to talk to you, young man," she said in her sternest voice. "I do not allow dogs in my unit, do you understand that?" And then she ran over and gave him the biggest hug. "Welcome back, young man. Welcome back! And you better take care of that girl out there because she never left your side. Do I make myself perfectly clear?"

"Yes ma'am," Colt said with a smile. "I will."

If you look hard enough, there is always a rainbow. Thank God.

The end

PS- Give the dog a bone!